The Redemption of Roman

T. Ashleigh

THE REDEMPTION OF ROMAN

DEDICATION

To my mama. Your support of my writing means the world to me. I don't know what I would do without your constant encouragement and positive influence.

BLURB

He walked into my life when I wasn't expecting him. Tall, dark, handsome, and everything I didn't know I wanted. He made me feel so many things, so deeply, so quickly.

That was okay, because I was happy.

We were happy.

Until we weren't.

He took everything I thought we were and shattered it. I don't even recognize the man I call my husband anymore. My mom used to say that every good comes from evil and evil comes from good. It took me a long time to understand the truth of that testimony but I understand it now.

Roman was my hell and I was his redemption, but as with everything there are two sides to every story.

This is ours.

Are you ready?

The Redemption of Roman is a full length standalone mafia MM novel with material that may be difficult for some readers. It's recommended for 18+ due to language and sexual situations . Please read trigger warnings before proceeding.

TABLE OF CONTENTS

ALEX

Prologue

I read an article once about perception.

It was similar to the game telephone. I'm sure you remember it from grade school but in case you don't, it goes like this. A group of people get together and the person who starts comes up with a sentence. Then you whisper that sentence to the next person and on and on it goes until it gets to the end. The last person says the sentence aloud and you usually find that it isn't anywhere near what you started with.

This leads to the breakdown of how people view, hear, and see things differently. It's amazing when you really think about it.

People strive to be the same as everyone else. You are taught from a young age by bullies that being different is not a good thing. Though when it comes down to it we are all different, everything about us, because of perception, and individual identity.

The article goes over the dimensions of perception versus reality. About how perception is the way a person understands something and reality is the truth and actual existence of something.

I have always struggled with this concept because who is to say that my reality and your reality are the same? I guess at the end of the day that's how I justified it all. How, after everything, I can still sit here and not hate him for everything he has done.

My mom used to say that every good comes from evil and every evil from good. It took me a long time to understand the weight of that testimony.

The road to Hell was built on good intentions and the path to redemption is difficult but not impossible to follow. Roman was my Hell and I was his redemption.

There are two sides to every story...

This is ours.

guy chuckles again and I snatch her beer from her, downing it in one go.

"Alright, enough. Let's go. You are done playing matchmaker tonight." I set the glass down harder than necessary before I all but drag her to the dance floor.

"Are you trying to have me kidnapped?" I eye her with fake disdain.

"I would never," she says, hand flying to her chest in mock horror. "Besides I would be lost without you." Before I can respond I slam into a hard chest.

"Shit, sorry. I wasn—"

I'm at a loss for words. *Holy fucking sexy ass man.*

This man looks like he walked right out of my every fantasy. Perfectly trimmed and styled, midnight black hair. Eyes so blue I swear he can see straight into my soul. He's tall too, around six-foot-three. I can't make out his definition, but I can guess he's packing a delicious body under that designer suit.

I scan my eyes from his head to his toes, appraising every inch of him I see. *Hello, handsome, where have you been all my life?* God, am I drooling? I feel Lacey nudge my arm and it pulls me from my stupor. Fuck. I snap my gaze back up to his devilish smirk and I can feel my cheeks flame with embarrassment at being caught checking him out. Damn it.

"S–Sorry, I didn't mean to run into you." Great, now here I go stammering. His eyes light up with amusement and I can feel my face burning hotter with each passing second.

He shakes his head. "It's no problem. I've been hoping you'd run into me all night." I gulp suddenly, my mouth feeling dryer than the Sahara. *What now?*

"You–I–But–What?" Right, because that made sense too. I am a disgrace to all gay men everywhere.

Lacey shoulders her way in front of me. "Please ignore our sweet, little baby here." She sighs in exasperation, patting my chest a little harder than necessary. "He can actually speak properly. Am I right to assume you bought us our drinks tonight?"

harder into him, trying to fight the whimper that's bubbling up my throat when he nips at my neck. He spins me around again, lifting my chin to meet his eyes. "Want to get out of here?" he says into my ear.

Is that even a question? I don't think I have ever been so keyed up in my life. "Please." My voice comes out in a husky plea.

He groans, shuts his eyes, and leans forward, his words whispering across my lips. "Come on." He reaches down between us, adjusting his erection, and my eyes zero in on the movement. Yes, this is exactly what I need. One night. One good fuck. I have a feeling he is going to give me more than what I bargained for though.

ALEX

Chapter Two

This hotel room is way fancier than any other I have been in. I really shouldn't be surprised. I noticed several details about this man on our ride from the club. First, he is wearing an Armani button down, with gold cufflinks. His slacks are definitely designer, and I know a pair of Salvatore Ferragamo loafers when I see them. He has several pieces of jewelry, all real gold and diamonds. And then there was a car and driver waiting on us as we exited the club.

I don't know who he is, but I know he comes from money. I wonder what he does for work? I should have asked more questions, but the moment we were tucked into the back seat of his car, I was on him like white on rice. Kissing, sucking, biting any place I could get my mouth on.

The click of the lock sounding through the room brings me back to the present and I whirl around to see him leaning heavily against the door, watching me with animalistic hunger. He beckons me over with a finger. "Come here."

Screw it. I can ask questions and check out the room later. I walk over to him, never breaking eye contact.

Fuck, he is sexy. His hair is all mussed from me running my hands through it and his lips are swollen from my kisses. He has a calmness about him, like a cheetah before a hunt, but I'm not scared. I am intrigued. Ready.

I reach out and start undoing his shirt buttons, fighting back a groan as his golden skin is exposed. I trace my finger down the expanse of his chest, through the split of his abs, and down his happy trail. When I reach his belt, I look up at him for silent approval.

He nods, heat shining through his blue orbs and I bite my lip. Oh yeah, it's game on. I drop to my knees, smirking as he releases a hiss. He wants this just as bad as I do.

I pop open the button of his slacks and release the zipper, his pants pooling around his ankles and I groan at the bulge hidden behind the black Calvin Kleins.

Leaning in, I inhale his spicy scent, sucking the head through the fabric of his boxer briefs. "Fuck, you're a tease," he growls, grasping my head and pulling me harder against him.

I look up at him through my lashes. "I just want to make it really good for you." I make a show of licking my lips as I rub my hand against the bulge.

He groans, his head falling back against the door. "It would be better with your lips around me."

I smirk at his desire. There is just something so powerful about being on your knees with a man standing above you, waiting on every bit of pleasure you have to give. "Well, since you asked so nicely." I reach up and grab the band on his briefs, sliding them down his legs and grab a hold of his cock, giving it a quick lick.

"Fuck," he curses and I can't help but smile.

Focusing on my task, I lick around the head slowly before sliding down a bit, coating his cock with my saliva. I pull back and pump him a few times, then go all the way back down. I continue teasing him for a few more minutes before bobbing, licking, sucking, and humming around his dick. His fingers thread through my hair, holding on to me as I work him over.

I look up, meeting his heated gaze. "You want it bad, don't you?" He fists my hair, slowing me, taking over while guiding me up and down at a slow pace. Then he pushes me all the way down and holds me there. I try to relax my throat around his girth, but I can feel the tears springing to my eyes.

"You look so good on your knees for me," he rasps, running his forefinger around my stretched lips, slipping inside and stretching them wider. I can feel my throat working the head of his dick and the tears that are sliding down my cheeks. "So damn perfect." His eyes hold mine with such fever that I worry I may combust before we even get started.

He pulls me off and I inhale sharply, trying to suppress a cough. Fuck, my throat feels used in the best way. Roman kicks off his pants the rest of the way and lifts me up, smashing his lips to mine in a hungry kiss. I wrap my legs around his waist as he carries me in the direction of the bed, never taking his lips off mine. He sets me down and grabs the hem of my shirt.

"Clothes. Off. Now," he grunts out against my lips. I untangle myself from him long enough to snatch my shirt over my head and remove my jeans before he's back on me, pushing me down onto the mattress.

His lips are soft and urgent and I swear, kissing alone could make me come. He moves down my jaw and collarbone licking, nipping, and sucking until he reaches my nipple. My whole body feels like an exposed nerve. I think I'm going to shoot off with just the smallest amount of friction.

I reach up and run my fingers through the silky strands of his hair, enjoying the feel of it through my fingers. "Please." I don't even recognize my own voice.

He smirks up at me, running his finger around my boxer band. "Please, what?"

"Suck me."

"Maybe I want to hear you beg?" he says with a smirk then resumes kissing across my stomach as I arch up into his mouth, seeking more of the pleasure he has to offer. *Fuck it!*

"Fuck, please. Please, Roman, suck my dick. I need it."

"Mmm, you beg so prettily." He rips my boxers off and inhales my cock in one motion. My hips lift up of their own volition and my back arches off the bed once more.

"Fuck, oh fuck. Yes." He bobs up and down, and I lose my mind. "Jesus Christ."

I'm no virgin, I've had a blow job before, but this man sucks me like he was born to do so. As if his number one goal in life is to get me off. I thrash, gripping the sheets as I push up into his hungry mouth. He pulls off me too soon and I whine at the loss.

"You are so fucking sexy," he croaks out, running sloppy kisses up my torso. His hand lazily pumps my cock, but it's too much. I'm right on the edge, barely hanging on.

"Roman, ah, I'm going to come," I choke out. He stops all movement and squeezes the base of my dick to stave off my impending orgasm. Fuck. I bite down on my lip, irritated at the loss, but glad this isn't over yet.

"Not until I'm inside of you. I want to feel you around me when you come." God that is so hot. My whole body shivers at his admission.

"Fuck, do it now. Want you now." I shift my hips, trying to rub against him, but he moves before I can take the edge off. Climbing off the bed, he goes to his pants, pulling out a packet of lube and a condom.

"On your stomach." He orders and I do so quickly, groaning when I feel the slide of lubed fingers.

"Please," I whimper, sounding like a needy whore, but I could care less. I am so gone for this guy. He slides his finger into my ass, slowly at first, then working up a rhythm before adding a second and third finger. I let out a groan as he works me over.

I push back onto him. "Come on. I'm ready," I beg, and he groans again, removing his fingers, and tearing the condom wrapper open.

My body is vibrating with desire and I am practically humping the mattress at this point. Lifting me up onto my hands and knees, he lines his dick up with my hole, sliding around my puckered entrance slowly, teasing me. "If you don't get inside me in the next second, so help me God

I will—" The words die on my lips as he surges forward, slamming his cock home in one brutal thrust. *Fuck, it hurts so good.* The groan that leaves me is inhuman, but I am too far gone to care.

He works my body like a violinist with a bow. His bruising grip on my hips is rough, but it doesn't matter. The only thing that does right now is this. Him and me, and the orgasms we're chasing.

Roman's hands slide up the length of my back, stopping on my shoulders. He grips them for leverage, slamming home so hard I slide up the bed. I grasp the sheets harder, meeting him thrust for thrust. "Fuck, yes, please. God. So close." Reaching around, he pulls me up so my back is flush with his chest. I can feel our sweat combining this way and I tilt my head back to lick the skin I can reach, needing to taste his desire.

I groan when the salty flavor of him explodes across my tongue. "Fuck yes, so good. Your ass is strangling my dick," he growls out, moving his hips faster while running his nose along my throat. "You want to come? You ready to come on my dick?" he taunts, pumping in and out of me in hard thrusts. I whine and arch my back more; pushing down, trying to get him deeper inside of me. His hand slides down the front of my belly and wraps around my cock. "Come for me," he whispers into my ear, as he jerks me. He pumps me twice and that's all it takes. I explode, my whole body shuddering and the room dims as stars burst behind my eyelids.

"Jesus Christ," he groans loudly, his hips losing rhythm as he orgasms. We sit like that for several minutes, me leaning back against him, and him holding me to his limp frame before he kisses my sweaty temple, turning my face toward him, and giving me a chaste kiss on the lips.

He maneuvers me onto my back on the bed and kisses me again softly. "Shower?" he asks, fingers running over my sweaty chest. I nod, sighing happily and close my eyes, letting the euphoria wash over my sated body. *Holy Christ. I needed that.* I look over at him as he stands from the bed.

Fuck, he is so sexy. Sitting up, I take a moment to appreciate the way his shoulders flex as he stretches. I run my gaze down the planes of his tattoo-covered back before stopping on his biteable ass. I definitely lucked out with this one.

He turns back to me and I slowly trail my eyes up his torso, unashamed of my perusal. His face is turned up in amusement when my gaze finally meets his. "See something you like?"

I bite my lip suggestively. "Oh yeah. Have you seen you?"

Shaking his head he lets out a raspy chuckle. "You are something, huh?" He turns away from me and walks into the bathroom.

"You have no idea!" I call out to his retreating form, falling back onto the bed, and enjoying the feel of the pillowy mattress.

"You better not fall asleep in there. I got something else planned for you!" he shouts once the shower is running.

I jump out of bed and hastily advance to the bathroom. There, under the steam in all his glory, is a very naked, very soapy, Roman. I feel my dick stir again as I drink him in. Biting my lip, I lean against the counter as I take in the view.

He turns to me, smirking through the rapidly fogging glass. "Come on, Alex." He slides his hand down his abs and I curse the fog for blocking my view of him. "Don't you want to play with me?"

I purse my lips in thought. I should really make the most of this night. After all, it is just a one time thing. Decision made, I stalk towards the shower, pulling the door open and step inside. My eyes rapidly move over his body as I take in every inch of him, this time no obstruction in my way.

Leaning forward, I lick a few droplets of water that have settled on his collarbone, then run my tongue across the expanse of his chest before stopping on his nipple, giving it a few nips.

His groan causes me to smirk as I run my lips over the assaulted skin teasingly. I make a show of kissing and licking down his torso before dropping to my knees. I reach forward and run my finger across the head of his dick. "Do you want my mouth here?" I ask, voice husky.

He stares down at me, eyes burning with heat. "Suck me," he demands. I smirk, lean forward and run my tongue across the tip.

"As you wish," I whisper, then swallow him down eagerly. I bob, stopping to suck on the tip.

He groans, grabs my hair, and rocks his hips forward, fucking my mouth. "God, your mouth feels so fucking good."

I hum around him. His praise going straight to my dick. My hand wanders down, pumping my cock in time to his thrusts.

I bask in the sounds he is making, loving the way he's taking his pleasure from me. My hips rock into my fist harder, chasing my release.

"Fuck, yes," he growls out, thrusting deeper, causing tears to spring to my eyes. "Look at you. Damn, it's so fucking sexy watching you choke on my cock."

Jesus Christ. My eyes shut involuntarily as my orgasm slams into me. I feel Roman's body stiffen as his release floods my mouth. "Fuck," he groans, shuddering as I swallow around him. His hands go lax in my hair as I slide off of him and plant a kiss to the softening head.

Our heavy breathing mixes with the sound of the running shower as we calm down. Roman pulls me to stand on shaky legs and walks me back until I hit the shower wall. He rests his hands next to my head, caging me in. His lips seek mine and we kiss lazily, lips barely brushing as we pant into each other's mouths.

I sigh, enjoying the weightless feeling from just having had two orgasms. My stomach chooses that moment to growl loudly. A chuckle escapes my lips as I rub my belly absently. He pecks me once more before grabbing the small bottle of shower gel.

"Come on, let's get you cleaned up and I will feed you," he says, lathering up a cloth and running it over my chest.

"Oh, you don't have to do that. I can grab something when I leave." I grab the cloth and take over washing myself. He arches his brow, eyes searching mine. For what? I have no idea.

"After all that, I think I can at least get you dinner." He rinses off quickly, stepping out of the shower and grabbing a towel from the rack. "Room service?"

I ponder it for a moment before giving him a nod. "If you insist." He throws me one last smirk before exiting the bathroom.

"Thanks for dinner," I say, setting the plate down on the nightstand.

"Feeling better?"

I turn towards him, smiling broadly. "Yes, thoroughly fucked and well-fed. Can't get any better than that." I fall back onto the mattress, stretching out my limbs.

After the shower, I had pulled my boxers back on before crawling onto the bed while Roman and I waited on our food to arrive. The kitchen was closed, but he managed to get them to bring up two club sandwiches.

Must be nice to have the money to sway people to do whatever you want. We ate our food sitting in bed, having a minimal conversation between bites. I'm now full and sated, and in the most comfortable bed I've ever been in. I sigh, nestling my head back into the pillow. "So, I take it you do this often?"

He turns towards me then, eyebrows arched in question. "What's that?"

"Bring men back to a hotel, fuck them, buy them dinner, and send them on their way."

He chuckles, shaking his head. "Yes, to the fucking; though most people leave after the first time." That surprises me.

"Why is that?" I ask, my voice riddled with curiosity.

He shrugs. "I'm not a nice guy?"

"You don't seem that bad to me." I shift, trying to see his expression better.

"You got that from a few orgasms and some dinner?" His voice comes out gritty.

"Please." I wave him off. "I've had an asshole one-night stand before. You are far from him."

He lets out a sigh. "Looks can be deceiving."

"So, tell me something about you then." I roll onto my side, resting my head on my hand.

He turns to meet my gaze, face a blank mask. "Nothing to tell." He clearly doesn't want to talk, but that only makes me even more curious about the man lying next to me.

"Seriously, that's what you are going with?" I gesture around the room. "You have a story. I want to hear it. Not like everyone can just afford to bring their one-night stands to this fancy kind of hotel. So, spill." I reach over and poke his chest playfully.

He just eyes me with something like disinterest and I huff, rolling onto my back.

After a few minutes, he says, "You know, most people would rather run the other direction than talk to me." I frown, staring up at the ceiling as his words settle over me.

"What makes you say that?"

"I'm not a nice guy," he says this again, as if it's the most obvious thing in the world.

I scoff. "As you've already said."

"It's the truth." His voice holds so much conviction, yet I don't believe the words.

"Well, I'm not scared," I whisper, biting down on the corner of my lip. The next thing I know, his weight settles over me and a surprised squeal leaves my lips.

He looks down at me, face scrunched up in confusion, as his eyes ping-pong back and forth between mine. I want to ask him what's wrong, but the words die on my lips as he kisses me. The kiss turns heavy and before I know it, we are wrapped up in each other once more. Sweaty, writhing, and groaning to orgasm.

Once we are done, Roman leans down and kisses me again before getting out of the bed to dispose of the condom. I don't know how long before he comes back, because sleep finds me all too quickly.

ALEX

Chapter Three

"And you just left him a note?" Lacey asks while sipping on her margarita.

It's Wednesday, four days since I left Mr. tall, dark, and handsome in his hotel room. I haven't had a chance to see Lacey because of school starting and now I'm being bombarded with twenty questions.

"I didn't want to make it awkward. We had good sex...hell, great sex. Best sex I ever had. Why would I want to taint that with the weird morning after?" I confess taking a giant sip of my own drink.

"What did the note say?"

"Why am I being badgered with all these questions? I wasn't the only one who had a guy that night? What about you and Sawyer?" I waggle my eyebrows at her.

"We actually didn't do anything but talk, thank you very much. I got his number, but I haven't talked to him yet." She shrugs noncommittally. "He was nice, but I didn't really see it going anywhere." Taking another sip of her margarita, she turns towards me with a hawk-like expression. "Now, you, spill."

I sigh loudly. She's relentless. "I basically told you already." I shrug. "It wasn't a big deal."

"Humor me. What did the note say?" Lacey asks again, this time pointing her fork at me before continuing on with her salad.

"I said sorry for leaving, thanks for a good night. Take care," I say with another shrug.

The fork drops to her bowl with a loud clink.

"You are lying. Your face gets all red when you lie." She points an accusing finger at me. Why won't she just let this go?

"It's freaking embarrassing," I mutter, folding my arms over my chest as I stare a hole into the table to avoid eye contact.

"What did you do?" she asks excitedly. I groan, slamming my hand to my forehead.

"I basically told him if we were meant to be, it'd be like kismet." Crickets...

"You did what now?"

"You heard me." I glare, and she bursts out laughing. Her ugly laugh. The one that draws so much attention. I bury my face into my hands. She keeps trying to speak, but is laughing so hard it's basically just hiccups and broken syllables.

"Go ahead, laugh it up. I'm so glad you think this is so funny," I grumble. She snorts, earning a withering glare. "God, see, this is why I didn't want to tell you."

"I'm sorry," she starts, breathing several times, trying to get her giggles under control. "Gah. I just...okay. Okay. Sorry." She fans her face, and inhales slowly. "I wasn't expecting that. Just, please, tell me what you wrote. You are probably making it seem worse than it actually was."

I groan loudly, thinking it over in my head. "I really don't remember it word for word. But I basically said thanks for a great night. I won't embarrass myself by leaving a number that you will probably never call, and I didn't want to have the awkward morning after. I figured if it was meant to be we'd cross paths again someday. Have you ever heard of serendipity? Take care. -A."

"You did not... *Serendipity*? Really Alex?"

"It's a great movie. Besides, what are the chances that I will actually see him again? We live in Vegas for fucks sake."

"Well, according to you and kismet..."

I ball my napkin up and toss it at her face. I'm done with this conversation.

"Eat your salad."

This week has seriously been the longest of my life. It's January and my last semester of school before I finally have my degree in business management. So, needless to say, it's been a busy first week back.

I walk into my apartment before heading to my bedroom. It's Friday and I have to work tonight. I'm a bartender at Drought; a newish bar and club on the strip. It's not anything glamorous, but the tips are good and the hours work with my school schedule.

My phone chirps, informing me of an incoming text and I swipe to read it.

Lacey: Almost to your house. Can you keep the door unlocked? Have a lot of stuff to carry up.

Me: Already open, just let yourself in. Do you need any help?

Lacey: You know you shouldn't just leave your door open like that right? Not safe...and nope. I will be fine. Xo

Me: Yeah, yeah. Okay, mom... See you in a bit. Xo

Lacey and I work together, that's actually how we met. We hit it off immediately and have been attached at the hip ever since. She has been the greatest friend, and I honestly don't know what I would do without her. She is my rock.

"Honey, I'm home!" Speak of the devil. I meet her in my living room, assessing all the stuff thrown onto my couch.

"Is all of this really necessary? I already have the outfit."

She rolls her eyes. "Most of this is for me."

"So, why didn't you just get ready at your house?" I pick up the wig and eye her curiously. "You can't possibly be considering wearing this?" She snatches it from my hands.

"Of course not. It's a practice dummy, I wanted to attempt something before I tried it on myself." I nod as if I understand the workings of her mind.

First things first, Lacey is in cosmetology school. She always has cases full of products and other accessories like makeup, shampoo, scissors, and hair dye.

Second, tonight is '80s night at work. I know it sounds lame, but honestly, it gets us a lot of business. One Friday out of the month, my boss, Pat, hosts a themed night. He was on the verge of closing and decided to do this as a last hurrah, and ended up hitting a landmine. It's a huge hit and we are usually filled to capacity with a wait out the door until close.

"Why didn't I just come to your house? It would have saved you so much effort. All I would have brought was my outfit."

"My roommate's family is visiting, I figured it'd be easier to come here considering I already had a full house. Plus, they were doing some kind of seance." Lacey's roommate, Helen, is... Eccentric? They are a part of a Wiccan group, which is completely badass if you ask me, but not something a lot of people understand.

"Makes sense. So, are you ready to get this show on the road, Madonna?" She thumbs around on her phone and connects to my Bluetooth speaker. A few seconds later, *"Like a Virgin"* by the goddess herself starts playing.

"We are now. Let's do this."

ROMAN

Chapter Four

I'm not a good man and I never claimed to be. I am the kind of man who takes what he wants without the fear of consequences. As an underboss to one of the three crime families in Las Vegas, I cannot afford to show fear or weakness. That's the kind of shit that will get you killed.

My name comes with a little bit of a stigma. Wicked, brutal, savage, barbaric, but my favorite of them all is inhuman. I was once told I came straight from the seed of Diavolo himself, with no regard for human life. I guess when you've been through the shit that I have, your view on the world is a little skewed.

Skewed? That's putting it lightly. Fucked would be a bit more accurate. Don't believe me? Well, how's this for a bedtime story?

Once upon a time, there were four crime families in Vegas. The Giulianis, Rossis, Morellis, and Stephanos. The four families settled in Vegas, splitting lines and territory between them. They each made established names for themselves amongst the community and lived in a peaceful understanding for many years. Until one day a new underboss was initiated into his role.

Angelo Rossi.

The young Rossi was pushed into the role after the tragic death of his father and grandfather.

Angelo was blinded by power, thriving off the leadership, and all the perks that came with it. He decided having one-fourth wasn't enough for him. He wanted a little more of what Vegas had to offer. After generations of peace, a territory battle broke loose.

My mother was nine months pregnant with me when she was kidnapped by the Rossi Family. They took my mother and the Giuliani heir as collateral.

Angelo wanted power and he saw my pregnant mother as an opportunity to make a move. Greed makes people do stupid things after all. But what he failed to realize was just how callous my grandfather could be.

In our family, war has casualties. You learn to never get attached to anyone. Love makes you weak and marriage is usually arranged, but in name only. Apparently, Angelo Rossi didn't get the memo when he took my mother and was extremely surprised when my grandfather didn't buckle under his demands.

Unimpressed with Rossi's attempts to take over, the other three banded together with the intention of taking Angelo out.

My father and his men went on a rescue mission. The most important thing was ensuring the next in succession was alive and well. By the time they found my mother, she was practically dead. With barely a pulse, she had been bludgeoned almost beyond recognition. My father used his hunting knife to cut me from her womb. Disregarding the life of the woman who bore me.

I came into the world with bullets flying around me and bathed in layers of blood that wasn't mine.

Born in blood and coated with violence. They say it was the main indicator of how strong I was. A pure Giuliani heir. And it was on that day, four families became three.

The knock on my office door pulls me from my thoughts, and my hand automatically slides to the gun on my holster. Instinct.

"Boss?" Sawyer calls out.

"What?"

"Dominic is here to see you." I glance quickly at my security screen, pleased to see Dominic is alone.

"Let him in."

The door swings open and in walks Detective Dominic Valentina with Sawyer not far behind him. My hand never leaves my holster.

"Don't shoot." He holds his hands up in mock surrender. My face remains neutral. "Keep up with those jokes and I'll bust a kneecap to prove a point," I grunt out. Dominic Valentina is one of the only men who can look me in the eye and not flinch or show fear. In a way, he is just as fucked up as I am.

We have an understanding: he helps keep my nose clean, and I, in turn, give him access to my...let's just call them resources, when necessary. Aka my cleanup crew.

I gesture to the empty chair. "What did you find?" I ask, leaning forward to take the folder he has to offer. He hands it over before plopping down in the seat.

"Alexander Pratt, twenty-four years old, five-foot-eight, and one-hundred-seventy pounds. His favorite color is red, he enjoys long walks on the beach and—" I snatch my gun from my shoulder holster, cock it, and point it at his head.

"Don't fuck with me." My voice booms in the small space, but he doesn't even blink. A smirk plays across his lips as he once again holds his hands up.

"Sorry, sorry. Bad joke." He's lucky. If this were any other man, he would be walking out of here with one less appendage than he came in with.

"I have killed men for far less, Detective. You shouldn't test my boundaries," I mutter through clenched teeth.

His face morphs into a serious one. "I apologize, I meant no offense, Boss."

I sit in limbo for several moments before I lower my gun with a nod. He lets out an audible sigh, relief flooding his features.

I gesture towards the folder. "What did you find?"

He flips through the documents, shaking his head slightly. "Really not much to tell. He was born and raised in Vegas. Family is minimal. His father hasn't been in the picture since he ran off with his secretary when Alexander was four. Not that he was ever really a father to begin with. His mother owned a café until two years ago when she died. She left everything to Alex. Her home, café, car. Her parents disowned her when she became pregnant with him at fifteen. It looks like he sold everything." He takes a breath, then continues.

"I can't tell what he did with the money, but my guess is school. He has four more months of college, then he will have his business degree. He doesn't have a lot of friends, from what I can tell. He isn't very active on social media either, though his friend, Lacey, posts a lot of pictures of them together on her account. He works at Drought, the club on the strip; Thursday, Friday, and Saturday nights. Oh, and his bank account currently has seven-hundred-eighty-four dollars in it." He finishes with a sigh. I nod, flipping through the folder.

"So, not currently dating anyone?" Not that it would matter if he was. From the moment he walked into my club Saturday, I knew I had to have him.

He was perfection. Built like a swimmer, lean muscles and movements refined, almost shy. His hair was so blond it could be mistaken for white. I couldn't make out his eye color from the distance, but later found out they were an enchanting green. His smile was huge with a touch of bashful innocence behind it. He was pure temptation.

It wasn't his looks that drew me to him though. It was his presence, the energy he carried. I just sat there staring. Watching his every move, recording him to memory. He had me enchanted and I was under his spell. He was an enigma and I was curious to know more.

I chalked it up to desire. It's been a while since I had a good fuck. I figured once I had him, the spell would be broken and I could move on. Wrong, I was so wrong. He lit something inside of me that I didn't even know I was capable of feeling. I was struck with raw, visceral need. To own. To possess. To claim. Those are very ominous feelings in a man like me.

He shouldn't have let me have him. He should have walked away. So innocent and pure, he just couldn't see the wolf in sheep's clothing coming for him. When I woke up alone after our night together, I was startled at the loss I felt from his absence.

I am so used to kicking people out; so the fact that he left on his own accord bruised my ego a bit. It also brought on an intense feeling of anxiety at the thought of never having him again. I felt like he was changing something inside of me and that was a very dangerous concept. I knew I had to let him go. I had every intention of doing just that.

I didn't have enough information on him to find where or who he was. My security footage led me to a dead end. Hell, he didn't even sign his *Dear John* letter. A smile plays over my lips at the thought of his note. Serendipity? I laughed at that. I am not a man who believes in fate, destiny, or second chances. The thought alone is ludicrous.

Which is why I can't explain what happened that night when I went to sleep and dreamt of him. He was so alive and vivid. It was like our meeting all over again. Yes, I know. Sappy shit for a man like me, but it's the truth. Except this time something happened. Something I had forgotten about in my haste to get him in my bed.

Lacey said his name. She called him by his name. Alexander James Pratt. So, let me ask you, is that destiny? I don't fucking know, but I didn't give it much thought either.

I immediately grabbed my phone and called Dominic, not caring about the time. Because if I call, they answer. So, now here we are. Five days later, sitting in my office, and going over a folder on the man that will be mine. Dominic clears his throat, pulling me from my wandering thoughts. "No, he doesn't have anyone in his life romantically."

Nodding, I shut the folder and tuck it into my desk. "Thank you for getting this to me." I glance down at the watch on my wrist. "I have other matters to attend to now. Sawyer will see you out." I wave towards the door where Sawyer is leaning. He nods and stands, my dismissal obvious.

I sigh and lean back in my chair, running a finger absently over my lips. My mind once again gets lost in thoughts of big, green, doe eyes. I stare at the wall, a plan forming in my mind. Looks like it's time to hunt him down.

Alex will be mine; he just doesn't know it yet.

ALEX

Chapter Five

It's fucking hot in here. My windbreaker is sticking to me like a second skin and I'm about ten seconds away from going to the back and changing out of this ridiculous outfit.

Lacey yells out a drink order to me as I lean over the ice well and grab out the bottle of beer.

"Why in the hell did we think this was going to be a good idea?" I whine, setting the bottle on the bar and sliding it over for her to grab.

Lacey is decked out looking like she just walked off the set of an '80s music video. "I don't know, but I have never regretted my shoe choice more."

I glance down to her high heels and frown.

"In what world did you think that was going to be a good idea? It's Friday night for fucks sake."

I don't know why I didn't think to warn her of that earlier.

"Hey, no judging! It seemed like a good idea at the time. I mean, I go clubbing in heels, so I didn't think this would be much different. I was very wrong," she says with a grimace.

I can't really say much though; out of all the outfit choices that I could have come up with, I settled on a pastel, multicolored, windbreaker sweatsuit. I guess her and I both made dumb wardrobe choices tonight.

"We need to remember this for the next themed night. Comfort over fashion." I glance down at my white converse.

"Well, at least we have a full staff tonight," Lacey mutters, before grabbing the beer and heading in the direction of her table.

"Can I get a double shot of tequila and three shots of whiskey?" I nod to the guy and set off to make his drinks. The club is busy, as expected, and I get lost in the grind of mixing, shaking, and slinging. That's probably one of my favorite things about bartending, once you get your groove, time flies.

The bar slows down slightly when Pat, my boss, sends me on a fifteen-minute break. I step around the bar and nod to Costa, the other bartender, letting him know I'll be back shortly. I'm almost to the door leading to the staff locker room when I hear the DJ call out to me over the loudspeakers.

"This is a special song request for Alex, your bartender tonight. Alex, can you please make your way to the dance floor and show us what you got?"

Lacey pops up in front of me, practically pulling me to the dance floor. I am struggling against her hold, shaking my head vehemently, but she is not having it.

The opening thrumming to "Footloose" starts and I can't help but cringe.

Lacey and I have been practicing a dance to this song that we saw on YouTube. When I say practicing, I mean wine...lots and lots of wine and messing around. Needless to say, I already know this is going to be a disaster in the making.

I grab her and pull her to me, then do a twist with her as the words start. We are laughing and the audience has made a circle around us as we dance. I do a half-assed version of Kevin Bacon's backflip, it's more of like a cartwheel but whatever. It's not like I have that much room on the dance floor anyway.

People are now joining in on our fun and I can't help but smile at Lacey. As much as I dreaded this, I have to admit she brings out the best in every situation.

I feel a hard body at my back, too close for it just to be an accident. I take a step forward to give them a little more space, but whoever it is, is very persistent and steps forward with me. I whirl around, prepared to tell them to kindly fuck off, but freeze when my gaze lands on a very familiar face.

Roman.

Wow, we found each other.

"Hi," I say lamely, I don't think my brain has caught on to the situation yet.

"Hi," he says back, a smirk playing on his lips.

I stare at him for several seconds before my brain switches back on.

"What are you doing here? I mean, not that you can't be here, but this doesn't seem like your style," I stammer.

He chuckles, running his fingers absently over my wrist.

"You would be correct. I can't say I've ever been here before. I was in the area; a meeting ran late, so a few colleagues and I decided to stop in here for a drink." He pauses, eyes scanning my body. "Now, imagine my surprise when I walk in and see none other than the man who has been the star of my dreams for the last week. You're a good dancer by the way." His hands are now gliding up my arms, almost like he can't not touch me.

A chuckle leaves my lips and I shake my head. "You lie, my dancing is mediocre at best. As for the other, I've been thinking about you all week as well." I give him a shy smile.

He offers me a satisfied grin.

"And yet, you left me." Sliding a hand up to my jaw, he tilts my head back so he can see me fully.

"I didn't want to make it weird," I mutter, getting lost in his eyes.

Why is he so damn sexy?

"As you said in the note you left." He chuckles, running his fingers down my throat. "What else did your note say?" He ponders it for a moment before continuing. "Serendipity, right? Well, I have to tell you I haven't stopped thinking about you since our night together and I think fate has decided that once just wasn't enough for us." His sinister smirk makes my stomach flip and I shudder as his fingers play with the zipper of my jacket.

"You shouldn't run from fate, right?" I smile broadly at him and lean up on my tiptoes to whisper in his ear. "I get off at three a.m. If you are still interested, pick me up." I bite down on his earlobe before pulling away and throwing him a wink.

"I'll be here, don't you worry." His eyes track me with raw hunger and I have to discreetly adjust my erection.

Only three more hours until closing time.

I think I have a problem. When I say problem... I mean addiction.

This addiction comes in the form of a sexy man. We can't seem to keep our hands off of each other.

This is our fifth meeting and I still don't know much about him. I guess that makes sense, we don't spend a lot of time talking. I always say I'll find out more, but the second he gets his hands on me all thought flies out the window.

Like right now, we were supposed to be having dinner and getting to know each other better. Yet here I am, straddling his lap in the back seat of his car, riding his dick like a rodeo cowboy.

"Mmm. God, uh, that feels so good," I groan, arching my back as Roman leans in to suck on my neck. "Fuck, keep doing that." I arch more, leaning back to rest my hands on his thighs, grinding down on him harder.

He takes advantage of my position, sucking along my neck, collarbone, and chest. The noises leaving my throat are so loud that I would normally feel embarrassed, but right now I'm too far gone to care. I reach forward, releasing one of his thighs and grab my aching dick.

"You look so good like this. Desperate for me," Roman grunts out, and I groan once more. My head falls back as the sensations take over. "Yeah, baby. Come on me, cover me with it." My mouth parts in a silent scream and my whole body tenses as my orgasm slams into me.

I swear, every time with him is better than the last.

I pump my fist lazily, milking the last spurts before slouching forward and nuzzling my face into his neck. I hum, kissing and licking his sweaty skin.

"Mmm, I love how you taste." I kiss up his jaw, stopping to flick my tongue across his lips, then slide off of him and continue my journey down his exposed chest. His button-down shirt was ripped open haphazardly in our pursuit to get naked as quickly as possible and I think I may have torn off a couple of buttons in the process. I chuckle at the thought.

"What's so funny?" he asks, guiding his hand through the strands of my damp hair.

"I think I ruined your shirt." I smirk, running my fingertips through the mess on his abs as I settle on the floor between his spread legs. I raise my sticky hand to his lips and he sucks them eagerly, groaning at the taste of me.

I tease his nipple with my other finger and he growls. "Fuck it, I can buy another one."

I chuckle, lean forward, and make a show of licking some of the cum off his stomach. I discard the condom since he hasn't come yet and his dick is hard. I grab it in a firm hold, pumping it slowly.

"So goddamn sexy," he says, his hand tightening in my hair.

I look up at him through my eyelashes. "Do you want to come, Roman?" I give him a few more licks.

His breath stutters and he rocks up against my lips, seeking more. "You know I do."

"Are you going to beg me?" I ask, blowing on his sensitive flesh.

His chuckle is sinister as he shakes his head. "I don't beg, baby. You will suck my dick because you want to. Because you like pleasing me."

Why does that sound so hot? I take him back into my mouth and focus on making this the best blow job of his life.

Up, down, lick, hum, suck, spit. It's messy and dirty and I could care less.

I want to be dirty for him.

His balls are damp from my saliva and I roll them in my palm.

"Fuck yes. Just like that." He lifts his hips off the seat, holding my head still with his fist, and starts fucking my mouth in earnest. "I love the sounds you make when you're choking on my cock," he rasps, face flushed with desire.

His chest heaves with exertion and his muscles are strung so tight they look like they will burst through his skin. I run my gaze up the curve of his throat and meet his smoldering stare.

"Yes, fuck. Look at me. Watch me own your throat."

I hum then and he groans one last time, erupting in my mouth. His salty flavor covers my tongue and I swallow several times, trying to drink it all down. Some spills out onto my chin and Roman catches it with his thumb, sliding it back into my mouth.

He falls against the seat heavily, smirking down at me. "That mouth of yours is sinful." He pulls me up onto his lap once more for a needy kiss, eating my mouth out with his tongue.

I feel my body starting to respond to his desire. We do not have time for round two...yet. I push his chest, sliding off his lap, and pull my jeans back on.

"What are you doing? Get back here." Roman goes to grab me, but I dodge him.

"No!" I smack his hand away. "You have to feed me first. I am famished. You just worked up my appetite."

He laughs, waggling his eyebrows at me, and we quickly readjust our clothes.

"You were right, Alex."

I turn to him, face scrunched in confusion. "About what?"

"I do need another shirt."

After deciding to come back to my apartment considering Roman couldn't go into the restaurant with a torn-up shirt. I'm now sitting on my couch, devouring a carton of Lo Mein noodles as we talk. So far, conversations over the last few weeks have been really light. I know it sounds crazy because I barely know him, but I really feel like I have a deep connection with him.

Crazy how lust can trigger so many feelings.

"Do you have any siblings?" I ask. This seems like the easiest way to approach a conversation about family. I try to avoid this topic altogether usually because I hate opening up to new people about my mom, but if I want to know more about Roman, we have to start somewhere.

He shakes his head, wiping his mouth with a napkin before continuing. "No siblings. My dad is a very busy man and didn't have time for more children. He was lucky to even have me. What about you?"

"Same, I'm an only child. Except my dad wasn't ever around. He left my mom when I was young."

Roman turns to me eyes riddled with curiosity. "Why did he leave?"

The question takes me back a little, mostly because I'm surprised he even asked. Most people just apologize or give me a pitying look.

"My mom told me he had a better offer from his secretary."

"Ouch." He winces, taking a sip of his wine.

I would usually agree but... "That's life," I say instead with a shrug.

"That's a way of looking at it," he says as I lean forward to refill our wine glasses.

"Well, here's how I see it. I can cry about it, get upset, have a huge emotional breakdown over it, or I can pick up my life and move on. Honestly, it happened so long ago and it's so far in the past, that I don't even think about him much anymore."

That is mostly the truth. It still stings when I think about how my father moved on with his life as if my mom and I never existed, but what can you do? I, for one, think he missed out; I am pretty awesome if I do say so myself.

"What about your mom?" I ask, his body stiffens and I regret the question instantly. "Sorry, you don't have to answer that."

He waves me off. "No, it's okay. I just never know how to answer that question." He sighs, hesitating for a moment before continuing, "I never knew my mother, she died in an accident before I was born. Actually, she died on the day of my birth."

A gasp tears from my throat before I can catch it.

"Roman, I am so sorry." I can't even imagine how that must feel. Never being able to celebrate a birthday without the reminder of your mother's death.

"Don't apologize. It's not something that I went through. Yes, it happened to me, but I wasn't old enough to go through it or remember it, if that makes sense."

That breaks my heart for him.

"I can understand that. My mom died about two years ago from cancer. It kind of appeared out of nowhere. One day she was fine, and the next she just wasn't." I pause to wipe away a lone tear that has managed to escape. "I found her passed out on our kitchen floor and she wouldn't wake up. She had an inoperable tumor; there was nothing the doctors could do except make her comfortable. She died a few weeks later."

The room is quiet for a few beats before he says, "I'm sorry about your mom."

"No, don't be sorry. I like talking about her. Makes her seem real, you know? Like, talking about her means she was actually here. Death sucks." I pause, voice cracking. "It's like, once you're gone, people just kind of forget about you. They move on with their lives and you become just a distant memory. My mom was an incredible woman with the biggest heart I've ever known. She deserves to be more than just a picture on a shelf, or a memory in my head." I feel a few tears slide down my cheeks as Roman squeezes my shoulder.

I laugh awkwardly and bat the tears away. "God, I'm sorry. I didn't mean to get all heavy there. I don't even know where that came from. Ah, I'm such a sap."

"Don't apologize. I like seeing you like this, so open. I don't usually have the privilege of seeing people in their truest form. It's kind of refreshing."

I snort, rubbing the sleeve of my shirt over my face. "Yes, because red eyes and a snotty face is just so appealing." I roll my eyes playfully.

"Everything about you is appealing, Alex." Leaning over, he nips at my bottom lip before pulling me onto his lap and kissing me softly. I feel him graze the markings on my neck, as he whispers, "I like having my mark on you." I shudder under his touch.

"Yes, thanks for that by the way. I look like I was attacked by a vampire. I can understand one love mark, but damn Roman, there are six hickeys here."

He leans forward and nips at one. "I can't help myself. You just taste so delicious."

I laugh, shaking my head. "How am I supposed to cover these up before my class tomorrow?"

I moan as he licks over my pulse point. "You won't cover them. I want everyone to know that you're mine."

I freeze, eyeing him curiously. "Yours?"

"Do you want to be?" His expression is so intense I almost have to look away.

"Yes," I whisper and he closes his eyes, leaning his forehead against mine.

"Then yes. *Mine.* You are mine." He leans in to kiss me once more. This time differently, our lips slowly making love to each other. It's not long before the kiss turns into something harder and I'm grinding down into his lap. On a moan, Roman lifts me off the couch and walks me back to my bedroom.

The rest of our meal long forgotten.

ALEX

Chapter Six

I hurry through the front door of my apartment, tossing my things down as I pass the couch. Roman is supposed to pick me up in ten minutes and I am nowhere near ready for our date. I stumble my way down the hall towards my bathroom shedding my clothes as I do.

Note to self always set an alarm when doing a cram session in the library.

I turn on the nozzle in the shower not even bothering to let the water heat before diving under the spray. I grab my body wash doing a quick scrub down before rinsing off and jumping out. I snatch a towel from under the sink, brushing it over myself quickly, not even drying completely before I'm running down the hall towards my bedroom.

The clock on my nightstand reads five-fifty-seven p.m. and a loud curse passes my lips.

Three minutes.

Pulling on the first pair of boxers and jeans I see, I then scan the expanse of my closet for a shirt. I settle on a plain white T-shirt and an olive-green sweater.

Once dressed, I stride back to the bathroom to brush my teeth and put on deodorant. I'm running a comb over my still wet hair when someone knocks on the door. I hurry that way, snatching it open and am greeted by a smiling Roman.

"Hey, baby," he murmurs, leaning down to press a kiss to my lips before walking in and shutting the door.

"Hi, sorry," I mutter, grabbing my jacket from the couch. "I'm almost ready. Just need to put my shoes on."

He cocks his head to the side, humor dancing behind his eyes. "What happened here?"

I follow his gaze towards the mess in my apartment, face flushing at the sight. "Don't look," I lean forward to cover his eyes playfully. "I swear I am not usually this messy. I lost track of time when I was studying in the library. I barely had time to shower and change before you got here."

He chuckles, pulling my hand away and resting it on his chest. "You didn't have to rush, I would have waited."

"I didn't want to make you wait." I pull away from him and bend down to slide my shoes on.

"I could have taken a shower with you." His voice comes out a little husky and he runs his fingers through my almost dry hair.

I push his hand away. "Cut it out. We have plans."

He pouts. "Fine, party pooper."

I snicker, shaking my head, pushing him towards the door. "You are insatiable."

"Only for you."

The car pulls up outside of a giant gate and I turn to Roman in confusion. "Where are we going?"

A smile plays on those sinful lips. "My home," he says, causing my mouth to fall open in a silent gasp. I turn back towards the window as we pass through the gates. "You live in a gated community?"

His deep chuckle reaches my ears and I gaze at him, my eyebrows arched in confusion.

"What?"

He shakes his head. "Not a community. Just my house."

What now? When we drive down a pebbled driveway and pass a water fountain, my jaw drops in wonder.

Who is this man? I just sit here, mouth gaping, when we stop in front of a large house.

House?

No, this is a mansion. I open and close my mouth several times before turning back towards Roman with surprise.

"You live here?" I squeak, eyes pinging around trying to take it all in.

His eyes hold humor when he asks, "Do you like it?"

I sputter, "Like it? Is that even a question? It's gorgeous."

He opens the car door, nodding in the direction of the house. "Let's go in and I'll give you a tour."

I nod, stupefied, and hurry out of the passenger seat.

The place is stunning. Stone gray in color, with large pillars across the front. He grabs my hand and guides me towards the entrance, completely dazed.

"Wow," I whisper when we cross the threshold. His home is breathtaking.

He shows me around and I fight back several gasps along the way. Black with silver fixtures and furniture surround the rooms and halls. The floors are a pristine white marble and there is a grand staircase with a crystal chandelier at the top. He has a multi car garage...with I don't even know how many cars inside and a very large pool with a jacuzzi in the backyard.

"This is incredible," I mutter, eyes wide as I drink it all in. "I have never seen a house of this caliber."

"I'm glad you approve."

"That is an understatement. I want to live here." My eyes widen as I realize what I've said. My gaze snaps to Roman's as my face flames with embarrassment.

"I didn't mean–" He cuts me off, shaking his head.

"Don't even worry about it. I know what you meant." I chuckle, reaching up and awkwardly rubbing the back of my neck.

He reaches forward grabbing my hand. "Seriously, it's fine. Come on, it's time to see the kitchen. Are you hungry?"

"I'm always hungry."

We enter the kitchen and I practically groan as the scent of food hits me.

I glance around, noticing a woman is standing at the stove, stirring something in a large pot. Roman clears his throat, gaining the woman's attention, as she turns towards us, her smile widens across her face.

She looks to be in her forties, if I had to guess. Her hair is dark brown with a few strands of gray running along her temples and her smile is warm. Her rich brown eyes put me at ease and I immediately feel comfortable around her.

"Roman, I will have dinner ready soon." She steps towards me, arms outstretched. "You must be Alex. I've heard so much about you."

"Alex, I want you to meet Leta."

"Lovely name." I reach my hand out to shake her hand, but she bats it away engulfing me in her warm embrace.

"None of that," she says, leaning forward and smacking a kiss on each of my cheeks. "We will be great friends."

She pulls away from me and goes back to the cooking.

"Leta runs the house when I'm away," Roman says, and I smile at the fondness in his tone.

She shakes her head. "You give me too much praise."

"Hardly, this place would be a disaster if it weren't for you."

"I just make the food." She mumbles, her cheeks turning a little pink from the attention.

"And handle the other house staff," Roman adds.

She waves him off. "You flatter me, Roman." She turns towards me then, gesturing to the other room. "Go sit, food is almost done. I have wine set up for you on the table, go ahead and relax. I'll bring you the food once it's ready."

"Thank you, Leta." Roman places his hand on my back guiding me from the kitchen.

The dining room has a huge window with a nice view of the pool and backyard.

I sigh, sitting down heavily in the chair he pulled out for me.

"I love your home."

"Thank you." He sits down across from me, unfolding his napkin and placing it on his lap.

"How long have you lived here?" I ask before adjusting my own napkin.

His lips purse as if in thought. "I had it built about five years ago."

"Wow, that's impressive. I thought you just bought it like this. Did you design it yourself?"

He chuckles, shaking his head. "No, luckily I had a very talented designer."

"Well, they did an incredible job," I state, and sip the wine in front of me. *Damn, that's good.* I hum, taking another eager sip.

Leta comes in carrying two large plates. The sight alone causes my mouth to water and my stomach to growl. She sets one down in front of me and I can't help but sigh again. It has been so long since I had a home cooked meal.

"It's bolognese. Roman's favorite."

I smile up at her. "It looks so good. I cannot wait to devour this."

Her smile widens. "I hope you enjoy it."

"Thank you, Leta," I whisper, grabbing my fork eager to dive in.

"Yes, thank you indeed," Roman says.

"Of course, just yell if you need anything else." She turns, exiting to the kitchen.

I wait until Roman takes the first bite then I dig in. I couldn't stop the groan from spilling past my lips even if I wanted to. I close my eyes, enjoying the flavors as they burst across my tongue.

"Oh my God. This is amazing. I have never had anything this good."

He chuckles, "Leta is incredible in the kitchen. I am blessed to have found her."

"I have to agree," I say before swirling my fork in the noodles and bringing more up to my mouth. We eat in comfortable silence and I can't help thinking how nice this is.

"Okay. Marshmallow Stars or Berry Crunch?"

Roman turns to me, confusion evident on his face. "What now?"

"Twenty questions." I cross my legs, sitting up straighter on the bed. Unashamed of my nakedness.

"I don't follow," he says, earning a sigh from me. Lord this man.

"Well, we can't seem to keep our hands off each other long enough to talk, so I figured this would be the next best thing. It's the easiest way to get to know each other." I wave around at the crumpled sheets and bed we are currently lying in.

His laugh echoes around me and he leans up to face me. "Fair enough, I would apologize for that, but it would be a lie."

"Alright, so...which is it?"

"Neither, I don't eat cereal."

I gasp, and slap my hand over my mouth in mock horror. "That is a disgrace."

"It's kid food, I'd rather have a real breakfast." He shrugs unapologetically.

"Movies or TV series?"

He looks over at me. "I don't watch TV."

I gasp again, "Ever?"

"Nope."

I groan, falling back on the bed. "You are impossible."

"I don't have a lot of time for that."

He is such a mystery to me. "So, what do you have time for?"

"Work," he grits out. Finally, we are getting somewhere. "What do you do?"

He hesitates for a moment, laying down beside me once more. "I'm an entrepreneur."

Oh wow, I guess I should have expected something so seemingly daunting. "Yeah, I guess you would be busy then."

He looks lost in thought, eyes far away before he blinks, coming back to the present. "I don't want to talk about work." He reaches over lacing our fingers together. "Continue on with your questions."

I laugh, "Fine, then. Pizza or tacos?" I roll over onto his chest, nuzzling against him.

"Is that even a question?"

"What do you mean?"

"I'm Italian."

I lean up, propping my head on my hand, eyeing him. "Not all Italians like pizza, you know."

"Then they aren't really Italian."

I open and close my mouth several times trying to come up with a rebuttal. "That's... I don't even know what that is."

He shrugs as if to say, "it is what it is."

"What about you?

I ponder that thought, smirking as I stare at his handsome face. "Will you be mad if I say tacos?"

I squeal when he flips me onto my back, pinning my arms above my head, as he lays over me. I bite my lip and take in his steely expression.

"We are going to have to change that." He smirks, leaning forward to nip at my chin, eyes full of heat. He licks a path down my chest and I groan at the mischief dancing behind his eyes.

In the end I give in. I guess pizza is better.

ROMAN

Chapter Seven

My tires squeal as I pull into the parking lot of Drought. Alex is working tonight and I was expecting to pick him up later, but it's looking like I have business I need to handle first.

I have had my security detail monitoring Alex for the last few weeks just as a precaution. Thankfully so, because I just got the call that my uncle has been lingering around. How does anyone even know about him? I thought I was being discreet. Keeping my two worlds as far away from each other as possible. Apparently not as well as I thought.

I'm going to fucking kill him!

Hopping out of my car I stalk in the direction of where Sawyer has Giovanni pinned in the alley. I charge forward, reach up and grab my uncle by his throat before slamming him harshly back against the brick wall.

"What the fuck are you doing here?" I sneer, getting in Giovanni's face. My rage is surfacing as the anxiety waivers. When Sawyer called me to tell me Giovanni was sniffing around Alex, I have never felt terror like that before in my life. It felt like the walls were closing in around me and I couldn't breathe. My mind ran through all the possibilities of what my uncle could want with Alex. None of them were good. My mind kept skipping to the thought of finding him beaten, or worse, dead.

I shake my head to rid the images as I stare into Giovanni's cold expression. This man is not someone I would trust in any capacity. Family or not. If I could, I would put him down for simply breathing. He mocks confusion, but the smirk playing on his lips gives him away. "I don't know what you mean."

"Don't fuck with me," I snarl, spit flying past my lips. "I want to know why you are here."

"I was just curious," he says in a deadly calm voice. I fight back a shiver.

"About?" I clench my teeth together so tight I feel my jaw pop from the pressure.

"The reason you've been so 'busy' lately," he says, around air quotes.

"That is not your concern."

"Oh, dear nephew, everything about you is my concern." Giovanni pats my cheek roughly. "When Snitch told me he saw you meeting with the same man several times I was surprised—"

"You've had a tail on me?" I ask, cutting him off. He waves off my question and continues like I haven't spoken.

"I thought surely you wouldn't be stupid enough to get involved with anyone; but just to be sure, I had to see for myself. And oh, was I surprised. I must say nephew, I am disappointed in you. What would our enemies think if they caught on to this discovery? If they found out about your weakness?"

My heart starts pounding at his words. "He is not my weakness."

"Oh, but that's just not true, is it?" he chuckles, "I saw you. The way you touch him, look at him. It's so painfully obvious how infatuated you are."

"You will tell no one." I grab him roughly, shoving him back into the wall once more.

"I will tell whoever I please." He leans forward, venom spewing from his lips before breaking out of my hold.

"There is nothing to tell, he is a good fuck, nothing more." The words sound false even to my own ears, but I don't let it show. I can't.

His manic laughter reaches me as he staggers away. "You are a fool. I cannot wait for everyone to know about this." He taps his chin, eyes lit with excitement. "I wonder who will try to take him first? Who will succeed?"

I grit my teeth and pull my gun. "Let someone try to take him."

"Are you going to kill me, nephew?" He holds his arms out in surrender. "It won't matter, people already know about your little plaything. Alex, that's his name, right?" I flinch when his name passes Giovanni's lips. "Sweet, defenseless Alex. They will tear him apart, piece by piece and send the remains back to you."

I growl, cocking my gun and aiming it at his head. "Do it. I have nothing left here anyways." His smile is sinister.

I lower my arm. "Is that what this is all about? You have some score to settle?"

"An eye for an eye. You killed the most important thing in the world to me. Now I am going to get you back."

I scoff, "That wasn't my fault." I slam my fist to my chest. "You pushed that. You and my father. William and I would have never been in that situation had it not been for you."

"It was your fault!" He screams, voice booming through the alley.

"No, it was yours!" I point an accusing finger at him. "And your desire to rule. It was your hunger, your greediness that got your son killed."

He shakes his head taking a step towards me. "He was better than you. He should have been the next in line!"

"He didn't even want it! He was weak! He hated this life. Hated the drugs, money, violence, whores. He wanted more than any of this. But mostly, he wanted an escape from you."

Giovanni's face visibly pales. "You're lying."

"I'm not!"

"He wanted to be a leader. He told me." I shake my head exhausted with this conversation.

"He begged me," I whisper. "Did you know that? He wanted to get out from under your thumb so badly, he begged me for it. Made me promise when the time came, that I would make it quick."

"NO!" he cries, pointing an accusing finger at me.

"You know it's true."

"You shut your mouth you disgusting fucking faggot." *I'm so fucking done with this shit.*

A bullet flies from the chamber of my gun, nailing him in his knee cap. A loud howl sails through the air, as my uncle crumbles to the ground.

I walk to him, crouching down to lean over his writhing body. "I am not the reason William died, I may have been the executioner, but I did not pass the sentence." I spit on him. "You will call off your dogs, and leave Alex alone. If you come near what's mine again, I will end your miserable fucking life." I stand, smashing the heel of my shoe into his temple.

I turn towards Sawyer who hasn't moved since the ordeal started. "Call a doctor and take Giovanni to the underground. Make sure he understands my threat isn't to be taken lightly."

"You got it, Boss."

I walk to my waiting car and pull out my phone, going down the list until I see the name I want. *My Capo.*

"Boss?" Jimmy answers on the second ring.

"Is Snitch there?" I bark, squeezing the steering wheel, trying to ground myself.

"Yes, sir."

"Excellent. Chain him in the basement and have my knives set up. I will be there in twenty."

I don't even wait for a response before hanging up.

No one is going to take Alex away from me.

The basement is cold, with underlying smells of urine and blood.

The smell is heady and adrenaline courses through my veins at the thought of what's to come. My heart is thudding with excitement and my monster is at the forefront of my mind, ready to be released.

To maim.

To hurt.

To torture.

I remove my suit jacket and cufflinks, handing them over to Jimmy, then make quick work of rolling up my sleeves before I walk over to my torture table.

I can practically taste the fear pouring from Snitch's heaving body

"How are you doing, Snitch?" I ask, my tone conveying no emotion.

"Not too good at the moment, Boss," he mutters, face morphed in what looks like fear.

"Isn't that unfortunate for you?" I run a finger over several different blades, skipping over the ax and buzz saw.

"So many decisions. What should I choose?" The question is rhetorical, I don't expect an answer.

"No, please. Don't do this. It is all a misunderstanding. Let me explain," he pleads with me.

I grab a pair of brass knuckles, sliding them on, then take the screw driver. I assess it, verifying it's dull before turning to Snitch.

"What is it that you think you need to explain?"

He doesn't say anything and I squat down in front of where he is kneeling, chained to the pole.

"I think we are well past the point where an explanation will work don't you?" I squeeze the brass, flexing them around my fingers, as I wait for him to answer. His eyes track the movement of my hands and I can see his Adam's apple working overtime, as he tries to swallow.

I tsk, "No answer huh? Big surprise." I stand, pacing back and forth. "Who do you work for?"

His lip wobbles, but he manages to say, "You, Boss."

I stop, shaking my head as I release a chuckle. "Is that right?" I strike then, the brass connecting with his cheek, a sickening thwack sounds through the room. My monster sighs like a drug addict taking that first hit.

Blood dribbles down his cheek from the cut and I watch it slide down his face, before it falls, staining his shirt. "Yet, you follow Giovanni's orders."

"It wasn't like that," he rasps, pain evident on his face.

"It wasn't? What was it like then?" I ask, pulling my fist back and connecting with his other cheek. He releases a guttural cry.

"He threatened me, Boss," he screams. "Told me he would kill my mother."

I glance at his features, taking in his pained expression.

"Why didn't you come to me? I lost my mother too, surely you could have expected some kind of sympathy."

His eyes widen in surprise. "I was scared."

I scoff at that, bringing my fist back and slamming it into his chin, knocking his front teeth out. He screams, blood coating his mouth and spewing past his lips like a fountain.

"Are you scared now?" I ask in a sinister voice.

"Terrified," he chokes out around a mouth full of blood.

"Good, that's good." I rear back and slam the screw driver into his thigh, leaving it there so he doesn't bleed out too quickly. A scream tears from his throat and he rears back as if trying to escape my onslaught.

"Please. I will do anything!" Snitch begs, his snot and tears mixing with the blood, making a gruesome sight.

I laugh and swap out the brass knuckles for a carving knife.

"You see, that's the problem." I squat down in front of him once more, leaning forward so he can see me clearly. "I have a ton of people that would do anything for me. Loyal people who I know wouldn't betray me." I run the knife down the column of his throat, slicing through his shirt and skin, to the top of his groin.

"So, tell me, why should I spare your life when you weren't concerned about mine?"

"Please. I didn't have a choice. I couldn't let him hurt my mother."

I snatch his head back harshly, glaring down at him. "You take me for a fool." I growl, slicing through his left eyelid. He screams, begging and pleading for me to stop.

"I don't. I don't!"

"Your mother has been dead for years." His eyes widen as realization hits. "Let's try this again. Who. Do. You. Work. For?" I punch out each word through gritted teeth, and watch as his expression morphs from a devastated frown to a bloody smirk.

Grade A fucking acting.

I slam the carving knife into his gut, giving it a hard twist. "Who the fuck do you work for?" He cries out, blood spurting from his mouth. His skin is ghostly white as more blood pours from his stomach.

"You will find out soon enough," he croaks, gargling around the blood. "I hate that I won't be here to see them tear apart your little cock sucker. Tell me something, do you fuck him or does he fuck yo–" I snatch the blade from his middle before plunging it into his ear with one hard thrust.

A shriek leaves his lips before his broken body falls limp against the pole. Anger like I've never known before heats my veins. I need answers and I need them now.

I turn towards my men who are scattered around the room, their faces all a blank mask, not one of them fazed.

"In case that wasn't clear, I do all the fucking." I meet all of their gazes before continuing. "Does anyone have a problem with that?"

As expected, no one says a goddamned word.

PART TWO

RED FLAGS

ROMAN

Chapter Eight

My monster is pacing in his gilded cage. The ability to keep him locked away is getting harder to control. I have around-the-clock security on Alex, but even that doesn't seem like enough.

They will tear him apart, piece by piece, and send the remains back to you.

Those words keep circling around my head like vultures. The thought of someone other than me laying a hand on him makes me violent. My temper is short and my punishments grow harsher with each passing day.

Giovanni is under my watchful eye. That old fucker is stronger than I ever gave him credit for. I have seen bigger and braver men crack under far less torture. My fist is bloody, clothes saturated with a mixture of sweat, blood, and filth, but I don't care. I need to know who he told about Alex. I need to know who to keep an eye on.

His head lolls on his shoulders as he goes in and out of consciousness, like he's fighting to stay alive. If it wasn't for this information, I'd have killed the bastard already.

I smack his face, rousing him. "Wake the fuck up," I grit through clenched teeth.

"Am I dead yet?" he asks, his voice coming out in a broken slur. I'm surprised he can even talk at this point.

"Not yet, but it doesn't matter. Your death looks a lot like this." I grab his face, tilting his chin up so he can see me with his non-busted eye. "I know the devil is waiting to personally escort you to Hell."

He lets out a dry chuckle. "I will be down there waiting for you, my sweet nephew." He chokes, spitting out a mouthful of blood.

"Tell me what I want to know." I pause, trying to make him see reason. "If you do, then all of this will end. I will kill you quickly."

He snorts, trying to shake his head out of my hold. "Oh, you will? How generous," he sneers. "No, I think I will wait. After all, why ruin the surprise? It shouldn't be long now. Showtime is coming."

I snatch his hair back, feeling the strands rip from under my grip. He always knows the right words to piss me off. My jaw ticks and I take a few calming breaths, trying to reel in my anger. "Tell me who it is."

The bastard just lets out a maniacal laugh and I see red. Releasing his hair, I stand up, pull my gun from the holster and aim it at Giovanni's head.

"God fucking damn it!" I roar, voice reverberating off the walls around me.

I stand there, still as a statue, gun cocked and ready. My brain is all over the place and my emotions are running high.

Pull the fucking trigger. No! Don't! You still need him.

A knock at the door makes the decision for me and I lower my gun. "What?" I call out, turning towards Sawyer when he walks inside.

"Boss, I'm sorry, but your father wants you. He said there is a delay on a shipment and he needs you to handle it." *Always fucking something.* I sigh, rubbing my forehead. Well, at least I can release some of this pent-up frustration since I cannot kill Giovanni yet.

"Isn't this your lucky day," I say, smirking down at him. "You will live to see tomorrow after all. Don't get too comfortable though." I reach down and pat his cheek with false affection, applying a little more pressure than necessary. "I will be back as soon as I can."

With that, I leave him here to hopefully rot.

Walking into my office later that evening, I'm not at all surprised to see my father waiting for me. Sighing, I continue towards my desk and pull out the whiskey I keep there.

"Father." I sit down heavily in my chair and uncap the bottle before taking a long swig. The liquid burns my throat but I welcome the pain.

"You look like shit."

Roberto Giuliani, ladies and gentlemen. Brutally honest and callous to boot. Exuding more power than any man I've ever known.

At sixty years old, the only indication of his age is the smattering of gray through his midnight black hair. We look a lot alike. Same build, height, and facial features, but that's about where our similarities end. Aside from our personalities, our biggest difference is our eye color. Where my eyes are a clear blue my father's are a muddy brown.

Not that he's ever been a father. Nothing about this man is nurturing.

From the moment I was born, I knew exactly what I was. A necessity. I snort, eyeing my 'father' with amusement. "Thanks."

He presses on as if I hadn't spoken.

"Did you fix the shipment?"

"Had a slight hiccup, but I worked it out." I can't help the smirk that appears. "Only four dead bodies. Not as bad as I was expecting." Especially, considering how desperately I needed a fight.

He nods. "Clean up?" I want so badly to roll my eyes, but I hold back.

"Already on it."

He looks at me, expression darkening. "Still no break through with Giovanni."

I sigh, here we go.

"Nope. The bastard knows he has me by the balls. The only thing I can do is torture him until his body eventually just gives out." I take another gulp of whiskey. "Want some?" I ask, holding the bottle out for him to grab.

He shakes his head, declining my offer then doesn't say anything for several moments as I sit back, watching...waiting for what he has to say.

His body is relaxed and if it wasn't for the pinch in his eyebrows or the way he is running his hand absently through his beard, I would think he was simply lost in thought. I know better though.

He's scheming. Calculating.

"How could you have allowed this to happen?" he snaps.

And there it is.

I sigh, letting my eyes fall shut, leaning back into my chair. "I fucked around and caught feelings." I open my eyes, turning my gaze to my father. "I do not recommend it."

He slams his hand down on my desk, face screwed up in frustration. "You need to take this seriously. You are putting a target on our backs."

I scoff, shaking my head in astonishment. "The target isn't on your back."

"It may as well be. A direct attack against you affects me greatly."

Is he fucking for real?

"You're pretending that you care? I'm touched, truly."

He stands then, eyes blazing. "Stop acting like a petulant child. This is greater than the two of us." His words shouldn't surprise me and yet somehow they do.

"You only care about your precious line coming to an end." My jaw ticks and I inhale deeply, trying to stop myself from lashing out.

"We have come too far to get to where we are to be brought down by you and your sexual desires. This infatuation you have over some nobody kid." He bites out, face screwed up like he just tasted something rotten.

I stand then, leaning forward, my hands braced on the desk as I stare my father down with as much hate as I feel.

"Watch what you say about him." My voice is so low I would have missed it had I been him.

His face changes into something that looks a lot like pity before he says, "Think logically. This boy is a means to an end." I swear to God, if this was anybody else right now, they would be dead.

"You got a lot of nerve."

"I'm telling you the truth," he growls out.

I round the desk then, not stopping until I am inches in front of him.

"No, you are trying to lecture me about something you don't understand."

He doesn't back down or cower; he simply pushes on. "What kind of life could you possibly have with him, Roman?"

I don't have an answer so I remain quiet. Mouth shut, jaw clenched, and fists balled at my sides.

I wish I could tell him to fuck off. I wish I could hit him. I want to scream and shout to the world that Alex is mine. I want to walk out of here now and never come back. I want so many things. Yet, at this moment I know he's right. I know I can never have Alex the way I truly want.

I stalk away from him and then grab the bottle of whiskey from my desk. "Thanks for the pep talk, Father. Until next time," I say, not even glancing back when I leave.

Chapter Nine

I glance down at my phone for probably the hundredth time in two hours, sighing in frustration when I notice there is still nothing from Roman. We have exchanged minimal texts since he canceled our plans a few days ago and I have this uneasy feeling that he's pulling away from me.

I try to shake those feelings away since everything between us has been going so well.

Shoulders slumped, I look down at my phone again. Still nothing.

I want to text him, but I also don't want to come across as desperate. Even though that's pretty much exactly how I feel right now.

I groan and start rubbing my towel into the bar top harder.

Why is dating so complicated?

I mean he likes me. I like him. I should be able to just send a quick 'thinking of you' text without it being a big deal, right?

Maybe?

Fuck, why isn't Lacey working tonight? I need to vent. I need advice.

"Excuse me, can I get another beer?" the man sitting at the bar asks me, pulling me out of my emotional turmoil.

I quickly grab a mug and refill it before setting it down.

"Here you go, sorry about the wait. I was in a daze."

He chuckles, grabbing his beer. "No big deal, it happens to us all."

I glance down at my watch and groan, noting it's only been ten minutes.

Just text him, my mind screams at me. Decision made, I grab my phone once more.

Me: Hey, sorry to text you so late. Just thinking about you.

I hit send before I can second-guess myself and put my phone away.

Thankfully, the bar picks up and I'm able to put my inner struggle on the back burner for now. Time passes quickly and before I know it, we are closing. I grab a towel from the bucket and begin wiping down the expanse of the bar. My feet hurt and I'm ready to sit down.

"Is it too late to order a drink?" My head jerks up and I meet the steely, blue gaze of the man I'm becoming addicted to.

My hand freezes and I stand there drinking him in. I can't believe how much I missed him in just a few days.

"Hey," I say, smiling broadly. "What are you doing here?"

"I wanted to see you," he says, sitting on an empty stool.

Oh, fucking swoon. Just like that, all the worry I've been having vanishes. I feel my face flush and my heart kicks up at those words. I reach out and lay my hand down over where his are resting on the bar.

"I'm glad you came."

His eyes hold mine, something like lust dancing behind his gaze.

"Come home with me," he says, voice a little husky.

"Are you asking or telling?" His devilish smirk tells me all I need to know. "I just have to clean up here, and I should be able to go."

"Good. You can ride with me."

"I don't have any clothes."

"That's fine, you won't be needing them anyways."

I bite down on my lip to stifle a groan. "You can't say things like that to me."

He laughs before standing. "I'll be waiting for you in my car. Don't be long. I have things planned for you."

That's all the motivation I need. After the fastest cleanup known to man, I am practically sprinting out the door.

Roman is leaning against his car door, waiting on me when I approach. His gaze appraising me with so much heat.

I do the same thing, eyes eating up every inch of his suit-clad body. Damn, he is a sight for sore eyes.

"Keep looking at me like that and I will fuck you right here in the open where anyone could walk by and see. I only have so much control," he rasps, eyes blazing.

And fuck me, if he tried, I'd probably let him.

I swallow, tongue feeling thick. "Well, then what are you waiting for?" My voice comes out husky. "Let's get out of here."

I don't think I've ever seen him move so fast.

"Oh, what about this one?"

"Looks great," I say, earning a scoff from Lacey.

I look up from my phone only to stop when I take in her expression. "What's wrong?"

"You weren't even looking," she bites out in frustration, folding her arms over her chest, scowling at me.

Guilt takes over when I realize she's right. "Sorry, show me again."

She pulls a dress from the rack and holds it up against her front.

"So, what do you think?"

I open my mouth to answer and my phone buzzes. I glance down and see another text from Roman.

"Roman again?" She sighs, slipping the dress back onto the rack.

"Yes. Just checking on me to see how my day is going." I shoot him a quick response and stuff my phone back into my pocket. "Okay. I put it away. Let's try this one more time."

"As sweet as it is that he is checking on your day and as happy as I am that you've found someone, he needs to back off my friend time. I feel like I haven't seen you at all lately."

"I know, you're right. I'm sorry."

She shakes her head, waving me off.

"No. Don't be sorry. I'm not mad or anything. I get it, trust me. Everything is fun and new right now and from what little you've told me the sex is nuclear." My face burns and I glance around to make sure no one heard her. "I just miss you, is all."

"I miss you too. You're right though. I will do better with it."

"Stop, it's fine, really. Anyways, will you answer me, please? I need an opinion because this is important." She holds the dress up one more time for me to see.

I look it over, scrunching up my face as I take it in. "No, it's too peachy, it washes you out." I walk over to the rack, skimming over a few before stopping on a deep purple, maxi dress. "Here, go try this one on."

"I knew you could help me pick out the perfect dress," she quips, pulling me in the direction of the fitting room.

I plop down in the chair as she enters the room.

"Let me see it once it's on!" I call out just as she shuts the door.

My phone buzzes in my pocket and I pull it out, surprised when I see the message notifications.

Roman: I am glad you had a good day.

Roman: You having fun with Lacey?

Roman: Did you buy anything?

Roman: What store are you at?

Roman: Are you still there?

Missed call: *Roman*

Shit, I didn't even feel my phone going off.

I call him back, but it goes straight to voicemail. Hanging up, I shoot him a text.

Me: Hey, sorry, I didn't see your messages until just now. Yes, I'm having fun with Lacey, no I haven't bought anything. We are currently at Fancy Gem, that new dress shop at the mall. Hopefully finishing up soon if Lacey ever decides on a dress.

Roman: I was starting to think you were too busy to talk to me.

My eyebrows shoot up and I frown in confusion.

Me: I'm sorry I made you feel that way but that isn't the case at all. Just got caught up helping Lacey.

Roman: Keeping you busy, huh? I just wanted to ask if you like seafood.

Me: Oh, yeah! Love seafood. I could eat it every day.

Roman: Excellent. Wanted to talk to you about something. I asked Leta to make a surprise dinner for you. I think you will enjoy it. What time should I pick you up?

Aw, how sweet is that?

Me: What day?

Roman: Tonight? Should I not have told you? I guess I just ruined the surprise, huh?

Me: Oh, no it's not that... It is really thoughtful of you to have planned something special but I can't come over tonight. I have plans with Lacey.

I see the bubbles stop and start several times before they disappear. I wait, but no message appears on the screen.

Lacey steps out of the changing room and I stuff my phone back in my pocket.

"Wow. That looks great."

And it does. The purple looks good against Lacey's skin tone. It's formfitting against the curve of her body. She will definitely be turning heads in that.

"You think?" She turns to the mirror, leaning up on her tiptoes, admiring her butt. "Oh yeah, this makes my ass look so damn good." She wiggles her hips, tossing me a wink over her shoulder.

I laugh, shaking my head. "I'm envious of your confidence."

She strolls over to me, plopping down on my lap, tilting my chin to meet her gaze.

"My sweet little baby, you have no idea how precious you are. Repeat after me." She clears her throat loudly like she's about to give the most important speech in the world. "I, Alexander Pratt." After several seconds she nudges me. "Repeat it back."

"Oh, right. I, Alexander Pratt."

"Am handsome, confident, and alluring."

I roll my eyes. "Am handsome, confident, and alluring."

"Anyone would be lucky to have me."

I snort, face flushing with embarrassment. "I am not saying that."

She sighs. "Fine, then repeat this one. Roman is lucky to have me." She arches her eyebrow with a huge grin and I can see the hidden meaning behind them.

"I plead the fifth." I hold my hands up in a placating gesture.

"One of these days, you are going to crack and tell me everything I want to know."

I open my mouth to respond but am cut off by my phone buzzing.

Lacey hops off my lap and I pull it out to see Roman's name lighting up on the screen. I go to answer it, but I'm not fast enough so it goes to voicemail.

"Go ahead and call him back. I'm going to change back into my clothes. Do you want to grab some food after I pay for this dress?"

"I could eat."

"Yes, I am craving some pizza." She pumps her fist in the air, then shuts herself back in the changing room.

I click on Roman's name to call, just as my phone rings again.

"Hey, sorry I was just calling you back."

"Why didn't you answer your phone the first time?" he barks through the line.

I pull the phone away from my ear, momentarily stunned by his tone.

"What?" I somehow manage to say.

"I called you but you didn't answer."

"I— Sorry, I was talking to Lacey."

"Oh, so you are too busy for me?"

I sit there silently, unsure of how to proceed.

"No, I already told you that." Several beats pass and I can feel my anger rising. "What is wrong with you?"

I hear a loud sigh through the phone before he says, "I don't know, besides the fact that I made all these plans to have this special dinner made for my boyfriend, only for him to turn around and tell me he can't be bothered to come because he is too busy."

What the fuck is happening right now?

"I'm sorry if you're mad—"

He cuts me off. "Oh, I'm not mad, it's fine. Don't even worry about it."

I can feel my anger rising and I take a few breaths, trying to calm myself.

"What is wrong with you, why are you acting like this?" I can hear a slight quiver in my voice and I mentally smack myself for it.

"Me? Nothing is wrong with me. What is wrong with you? I was trying to do something nice for you and you don't even care."

"That's not true. I didn't know you had something planned. If I had, I would be there. You know that."

"Right."

The line goes quiet and I listen to his harsh breaths puffing through the line.

"Don't be mad."

"Not mad," he says back almost too quickly.

"You are, I can tell by the sound of your voice."

"I have to go. I'm at work, where people actually value my time."

He hangs up.

I sit still for several stunned seconds, just staring at the blank screen.

What the fuck just happened?

"You ready to go?" Lacey asks but stops when she sees my face. "What's wrong?"

"I'm not really sure. I think I hurt Roman's feelings, and then he turned into a grade A dickhead." I fold my arms over my chest, leaning back heavily into the chair.

Her eyebrows scrunch up in confusion. "What happened?"

I give her the rundown, but leave a few things out because I don't need her going all mama bear on me right now.

"I think you should go have dinner with him," she says after several beats.

An uncontrolled gasp slips past my lips as I stare at her. "I don't want to go have dinner with him. He was an ass."

"Yes, he was. Which is why I was going to say make him grovel a little and have hot make up sex," she says, a sinister smirk playing across her lips and she winks.

"God, is everything about sex with you?"

She nods her head, then her face turns serious. She reaches out and cups my hand.

"I'm not saying he is right, because he's not. I think he could have gone about that in a completely different way." She stands, pulling me up with her. "I'm thinking this dinner was important to him for whatever reason. So, I'm saying go have dinner, hear what he has to say, and then tell him how you feel."

I ponder that thought as we head to the counter so Lacey can pay for her dress.

"Okay fine. I will call him back and see if he still wants to have dinner, but if he is a dick again, we are going to get pizza instead." Yeah, because fuck him if he thinks I will deal with that shit.

"Sounds good, babes. Just let me know."

"I will." I give her one last hug before we make our way across the parking lot to our cars.

"Hey, Alex. Call me after and tell me how good the make up sex was!" she yells to my retreating back.

Fuck me. I can feel my cheeks burn as several eyes swing my way.

I throw up my middle finger and her cheerful laugh meets my ears.

Bitch.

ROMAN

Chapter Ten

I slam my phone down on my desk so hard I'm surprised the screen doesn't crack. I overreacted. I knew I was during the call, but I just couldn't stop. I was pissed. I'm still pissed and now I'm not even sure who I'm actually pissed at. Between my father's disapproval of my choice to keep Alex under my protection and Giovanni's threat lingering in the background I'm on edge, and that's putting it lightly. I grit my teeth, lean my head back in my office chair, and stare at the ceiling.

I need to calm down. I inhale and exhale several times, trying to release some of this anger. I shouldn't have even been upset with Alex. It's not like he was wrong in what he said. I didn't ask him to come over. I just assumed he would. I scoff at my own thoughts because why the fuck wouldn't he be coming over?

All of my free time revolves around him. Granted it's not a whole lot of free time, but fuck, I'm a busy man. He should understand how valuable my time is by now. Besides, I had something important I wanted to talk to him about tonight.

I stop that train of thought because I'm getting worked up all over again. I need to hit something. I wonder if Jimmy has anyone at the ring tonight. My thoughts are interrupted as my phone dings.

Alex: Hey, can we still have dinner? I think we need to talk.

Fuck, he wants to talk. Nothing good has ever come from those words.

Is he going to break up with me? Tell me we are over? Like fucking hell he is. He is mine. I'm not letting him go.

Me: Yes, we do. Pick you up in an hour?

Alex: I can meet you at your place.

Fuck me. He *is* trying to break up with me. I grind my molars together, trying to refrain from throwing my phone across the room.

Me: Let me come get you. You can stay the night. You know I don't like you driving really late.

Alex: I need to drive because I have to be at school early tomorrow.

Well, that's good. At least he doesn't want to drive so he can leave me.

Me: I don't mind.

Alex: You're sure? It will be early.

Me: Since when am I not up early?

Alex: Fair point.

Me: I will see you soon.

Alex: Okay.

I smile before leaving my office. I won that round.

The ride back to my place was uncomfortable to say the least. I could tell Alex wanted to talk, but when I tried to start a conversation, he was short with me.

Leta left the meal I requested for Alex, and I tell him to go ahead and sit at the table while I prepare our plates. I would have had us served properly had he let me pick him up earlier.

Don't even go down that road, Roman.

I quickly get our food together before heading into the dining room. I set his bowl down in front of him, shooting him a wink. "Would you rather have white or red wine?"

He ponders that thought for a second. "White please, I think it would go best with the seafood." He offers me a shy smile. He is too adorable.

"Good choice." I lean down and place a kiss on his head before going to grab the wine.

I open a bottle and grab two glasses, then walk back to a waiting Alex. I sit down at the table and pour us each some wine. I slide his glass over to him, tilting mine up and we clink them together.

"Cheers."

The first sip is sweet and a little tart with the perfect amount of bite to it. Definitely will pair nicely with the seafood. Unfolding the napkin I set it in my lap. "Dig in and let me know how you like it."

He shoots me a beaming smile, dipping his spoon into the food to take a bite. He closes his eyes, groaning as he chews. "Damn, this is really good, what is it called?"

I smile, taking a bite of mine before answering. "Cioppino Stew. Leta makes it when I get a craving for seafood."

"I can understand why you like this. I have never had anything like it, the flavor is delicious." He continues eating, humming around mouthfuls.

"I'm glad you're impressed." I take a sip of my wine, nodding in his direction. "What did you want to talk about?"

He hesitates for a second, setting his spoon down. "About our conversation earlier." He looks down at his lap momentarily before looking back at me.

"I figured as much. I shouldn't have responded the way that I did. I overreacted." I try to shrug it off but he isn't letting it go that easily.

"What was that, though?" He folds his arms over his chest. "You were so... mean?" Leaning forward, he rests his hands on his head. "God, that sounds lame, but I don't know how else to put it. You were callous almost." He says, leaning back once more, his face mashed up like he just sucked on a lemon. "I have heard you like that a few times when you've been talking to other people, but never with me. I guess it just surprised me."

I ponder that thought, trying to come up with an explanation as to why I reacted the way that I did, but what can I possibly say? He doesn't know about the business or my uncle. He doesn't even know what kind of danger he is in, telling him would only cause more issues that I'm not ready to deal with currently.

I set my spoon down and nod. "You're right. I acted awful towards you and the reasons why are inexcusable." I sigh, bringing my laced fingers under my chin, and lean my elbows onto the table. "I should have understood that you were spending time with your friend. I am sorry, baby, I just missed you and wanted to spend time with you." I reach across the table, hand outstretched towards him. "I had this whole evening planned out, and I ruined it."

His eyes soften and he slides his hand in mine.

Thank fuck, I said the right thing.

"You are forgiven." He stands slightly and leans forward to smack a kiss on my lips before settling back into his chair. "Next time though, I won't be as forgiving. I understand things happen and couples fight, but that was close to crossing a line." He points an accusing finger at me.

I put my hands up in surrender. "I'll work on controlling my temper." And in that moment, I mean it. He smiles, picking up his spoon and going back to his food.

We sit in a comfortable silence for a minute, eating and enjoying the wine before I decide to ask him the question that's been weighing on my mind. "I wanted to talk to you about something."

He arches an eyebrow. "Okay, shoot," he says, taking a drink of wine before setting the glass down.

I inhale deeply, looking him deep in the eyes. "I want you to move in with me."

He chokes on his wine, coughing and sputtering as he smacks his chest roughly.

"Are you okay?" Maybe I should have waited.

He waves me off. "Back up. What did you say?"

"Move in with me."

"Have you lost your mind?" His voice holds humor.

"No, I want you to move in with me."

He shakes his head. "I can't."

"Why not?"

His face is scrunched in frustration. "We haven't been together long."

"What's that got to do with anything?" My own frustration is evident in my tone. I genuinely do not understand his hesitance.

"Moving in together is a really big deal, Roman. Most people only do that if they are really serious about each other."

The fuck does that mean?

I feel my face flush with heat. "Are you saying you aren't serious about me?"

He fucking better not be saying that. I will take him to my bed right now and show him how fucking serious we are.

He shakes his head and sighs. "That's not it, I just mean it's really fast, why rush it?"

"Why postpone?" I fire back.

He has no point. Yes, we haven't been together long, but I know how I feel about him, and I know how serious this is for me.

"So, we can get to know each other more."

I stand, pulling him out of his chair and dragging him back into my lap.

"I know you plenty." I nuzzle his jaw, kissing a path up to his ear, and giving it a nip.

He moans, arching his neck to give me better access. "That's not fair, you know I can't concentrate when you do that."

I do know, that's the point.

"Move in with me." I unbutton his jeans, barely sliding my hand inside, and start rubbing circles over the head of his dick.

Mouth falling open in a silent cry, he tries to push up into my hand. His head falls forward onto my shoulder. "Touch me." His breath whispers across my neck.

I almost have him.

"Move in with me." I push him to stand, making quick work of his boxers and jeans. I sweep my hand across the table, sending everything crashing to the floor.

I need to have him now.

I lift him and set him on the table before smashing my lips against his. This kiss is nothing but fire, hunger, and need.

He yelps at the sudden change and I take advantage of his open mouth by shoving my tongue inside.

Fuck, he tastes delicious, *like mine.*

Fucking mine.

I push him back so he's lying flat across the table and I lift one leg, resting it on my shoulder.

I make a show of licking and sucking on his ankle, slowly working my way across his calf and knee.

"Move in with me." My voice is husky, full of desire, as I watch his body writhe on the table.

He groans and lifts his hips off the table as I run my fingers across his inner thigh. Shivering violently, I watch him, mesmerized as goose bumps litter every inch of his skin.

God, he is delectable.

"Please, Roman, please. Fuck, I need it," he begs, propping his other leg onto the table's edge.

"That's right, baby, beg me." I lick the inside of his thigh before dropping down to my knees. "What do you want, Alex?"

"I want you inside of me. I want to feel you." Spreading his legs, exposing his hole to me, I run my finger along the puckered skin, reveling in the sounds leaving his lips. "Beg me." I lean forward and flick a teasing lick over his entrance before pulling back again.

He groans frustratingly. "Roman, please, please, make me come. I need it so badly, please."

I dive in then, eating out his ass with hard licks. The noises leaving his mouth only egg me on as I lick, suck, and probe his sweet little hole.

I reach my hand up and tap two fingers against his parted lips. "Open wide, and get them nice and wet for me." I shove them deep and he sucks eagerly, lapping at my fingers like a lollipop.

The things he does to me. I have never felt the desire to claim someone so fully before.

It's intoxicating.

I pull my fingers free, making quick work of opening him up for me, getting him nice and ready to take my dick.

He is whining and writhing, his body vibrating with the need to come.

Not yet, baby.

I get to work on my own slacks, not even bothering to fully remove them. I spit on my hand, coating my dick before I tap the head of my cock against his hole. "Are you ready for me?"

"Yes, please, fuck." I smile, slowly teasing him. I slide in the head only to pull back out.

"You want me in here?" I stop halfway inside and rub the spot where we are connected with a finger. He feels so fucking good.

"Roman, please." He's practically crying with the need to come and fuck if he isn't a sight. Laid out naked on my dining room table, begging to be stuffed full of me. I spit on my dick one more time, then push in.

I go slowly at first, building up a rhythm, getting more forceful with each passing thrust. Sweat coats my body, as I pump into him vigorously. His face is slack, mouth parted, eyes closed as he claws at the table, trying to find leverage.

The sight just makes me want to go harder. I have never had sex like this, never needed someone this badly.

Own. Claim. *Possess.*

I reach up, jerking him in tandem with my thrusts.

"Oh, fuck. Fuck, going to come." I slow down and remove my hand. His eyes snap open and he leans up onto the table, glaring at me. "No, why?" he whines.

Victory is close and I want to beat on my chest like a caveman. I toss him back a sinister smirk. "Move in with me." I slowly roll my hips, trying to find that spot inside.

He groans, falling back once more. "Roman, ah. I'm so close."

Hook.

"You want to come, baby?"

"Yes!" he exclaims.

Fuck, he is a sight. Face flush, pupils blown wide, and legs quivering with the need to come. God. I have never wanted anything in my life the way that I want him.

He reaches down to pump his dick, but I smack his hand away before he can.

Line.

"Tell me you will move in with me. Tell me, baby, and I will make you see stars." A choked sob leaves his lips as he arches off the table.

Sinker.

"Yes, yes. Fuck yes! I'll move in with you, you fucking bastard. Now make me fucking come."

No problem, baby.

I slam home in one brutal thrust, fucking him so hard that the table moves under my assault. I grab his dick and pump him roughly, ready for all he has to give me.

The scream that leaves his lips is riddled with ecstasy and stream after stream of cum shoots out of him. The sight of his cum-covered stomach and convulsing body is enough to send me over the edge.

I let the sounds wash over me and my head falls forward as my orgasm barrels through me. I pump twice more before exploding into his waiting body.

God. Fucking. Damn it. This is everything.

Desire in its truest form. So intoxicating.

I lazily pump my hips as I come down from my high and contentment washes over me. I look down at him, covered in cum and face blissed out. He is so damn beautiful.

I lean forward to kiss his lips slowly, thoroughly. He releases a sigh and wraps his arms around my neck, pulling me down onto him. I go easily, not caring about the sticky mess between us. I lean back slightly to look at him.

"So, should we get you moved in on Saturday?" I ask, a smirk playing across my lips. He reaches up, swiping the fallen hair off my forehead.

"You're evil, you know that." His voice is teasing, but the truth to those words hits me deep.

Oh, baby, you have no idea.

ALEX

Chapter Eleven

I groan, standing to stretch my sore back. Roman was not joking when he said he wanted me to move in as soon as possible. At the time, I told him it was unrealistic to get it all taken care of in a matter of days, but he assured me that money could buy anybody's time. I guess he was right.

He took care of everything, as expected, but I drew the line at letting someone else pack up my things. First off, I don't need anyone going through my stuff. Second off, the thought of some random person in my underwear drawer makes me shudder, because...gross.

My living room is stacked high with boxes and clutter. A lot of this stuff is going into storage or Lacey's house, considering I won't be needing it at Roman's. I guess that's one of the perks of having a wealthy boyfriend.

I can't pretend to not be excited though. Roman's house is amazing. I'm mostly looking forward to trying out that pool.

My mind wanders to thoughts of Roman. I bet he looks really good in a pair of swim trunks.

I envision him climbing out of the pool, shorts hanging low off his hips. Water droplets running down his chest and happy trail. I bite my lip, instantly going hard.

Nope, stop it. You are too busy to be lost in dreamland.

The knock on my door pulls me from my thoughts. "Come in! Beware of all the boxes," I call out to her.

"Jesus Christ! How are you even fitting in there?" Lacey yells back from the open door.

I laugh. "I know it's a mess, but Roman said the movers will be here soon to start taking some of this stuff down."

She cringes, glancing around the space. "Well, I came to help you, but it looks like you already have it taken care of. Want me to start taking some of the 'Lacey' boxes down to my car?" she asks, gesturing towards a section of boxes.

I nod. "Yeah, if you can grab them. If any are too heavy, just leave them. I can have the movers bring them down for you."

She flexes her arms before giving her nonexistent bicep a kiss. "I don't need help, I got this."

I wave my hand, dismissing her. "Yeah, yeah. You're a little nuts, do you know that?"

She gives me a devastating smirk. "You are what you eat."

Yep, I walked right into that one.

"Oh, go take those downstairs." I fake scowl before pointing in the direction of the door.

Her laughter bounces around me before she grabs a box.

"You love me!" she shouts before exiting the apartment.

You have no idea how much.

The movers arrive soon after that and they get started on emptying my apartment. It doesn't take them long to finish and before I know it, it's just Lacey and I standing in an empty living space.

She sighs, glancing around. "This feels weird."

I can only nod. "It really does."

I only moved in here a few months after my mom died. After two years it kind of feels like I'm leaving a bit of myself behind here.

I walk around each room one last time, verifying that nothing has been left.

Lacey slides her arm through mine before turning to me with one of her brilliant smiles.

"If you aren't sure about this, you can still back out. It's not too late." She pokes me in the chest and I shake my head, smiling at her antics.

"Let's go," I say, leading her towards the exit.

As we walk to the open doorway, I glance around the empty space one last time before flicking off the light and shutting the door behind me.

I'm actually really excited about what's to come, regardless of how hesitant I was when Roman asked.

Cheers to new beginnings.

I'm sitting on the floor of Roman's bedroom, clothes thrown around me haphazardly, as I try to make room in his dresser and closet for my stuff.

For a man who doesn't do anything but work he sure owns a lot of nonwork clothes. We are going to need another dresser. I stand, taking a few of my dress shirts to hang them in the closet, and yelp when I feel strong arms come around my waist.

I squeal, smacking Roman on the arm. "Jesus, you scared me. I wasn't expecting you back yet."

He eyes me curiously. "It's past midnight, Alex."

My gaze snaps to the clock on the nightstand. My eyebrows shoot up in surprise. "I must have lost track of time. I didn't realize it was so late already." I turn, wrapping my arms around his neck, and peck him on the lips. "How was your day?"

"Better now that I'm here." He nuzzles my jaw. "Sorry, I couldn't be there to direct the movers. I take it they were professional."

I nod. "They were, and they made the extra stops I needed too. Thank you for arranging all of that as well."

A megawatt smile lights up his face. "It was my pleasure." He looks around the room, eyebrows shooting up to his hairline in confusion. "What happened here?"

I blush, turning towards the mess. "I'm sorry, I know it's a mess." I run my hand through my hair, "I was trying to have all of my clothes and stuff put away before you got home. I just underestimated how many clothes you actually had. I think we are going to need another dresser."

"Say that again."

I frown. "We need another dresser?"

He smirks, shaking his head. "No, the other part."

"Sorry for the mess?"

He scoffs, leaning down and running his nose across mine. "No, where are we?" he whispers against my lips.

I think about it for several seconds before realization dawns on me. "Home?"

He beams. "Yes." His voice comes out husky, and the sound of it makes my dick twitch.

"Home. I'm home."

"Yes, you are. And I know just the way to celebrate." He waggles his eyebrows at me.

"Oh yeah, I bet you do." I squeal as he picks me up and tosses me onto the bed.

I sit up. "What about all the clothes and the mess?" I gesture around the room.

"We will get it tomorrow." I go to protest, but Roman removes his shirt, showing me those abs I love so much and all thoughts of unpacking fly out the window.

We can definitely deal with that tomorrow.

ALEX

Chapter Twelve

I yawn for what feels like the hundredth time before taking another sip of my double shot espresso.

Why did I let Roman keep me up so late last night?

Well, you weren't complaining at the time, were you?

I laugh out loud at my inner turmoil earning a few curious glances.

Lovely.

It's four-forty in the afternoon and I'm sitting outside Java Cha-cha, near campus, waiting for Randal, Roman's driver, to come pick me up. He says now that we are living together, I should be taking advantage of his driver.

I can't believe I am living with Roman. I never would have thought a one-night stand could turn into this.

I love him. I love him so much and I don't know how to tell him. We definitely did this whole relationship thing backwards. I mean who moves in with someone before they drop the L-word?

Right... That'd be me, ladies and gentlemen of the jury.

I have known for a while; it just hasn't ever felt like the right time to say the words out loud. I have come close during sex a few times but managed to stop myself before it was too late.

I'm nervous about how Roman will react to my declaration. It seems silly. I know he is the one who asked me to move in with him, but what if he isn't emotionally ready for my truth? You can want to be with someone physically and care about them without being truly, emotionally invested.

That's not the only reason I'm scared to tell him. Roman hasn't had a traditional upbringing. We don't talk about his family much but from what little I have gathered, his relationship with his dad is full of tough love, light on the love.

And I mean light like a feather.

In all of our time together, I have yet to meet him. Don't mistake me, I am not in any way, shape, or form in a hurry to meet daddy dearest. I just think it's kind of strange to be at this level in our relationship and to not have met the parents.

Although, nothing about our relationship has been typical this far. Anyways, I will tell him soon. Once the timing is right.

I take another sip of my drink as someone plops beside me on the bench. "Hey, what are you still doing here? I thought your classes were over a while ago?" Thomas, one of the people in my study group, says.

I shrug, turning towards him slightly. "They were. I was just in the library, trying to do some more studying."

"Right, finals are coming up. I need to do some more studying too. Are you nervous?"

I shake my head. "Not really, I do pretty well when it comes to testing. You?"

He hesitates, releasing a chuckle. "Oh, no. I flounder. I don't know what it is about timed testing that makes me panic, but I can go in being one-hundred-percent sure of the material and still blank out."

"I know what you mean. It's like having a dream where you're being chased but are unable to run away." I mock shiver.

He laughs. "Ah, I hate that. It's like your whole body is being weighed down with slime. You know they say you can't count in your dreams. I don't know what truth there is to that, but my friend did a course study on dreams for his final project and I was surprised by all the information he found."

I arch my brow. "Well, the next time I fall asleep I'll be sure to try and count."

He barks out a laugh before nudging me with his elbow. He leans back into the bench, crossing his ankles.

"You will have to let me know if it's true or not."

I go to respond, but a throat clearing has me snapping my gaze to the side. "Hey, Randal." I stand, grabbing my bag. "Thanks for picking me up."

"No problem, Mr. Pratt. Who is your friend?" He gives Thomas a once-over before turning his gaze back to me.

"Right, sorry. This is Thomas, Thomas this is Randal." I point between the two of them. Thomas extends his hand out to shake, but Randal doesn't take it, instead, he eyes it with distaste.

I frown at the blatant disrespect before turning to glance at Randal's face. He eventually reaches forward accepting the offered hand. I arch my eyebrow. "Is everything okay?"

"We need to get going, Roman is expecting you."

"Oh, right." I turn back to Thomas. "I will see you Monday?"

His eyes ping-pong between us. "Yup. Have a good weekend."

He obviously caught onto the eat shit vibe Randal was giving.

"You too," I mutter, waving.

The walk back to the car is quick, and Randal goes to open the door, but stops with a hand on the door handle. "You know, Mr. Giuliani is not a man who likes to share."

I'd think he was joking if it had not been for the seriousness of his tone. My eyebrows shoot up to my forehead in surprise.

"Excuse me? What is that supposed to mean?" I grit out.

He holds a hand up. "I apologize, I meant no offense, Alex. I'm just saying..." He looks away for a second before he zeroes back in on me. "Tread with caution, he can be very temperamental if he feels threatened."

He opens the door then. "Threatened? By Thomas?" I scoff. "He has nothing to worry about there." I slide onto the back seat.

He sighs. "Just remember what I said, Alex. I would hate to see anyone get hurt."

He shuts the door before I can even respond.

What the fuck just happened?

I walk into the front door and discard my bag and shoes. I can smell the fragrance of food wafting from the kitchen.

"Hey, Leta. It smells really good in here."

"Thank you. I'm making chicken parmesan with angel hair pasta."

My stomach growls loudly.

"I'm starving. I cannot wait to eat it."

She beams, pulling out a loaf of bread.

"Have you ever had Rosemary infused olive oil?"

That sounds delicious. My mouth waters at the thought.

"No."

She waves me over. "Here, we will call this, a sneak peek." She winks, breaking off a piece of the bread, dipping it in the oil, and passing it over to me.

I take a bite and groan as the flavors coat my tongue. "Holy crap. This is amazing. I'm going to need to borrow your recipe book," I say around a mouthful of bread.

She taps her temple. "No recipe books. I keep everything up here."

I smirk. "I wish I was this talented. I've never been good in the kitchen, though I can make a mean grilled cheese."

She scoffs. "That is not a meal."

"I take offense to that," I state, popping the last bite into my mouth, eyes closing of their own volition.

She rolls her eyes playfully. "I will get you right, sweet boy." She reaches forward and taps my cheek affectionately.

I smile then gesture behind me. "Have you seen Roman?"

"No, he was in his office with Sawyer." Again? I swear Sawyer is here every day.

"What does Sawyer do for Roman anyways?" I ask, and she gives me a curious look.

"He's Roman's personal security."

My eyebrows shoot up to my hairline.

"Security of what?"

Now it's her turn to look confused.

"Roman's security?"

I sit down at the barstool, leaning forward to get a better look at her.

"Wait, what? Roman has security?" I shake my head, surely I heard her wrong.

What would he need his own security team for?

"You didn't know?"

I shake my head with a little more force than necessary. "No."

"Forget I said anything." She waves me off, turning back to the stove.

"Wait, why would Roman need security?" I reach over to grab her arm, but she dodges me.

"It's not my place to say." Her face looks stricken and I cannot even begin to understand why.

What does that even mean? Why is everyone giving me answers like that today?

"But why would he—" The echoes of voices approaching stop me in my tracks as Roman and Sawyer step into the kitchen.

"Hey," he says, glancing between the two of us. "Is everything okay?"

"Yes," Leta and I say at the same time.

Great, because that doesn't make us look guilty. Roman arches his eyebrows at us. "Uh-huh."

"Sorry, I was hungry so Leta was just letting me sample dinner. It tastes delicious."

"I bet it does." He walks the rest of the way over to me, pecking me on the lips. "Her cooking is always superb." He rubs my arm slightly, kissing me once more before continuing. "I have to run out for a bit, there is an issue at one of my clubs that cannot be put off. Go ahead and eat. I will probably be gone for a while."

I nod, trying to hide my disappointment. "Alright."

He gives me another quick peck before turning and leaving, Sawyer in tow.

The food was delicious. I ate way too much, but it was worth it.

I'm currently lying in our bed with books scattered all around me, trying to wait up for Roman.

I really need to ask him about Sawyer. I tried to press Leta about it some more after he left but she was evasive. After my third attempt to get her to open up to me about it, I realized it was a lost cause, any information I was wanting would have to come straight from the source.

I sigh loudly, flopping back on the pillows, sending books, and notebooks crashing to the floor.

Damn it.

I slide out of the bed to retrieve my fallen items when I sense that I'm being watched. My head snaps up to see Roman leaning against the doorframe, hands shoved into his pockets and a stormy expression on his face.

"Hey." I stand, setting the books on my nightstand. "Are you okay?"

He doesn't respond, just stands there staring at me.

Staring through me.

"Roman?" I frown. "What's wrong?"

"Who the fuck was that guy you were flirting with today?" he seethes, taking a step into the room.

My eyebrows arch in confusion. "What guy?"

He takes another menacing step towards me, face flushed. "Don't play games with me. The one who was sitting with you when Randal picked you up today."

Realization dawns and I smile, trying to calm his anger. "Oh, Thomas, he is just some guy in one of my study groups." His eyes hold mine, searching.

"Some guy who seems to have no issues touching what belongs to me?"

I cock my head in confusion. "Touching? He didn't touch me."

"Really?" His expression is dark as he takes a few more slow steps towards me. "From what I understood, you were laughing and talking and he thought he could touch you." His voice is rising as his anger flares and I take a cautious step back, holding my hands up in a placating gesture.

"Listen, Randal didn't tell you the full story."

His eyebrows jump. "Randal didn't have to tell me anything. I heard it from security."

I stop retreating, staring up at him even more confused now than before.

"Your security team, how would they..." Realization dawns on me, and my spine snaps up as I straighten. "You have someone following me?" I practically sneer.

"It is for your own safety." He waves me off, as if he didn't just drop the biggest bomb on me.

"My safety? I'm safe. I don't need someone following me around, Roman!" I exclaim, anger fueling me.

He stands a little straighter. "Yes, you do, and that is not up for discussion."

I shake my head in bewilderment. "Roman, you cannot just decide that for me. I don't need a security guard. I only work, go to school, and hang out with Lacey. I am never around anything dangerous enough to need security."

An expression crosses his face and is gone too quickly for me to decipher its meaning.

"You will have security and that is final."

"It is not. You don't get to decide that."

"The fuck I don't!" he shouts, reaching forward, grabbing me by my biceps and pulling me towards him.

"You're being crazy," I hiss, wiggling from his grasp.

"You make me crazy! Tell me, why the fuck some prick thought he could touch you?"

I shake my head, looking him in the eyes so he can see the truth to my words.

"Roman, first off, he's straight. His girlfriend is in the study group with us." I count off on my fingers as I push on. "And second, he didn't touch me, at least not in the way you are thinking. He nudged me with his elbow and it was just for a split second."

He clenches his teeth so tight I can hear the bone pop in his jaw. "I should chop off his fucking arms."

"What the hell is the matter with you?" I push him against his chest but he doesn't move.

"You! You let someone touch you. No one touches you! No one but me! You are fucking mine!" He narrows his gaze, searching my expression. "You aren't to see him again."

"I may be yours, but I'm not your property, Roman." I push back from his hold and this time he lets me. "You can't tell me who I can and cannot see."

"Like fuck I can't. Anyone who thinks they can come in and take you from me is dead." He slices a hand through the air to prove his point.

I fold my arms across my chest, glaring at him. "Roman, listen to yourself. No one is going to take me away from you. No one but you if you keep saying crazy stuff like that. You need to calm down, this is ridiculous."

"Calm down. Calm down? I will not calm down, the nerve of that little prick, coming in and putting his hands on—"

"I love you, Roman."

He freezes, mouth opening and closing like a fish.

"What?" His voice is barely a whisper but I hear the trepidation.

"I love you; no one is going to take me from you, because I love you."

"You love me?"

"Yes, you idiot," I snap, poking him in the chest. "And now I'm mad at you because I didn't want to tell you like this." I wipe away a few tears before turning to go into the bathroom. I try to shut the door, but he catches it with his foot, pushing it open and staggering in behind me.

I plop down on the toilet seat, wiping my eyes with a tissue.

Fuck, I hate crying.

I'm not even crying because I'm sad. I'm crying because I'm *furious.*

How dare he! Coming in here with his stupid accusations and lack of trust.

"I'm sorry, baby. Please don't cry. I didn't mean to upset you. Fuck. I was just worried. I was told someone was getting close to you and I panicked. I don't want to lose you." He squats down in front of me, tilting my head to look at him.

He sighs. "I shouldn't have reacted like that. I just— There is no excuse, Alex. I panicked, okay. I don't have anything else to say other than that." He leans down, resting his head on my thighs.

"You have to trust me. Trust is the only way this is going to work between us." My lip wobbles and I bite it.

He lifts up looking me deep in the eyes, a sad smile crossing his lips. "My track record with trusting people isn't very successful."

"I'm not everyone else. I love you; I would never do anything to intentionally hurt you."

He shudders, leaning forward, resting his forehead against mine and I close my eyes.

"I don't know what I did to deserve you."

"I don't know, but you're pretty lucky."

He chuckles before kissing my eyelids, and then my nose.

"Very lucky." We sit like that for several seconds, Roman rubbing my back and placing soft kisses all over my face. "Forgive me?" he asks.

"I forgive you, just don't do that shit again." I poke him in the chest roughly. He cups his hand over mine where it now lays over his heart.

He shakes his head adamantly. "I won't."

"Come on, let's get to bed. It's late and I'm tired." I stand, stretching my arms over my head, trying to release the tension from my limbs.

Roman stands and lifts me up bridal style, carrying me to the bedroom and dropping me onto the bed.

He strips down to his boxers, climbing in beside me, and pulling up the covers.

He pulls my back flush against his front, wrapping his arm around my waist snugly. He kisses my temple softly, and murmurs, "Good night, baby."

"Good night, Roman." I hear his heavy breathing in my ear and as sleep overtakes me two things dawn on me at once. We never talked about him having security on me and he never said he loved me back.

ROMAN

Chapter Thirteen

It was a bad day. A bad day that turned into an even worse night. I feel like the line between my two worlds is slowly fading away, and soon enough they are going to crash into each other, but when that happens will there be any good left over?

What I am and what I always have been is just...dark. All I've ever known is blackness and rough edges.

How am I supposed to keep up this charade? Alex is starting to see my monster, see the hunter behind the mask. What will he do when he sees just how bad I am? Will he run?

No, I won't let him.

Besides, he won't run, he loves me.

Love.

Alex loves *me*.

My monster puffs his chest out with pride at the sentiment. I have never heard those words before in my thirty-two years of living. Only once has anyone told me they cared and the situation was very different than this one.

Hit, jab, swing, kick, choke.

I say those words over and over in my head. Or aloud? At this point, I don't know. My brain feels fuzzy and my vision's distorted around the edges.

I can feel the blood mixing with sweat as it runs into my eyes, making it even harder to see, but I don't quit. I can't ever quit, no matter how many times I'm forced to do this. No matter how much I wish it would stop.

"Keep going. He's almost down!" The shout comes from the crowd, but I know they aren't cheering for me. They are cheering against me.

A blow to my gut has me stumbling back. My stomach heaves and bile coats my tongue from the onslaught.

I want to give up, I want to stop this assault. I think about it for a second. But only for a second. I think about the peace of death. The peace of giving up and leaving this world. This fucked-up world that is full of nothing but pain.

Pain. It hurts, everything always hurts.

My thoughts morph to anger and now I'm mad. No, not mad, enraged. I think about the reason I'm even here, the people who have me here.

I focus on the rage, let it rush through my veins like venom. I can feel my pulse in my head. The thud, thud, thud, calming my nerves as a new peace settles over me.

Giuliani men don't fall.

Giuliani men cannot fall.

I inhale deeply, summoning all the strength I have left, and attack.

A roar leaves my lips but I don't hear it. I feel it, the vibrations of sound ricocheting around my chest before it courses up my throat and erupts around the ring.

Hit, jab, swing, kick, choke.

HIT! *I slam my fist into his nose.*

JAB! *My hand sails through the air, nailing him in his airway.*

SWING! *I cock my fist back once more, smashing him in the ribs with an uppercut.*

KICK! *My foot comes off the mat, sweeping his legs out from under him, as he hits the ground.*

CHOKE! *I fall down on top of him, wrapping my hands around his throat, squeezing.*

He beats down on my hands, trying to pull me off. His nails scratch along my arms, but I don't feel it. His body is squirming, hips bucking trying to throw me off, but I don't budge. I'm locked in. Focused.

TAP OUT! FUCKING TAP OUT!

He doesn't, he's too strong to. Tapping out means you're weak and when it comes to this you fight to the death or you're dubbed a pussy. The punishment from your family would be worse than death here. At least here you die with dignity.

Giuliani men aren't weak.

I should let him go; I should release him.

Giuliani men aren't weak.

I think about my grandfather's words as my grip around his throat tightens.

The guy's body goes lax and he stares at me. I stare back, watching the life leave his eyes.

Sadness consumes me for a moment and I let it. For just that moment, I say a silent apology to the God above, praying that he hears me. Praying that he will forgive me for this act. For all the other acts I have committed and will continue to commit.

"You can let go, it's over, son. You did it," my father whispers, pulling me off the other man.

No, not man.

Boy. Another boy. Like me.

My father drops to his knees in front of me, resting his hands on my shoulders, as he stares into my eyes.

"You did good, real good tonight. I'm proud of you, Roman."

He squeezes my shoulders and I wince, pain shooting through my body. I start to become aware of how badly I'm injured, the adrenaline is wavering and my limbs are screaming from the pain.

"Roman, I know this hurts. I know this is hard, but one day when you're in my position and you have your own son, I hope you think back on this moment. I hope you remember all the training, remember all the fighting, and how I set you up to be strong. To be undefeatable. I set you up to live, Roman." He stares at me, his eyes pinging back and forth between mine, looking so deep I think he can see my soul. "I hope you can understand that I do all of this because in my own fucked-up way, Roman, I do care for you and I don't want anything to happen to you. Our world is very dangerous, you never know who could be lurking, what friend may be a foe. So, I need you to be ready. I need you to always be ready." He leans in and kisses my forehead, unbothered by the sweat and blood.

He stands then, nodding to the doctor and trainer at the sideline before leaving. They come over and assess me, verifying my wrist is fractured and so are a couple of ribs.

I look back to the spot where I killed that boy, it now lies vacant and saturated with our body fluids.

I stare at it as they work on cleaning my wounds.

I'm fourteen years old. Fourteen years old and I already have a body count.

I shake away the memory and focus on Alex's sleeping face. I draw a line from his temple down to his cheek, soaking in his sweetness. Soaking in some of his warmth.

He loves me.

My heart beats wildly in my chest as I weigh in all of these feelings.

Love.

Is that what I'm feeling? It has to be love right?

I have no idea how we got here. I just know I'm glad we have. Alex gives me something that I never knew I could want or need. He is just so good. Too good.

I have to be more careful. I have to keep him safe. Loving me puts a bigger target on his back. One he doesn't even know is there.

I really need to tell him about the darker side of things, but not right now. That's just not an option. I can't risk losing him. I need him tied to me in every way first.

I'm so glad he moved in. At least here I don't have to worry as much about his safety. I think about my father's words once more.

"I do care for you and I don't want anything to happen to you."

Love means protecting what's yours at all costs. Love means keeping them safe no matter the means it takes to do it. Love means fighting for them or them fighting for you. Love means living. Love means family. Alex is the definition of love to me.

I love Alex.

I wrap my arms around him once more, leaning down and inhaling his scent, as the realization washes over me. I have to keep him safe. I have to protect him. No one can get to him, no one can take him away from me.

Alex is mine. He has been since the moment I saw him. It's time to make it official.

I have to convince him to marry me. The last step to making him completely mine.

ALEX

Chapter Fourteen

"I'm so nervous, I can't look." I hand my phone over to Lacey, as I take a bite of my peanut butter and chocolate sundae.

"You are worrying over nothing, babe. You got this. I know you do." She slides my phone back to me and I glare at it.

"I don't want to look," I whine, shoving more of the sundae into my mouth.

"Listen here, you're worrying over nothing. You studied your ass off, and you have been working towards this for years. You've got this. Now grab your phone and check your scores." She glares at me before taking a sip of her strawberry milkshake.

"Fine, but if this is passing, we are going out for celebratory drinks later."

"I wouldn't expect anything less." She smirks.

I grab my phone from the table, saying a silent prayer before hitting the University App. The results screen is taking forever to load and I strum my fingers impatiently.

"I PASSED!" I yell, jumping out of the booth and doing a quick victory dance.

"Woo-hoo! I told you!" Lacey says, getting up to join in on my dance.

"I can't believe I did it!" I screech, throwing my arms up into the air and doing a fist pump.

"I knew you could," Lacey says and I throw my arms around her squeezing tightly. "You are squeezing the life out of me!" she rasps.

"Sorry! I'm just really excited. I can't believe it." I grab my phone looking at the grades once more.

"Well, believe it, mister." She pokes me in the chest. "Now it's time to plan our evening out. What are we going to do? Where do you want to go?"

We sit back down and I ponder that thought for a moment. "I don't know. I want to dance; it's been way too long. I wonder if Roman will want to go, he hasn't been doing anything but work lately."

"Oh, how are things going with him?"

"Good, aside from the fact that he works twenty-four seven. The man never gets a break, even when he is home. He is always answering the phone or having to go in because of a situation. I didn't realize how stressful being an entrepreneur was. I'm glad I stuck to business management. I can handle running one place, but multiples? Hell no."

"Doesn't he have people under him who are supposed to take care of that stuff? Like managers?" She questions before sipping more of her milkshake.

I shrug. "I don't know how it all works. We don't really talk about his work stuff."

"You don't find that odd." She gives me a questioning look.

"Not really, I mean if you were constantly working would you want to talk about work once you had the chance to talk about something different?"

"I can see your point. I couldn't do that. That is one of the main reasons I want to do hair. I can make my own schedule, pick my clients, and work from wherever I please."

"I think I chose the wrong career," I mumble, finishing off my sundae.

She laughs. "See, I'm the real genius amongst us." Lacey wags her eyebrows at me.

"I'm so excited. All my hard work is paying off. I wish my mom was here to see it." I glance down at the table; wondering what my mom would think if she was here.

Lacey reaches across the table, grabs my hand, and I turn towards her.

"Your mom would be so proud of you. You know that right? I have no doubt that she is watching over you, smiling down at all that you are accomplishing."

My lip wobbles as I stifle a sob.

"I know, it just sucks. She should be here." I bite down on my lip.

"She is here, babe." Lacey touches her fingers to my chest. "She's always right here." Tears slide down my cheeks and I bat them away quickly.

"Way to get me all emotional. How does my face look? Red and splotchy?"

"You are perfect as always, my sweet little baby." She leans forward, pinching my cheeks.

"Ah, you are annoying." I swat her hands away.

She chuckles. "You love it."

I roll my eyes at her antics.

"Okay, Let's get out of here." We stand and make our way over to the door. "I'm going to head home and get ready. I'll ask Roman if he wants to go with us. His answer will be the deciding factor on where we end up going."

"Alright, sounds good to me."

We dispose of our trash and say our goodbyes before walking out of the ice cream shop.

I see Randal when I round the corner, but am surprised to find he's not alone.

They look to be having a heated conversation, so I approach with caution.

"Is everything okay, Randal?" Their heads both snap in my direction before Randal steps forward, almost blocking me from the other man? Or blocking him from me?

Just then, I see Sawyer and two other guys I don't recognize come into view, followed by a very pissed off looking Roman.

Oh shit.

"Thank you, Randal. We will take it from here. Can you please escort Alex home?" Randal nods, grabbing me and pulling me towards the car. I push back against his hold wanting to talk to Roman first.

"Roman?" He doesn't look my way. "Roman? Are you okay?" I try again.

He turns to look at me over his shoulder, the expression on his face is one I have never seen before. The man before me doesn't look like the Roman I know at all.

"Roman?" I say once more, voice breaking on the last syllable.

"Everything is fine. You go with Randal. I'll meet you at home soon, Alex."

"Are you sure? Because you seem—"

"I said go." His words crack like a whip and I freeze, taking in his stoney expression. "Randal, get Alex home." In a daze, I allow myself to be pulled and pushed into the car.

The last thing I see is Sawyer, roughly grabbing the man and shoving him into an alleyway.

ROMAN

Chapter Fifteen

I watch Alex get into the car, glad to see him gone and out of harm's way. For now at least.

I need to focus and I cannot do that with him here out in the open and not knowing he's safe. I follow Sawyer into the alley, trying to calm my racing heart. I've been on the edge of losing my fucking mind since I got the call about someone lurking around Alex.

Sawyer has the guy cuffed and down on his knees, execution style, when I make my way over to them. He's a little busted up from Sawyer already and yet he still sneers when he finally notices me.

"Is he ready to talk yet?" I ask Sawyer.

He shakes his head. "Not yet, but I was just getting started." He chuckles, sliding the silencer on his gun.

I turn back towards the beat-up sack of shit and squat down to meet his gaze. "We can do this the easy way or the hard way."

His face is coated in disgust. "What's the easy way?"

"I will kill you quickly," I say, holding my hand out for Sawyer to give me his gun.

A shudder racks his body and he releases a slight whimper.

Not so tough now, huh?

He doesn't say anything for far too long; so I make a show of cocking the hammer to prove a point.

"What do you want from me?" he asks, voice trembling as he speaks.

"Tell me why you are here."

"I was told to watch Alex, to keep my distance, and report back to my Capo with any information."

There are only three known Capos. One representing each family.

Jimmy is as loyal to me as they come, which only leaves two options. This is good information but not enough. I need to know who and why.

"And who is your Capo?" I run my gun across his temple for good measure.

He shakes his head slightly, trying to pull away.

"I can't tell you that." His voice is so quiet.

Like fuck you can't.

"What did your Capo want with Alex?" I bite out through clenched teeth.

"I don't know."

Okay then.

I aim the gun and pull the trigger. A guttural scream tears from his throat, as he leans forward, screaming out in pain.

"You crazy son of a bitch, you shot me in the fucking thigh!"

A manic laugh rips from my mouth, and I raise my gun to rest between his eyes.

"I'm about to shoot your fucking ear off if you don't tell me what the fuck I want to know." I move my gun to the side and give his ear a flick with the barrel for effect.

He says nothing, so I lean back and cock my gun once more.

"Okay! Okay!" he practically screams. "He wanted to know Alex's schedule. Wanted me to follow him to get to know his routine."

My anger rises with each word spilling past his lips and I fight the urge to just kill him and be done with this.

"How long have you been following him?" I start my pacing now, trying to calm myself the fuck down.

"Not long, only two days."

Two days.

Two motherfucking days this man has been following Alex and not one of my security personnel caught it? His personal fucking security team?

Oh, someone is going to fucking pay for that.

I turn to him then, seeing red.

"What did you report back?"

"I just went over what he does with his day. Said where he went to school, where he worked, if he drove, who he met up with, just that kind of stuff."

A manic chuckle leaves my lips. "Oh, yeah. Just that kind of stuff, huh?" I aim and shoot him in the shoulder.

Just because I fucking can.

The sounds of pain fill my ears and the scent of blood wafts in the air. I breathe it in and sigh. *Just another day in the life of Roman Giuliani.* He howls like a madman and I know we need to get this finished quickly before we bring any more unwanted attention our way.

"Why did you do that? I told you what you wanted to know!" he screams, agony morphing his features.

"You pissed me off," I state, once again pacing. "You followed him everywhere?"

He stares at me for several seconds. "Yes." I aim and pull the trigger, the bullet slamming into his other shoulder. I can see it enter and exit his body in a clean zing.

The animalistic moan that tears from his lips leaves me unfazed.

"Who is your Capo?" We stare at each other. I can see the sweat lingering on his brow, his color changing rapidly from a flushed red to a sea green. "Tell me who the fuck your Capo is!" I shout, voice ricocheting off the walls.

"Anthony Vinatelli." The words are whispered from his quivering lips.

Damn it, I shouldn't be surprised. Between the three crime families, the Morelli's are the ones who cause the most problems.

Fucking Morelli scum!

"Thank you for your help." I take a step back and cock my gun one last time, aim at his head and pull the trigger.

His blood coats the ground and wall like a painter's masterpiece.

I sigh, turning towards Sawyer. "Call the cleanup crew and get them to come down here and clean this mess up." I turn to walk back to my waiting car when I hear Sawyer's voice explode with fury from behind me.

I turn to see him, face red and a vein protruding from his forehead. It's pulsing so hard it looks like it will burst.

"What is it now?" I ask, knowing by his expression I am not going to like it.

"Boss, that was Jimmy, he just arrived at the ring to check-in and..." He hesitates and I can feel my hackles rising.

"And... What, Sawyer?" I demand, annoyed with his hesitancy.

"He said Giovanni is gone."

My heart pounds wildly in my chest. "Gone? What the fuck do you mean gone?"

He shakes his head. "I don't know, sir. Jimmy just arrived at the ring and said two of the guards were unconscious and the other two were dead. He went to the basement to check and Giovanni was just gone."

"Someone got him out?" I spit, fury rising. How is that possible? I had it heavily guarded.

"He doesn't know, Boss. He is waiting for me to review the camera footage."

I throw my hands up. "Where the fuck were all the other guards?" I sneer, jaw tight. One job. They had one fucking job.

Sawyer looks away from me, almost like he doesn't want to answer. "Most of them came here on your order, or they are at your home protecting Alex, Boss."

Fuck he's right. This is my fault. I let my panic for Alex's safety take over and I acted impulsively.

Fuck.

I freeze, all the color leaving my face as realization dawns on me. They were waiting on me to let my guard down. Giovanni told me something was coming, but how would he have known it'd be this?

A roar leaves my lips, and I slam my fist into the brick wall of the alley.

I hear the crunch and my knuckles scream from the impact. I pull my hand back and glance down, noting the blood that pools there. I can feel my body thrumming and I turn towards the now very dead body on the ground.

The diversion. The motherfucking bait. Time to pay a visit to Anthony Vinatelli, looks like I have a rat.

ALEX

Chapter Sixteen

I have been pacing the expanse of the living room for what feels like hours. The house is full of scary looking men, all in suits, and Roman still isn't back yet. I swear if someone doesn't tell me something soon I'm going to lose my shit.

I went ahead and canceled my evening plans with Lacey as soon as I got home. I lied to her. I have never lied to her before and I hate that I had to. But what was I supposed to say? 'Hey, so today after I left you, I went outside to the car and Randal was having a heated conversation with some guy, only to have Sawyer drag him away like a live-action James Bond movie?'

Yeah, I can see that going over well.

I sigh, picking up my pace, Roman's expression flashes through my mind once more. I have never seen him look like that before. He seemed ready to beat the crap out of someone or worse... I shiver at the thought.

Who was that man?

A hand lands on my shoulder pulling me from my thoughts and I jump slightly. I turn to face Leta's smiling face, and she hands me a cup of something.

"This is camomile tea. It will help calm your nerves."

She hands it over to me and I hold the cup, soaking in the warmth.

"Thank you." I sigh, taking a sip.

She squeezes my arms gently. "Have you eaten?"

I shake my head, my stomach feels sick at the thought of eating. "No."

She tsks. "That won't do. Come on, let's throw something together for you." She grabs my arm, pulling me towards the kitchen.

"You don't have to go to any trouble. I'm not really hungry anyways."

She glances back at me over her shoulder, a smirk playing on her lips. "Who said anything about me cooking? I was hoping you'd show me what's so special about your grilled cheese."

I can't help but smile at that. "I thought you said a grilled cheese wasn't a meal."

She waves me off, sitting down on the stool in the kitchen. "You say potato, I say tomato."

I can't help it. I laugh. Thick and hardy. "That isn't how the saying goes."

She shrugs, as if to say whatever and nods towards the cupboard behind me. "Now are you going to cook them or what?"

I hold my hands up in surrender. "Alright, alright. I'm on it." I grab the ingredients I need and get to work.

Two loaves of bread, a ton of cheese, and butter later, I have successfully fed every person inside of my house.

Who would have thought all these silent and brooding types would devour a whole platter of grilled cheese sandwiches. I gesture to the empty plate. "What did I tell you? Mean ass grilled cheese, right?"

"It was okay," she says, shoving the last bite into her mouth.

I arch my eyebrow. "Right, just okay."

She smirks. "Fine, it was good. It still doesn't qualify as a meal, but it can slide by as a snack."

I shake my head in amusement. "I guess we can just agree to disagree." I take her plate from her and start loading the dishwasher. Leta gets up from her stool, and we make quick work of cleaning up the kitchen.

"Thank you for the tea, and for making me eat, even though I had to cook," I say, rolling my eyes playfully.

She laughs, squeezing my cheek. "Of course. How are you feeling now?" She looks me over like a concerned mother and my heart warms a little at the thought.

"I would be better if I knew what was going on. No one will tell me anything." I fold my arms over my chest.

"I know it must have been really overwhelming for you to come home to a house full of people you didn't know. Not to mention, intimidating looking men. But, think of it like this; the fact that they aren't telling you anything is probably a good thing. It likely means there is nothing to tell. No news is good news." She leans over, giving me a gentle hug.

"Go upstairs, take a bath, and go to bed. It will make you feel better once you've relaxed some. By the time you wake up, Roman will be home. He will be able to answer any questions you have then. In the meantime, stop worrying too much over this." She ushers me out of the kitchen.

She is right. I know she's right. I just need to calm down and talk to Roman myself. With one last hug and a few parting words, I go upstairs.

I'm awoken to the sounds of water running in the bathroom.

I roll over and glance at the clock on the nightstand. It's three-forty-five in the morning. I guess Roman must just be getting home. I sit up, just as the bathroom door opens and out walks a towel-clad, dripping wet Roman.

Jesus, why is the man so damn gorgeous?

"Sorry, I didn't mean to wake you," he says, toweling off his damp hair. I gulp, greedily looking over every exposed piece of skin.

I rub my eyes. "No, it's fine. How are you?"

"I'm alright. It was a rough night," he sighs, dropping the towel to the floor. His eyes have dark smudges underneath them and he looks burnt out.

"Do you want to talk about it?" I bring my knees up to my chest, resting my chin on them.

"Not really, can we wait until after I get some sleep? I'm exhausted." He yawns as if on command.

"Oh, right. Of course. Whenever you want." I pull the covers back and gesture for him to join me. He doesn't even bother with clothes, just slides between the sheets.

"Thank you. We will talk tomorrow, okay? I just can't right now." He pulls my leg over his hip, placing a kiss against my temple.

"I understand." I lean in and kiss his cheek, snuggling into his side. "Get some rest. I love you."

He hums, his breathing already evening out with sleep. I close my eyes and rest my head on his chest.

The last thing I hear as I fall asleep is a whispered, "I love you too, Alex."

ROMAN

Chapter Seventeen

I'm a good liar. I'm an even better poker player.

So, I cannot fathom why right now, as I sit here staring at Alex, I am having a hard time coming up with an excuse for yesterday. I really don't want to lie. There is enough secrecy between us already, but what choice do I have?

It's not like I can tell him how I went and picked up Anthony, the man who has been having him followed, and pumped him for information before I beat him within an inch of his life now can I?

Fuck. That was a bust. Anthony was locked up tight. At least the Morelli's know they have a loyal Capo. Well, what's left of him anyways. I sigh, rubbing my forehead.

Alex can't know the truth yet. Him knowing will ruin everything. I need him tied to me first. I need the certainty that he can never leave me. Remember, I never claimed to be a good man. He will forgive me in the end. He will see I did this because I love him.

He has to.

This life won't be easy, but I have no doubt he can handle it. I will break him apart piece by piece and put him back together again. I will rebuild him, just like I was.

Alex is strong, he can get through anything.

Giuliani men aren't weak.

I stare across the table at Alex as he eats his breakfast.

He is so beautiful.

"Marry me." The words fly from my mouth before I even register that I have spoken.

Alex freezes, still as a statue, with his fork lifted into the air almost to his lips. His eyes are so big, he looks like a cartoon character. "What?" he whispers, as he sets his fork down.

"Marry me," I say with more conviction.

We stare at each other for several beats before he speaks again.

"Are you serious?" His voice cracks with the question.

"Yes." I nod my head.

"Roman, we can't get married." He shakes his head in exasperation.

I arch a brow at that. "Why not?" Why is he always so apprehensive?

"It's too soon."

I scoff, frustration rising to the surface. "No, it is not, we live together and we have been together for a while—"

"Six months is not a while, Roman," he cuts me off and I can feel my anger start to rise.

"Who cares how long it's been? When it's right, you know."

He sighs, folding his arms over his chest. "Roman, I'm not saying we can't get married eventually, but there is no hurry. Why can't we just enjoy each other for a little while longer? Get to know each other more."

"And why can't we just go ahead and get married, knowing that's the plan eventually anyway? You say this like we are some teenage kids trying to figure out how the world works. I'm thirty-two years old for fucks sake. I think I know what I want and when I want it, Alex."

My heart is pounding, my hands are sweaty, and my stomach is one giant knot.

"And that's awesome for you. I'm so glad that you have it all figured out, but I don't. I just graduated college. There are things I want to accomplish, like finding a job with my new degree."

"See, if we got married you wouldn't need to work. I have plenty of money, I could take care of you."

He shoots me a withering glare. "I didn't go to school for four years to have my boyfriend take care of me, Roman. I worked my ass off for my degree and I want to use it."

We will see about that, now won't we?

I wave him off. "Fine, so you get a job. Can you not have a job and still be married to me?"

"You are missing the point." He sighs in frustration.

I clench my teeth together, inhaling deeply through my nose.

"How? What am I missing? I just want a valid reason as to why we shouldn't get married right now."

"Because I'm not ready!" He practically shouts, throwing his hands up in the air.

"But why?" I counter.

"This is like déjà vu. We have been here before, this exact same setting just with a different question. You aren't going to bulldoze me into this, Roman. My answer is no."

Right, and that just pissed me the fuck off.

"Fine." I toss my napkin onto the table and stand to leave the dining room.

"Roman, wait, where are you going?" he asks as I walk towards the open doorway.

"Away from you."

He stands, dishes rattling under the sudden movement.

"Wow, that's just great. You want to get married, but you can't even have a conversation with me. We haven't even talked about yesterday, yet."

I turn back to him, hands balled into fists at my sides.

Breathe, Roman.

"No, because this isn't a conversation. This is a debate. I can feel a fight rising to the surface and I need to walk away before I do something I will regret." I go to turn, but stop dead in my tracks at his next words.

"Great, so just do what you do best, get mad and have a hissy fit," he spits out through clenched teeth.

What. The. Actual. Fuck?

I see red. Before I can stop myself I'm charging across the room. "The fuck did you just say?" I stalk towards him, and grab him by his biceps, walking him back several feet before slamming his back into the wall. *Roman, stop.* "A hissy fit?" I growl, pulling him forward slightly and slamming him back into the wall more forcefully.

Roman, let go.

"Roman, you're hurting me." His fragile voice breaks through the fog, but it does nothing to fizzle my anger.

"Good, think of this the next time you want to question my reasons for walking away." I let go before turning and stalking off.

I need to get as far away from him as possible before I do something I will regret.

***

Alex

I stand in shock, leaning against the wall in the dining room as I watch Roman's retreating form. When he is no longer in sight, my legs give out from underneath me, and I slide down the wall.

What just happened? How did that go so wrong?

I rub my arms and grimace at the soreness. Why did I provoke him like that? I replay the conversation in my head several times, and I realize how wrong I was to react the way that I did. After all, the man just asked me to marry him and I acted like he spit on me.

So yes, I know my reaction was distasteful, but fuck, what the hell did he expect? In all honesty, I hadn't even thought marriage was in the cards for us. Roman is such a guarded man I never expected him to want me in that deep, or hell, if he was even capable to let me in that deeply.

Fuck.

I swipe away a few tears as they glide down my cheeks. I feel like an asshole. I never meant to upset Roman, and now I have no idea how to go about fixing this.

Leta walks into the dining room then, immediately rushing to my side once she sees me.

"Are you okay?" she asks, concern etched on her features.

I manage a nod. "Yes, I'm fine, thank you."

She grabs my hands and helps me stand. "What happened?"

My lip quivers before I can control it.

"We had a fight?" A sob tears from my throat. "Oh, I think I messed up."

"Shush, shush, come sit." She pulls me to my abandoned chair and sits next to me. "Tell me what happened."

"It's so fucked up." I sigh, taking several calming breaths before unloading on her. I tell her everything. From him coming home very late last night and us not talking about the events of the day, to everything else leading up to the fight we just had.

She stays quiet as she listens, rubbing my arm soothingly. When I'm finally done, I feel even more emotional than I had moments before. I slump forward and rest my head in my hands, elbows braced on my thighs for support.

"Oh, sweetie." She tilts her head to the side, lost in thought. "Roman is a complicated man, but he does care so very deeply for you, that I do know."

"I hope so," I say, rubbing away a few more tears.

"I know so. I have never seen him with anyone the way he is with you. It's good to see him finally open up to someone."

My heart flutters at her words and I smile momentarily before sadness washes over me once more. "I told him no." I sigh in defeat.

"That's okay, you're allowed to not be ready. Maybe it's not the right time for marriage. It doesn't mean you can't still be together."

I bite down on my lip contemplating my next words.

"But I think it was the wrong answer."

"For you or for him?" she says curiously. I don't have an answer.

She nods, crossing her ankles and leaning back into the seat. "How do you feel now?"

I rub my temples. "I don't know. Confused? He had a lot of points that made sense." I contemplate my next thought. "Then he did a lot of shit that wasn't okay either... I don't know, with Roman it's always his way or no way."

"That sounds like Roman. He's not used to being challenged." She shakes her head in exasperation. "You aren't wrong to feel the way you feel though, he was out of line."

Yes, he was, but so was I.

"What if I said no for all the wrong reasons? I mean. I love him. I do want to be with him. He is so important to me." I sigh, looking up to meet her gaze. "What do I do?"

She pursed her lips as if in thought. "What is your heart telling you?"

"I don't know. My heart and brain are warring right now and I'm unsure of who the winner will be," I say jokingly, but it falls flat. I really have no idea where to go from here.

"Well, maybe you need to listen a little closer." She taps my heart. "You will figure it out, just breathe and listen." She stands, squeezing my hands before walking away.

This woman and her riddles. What am I listening for? A sign? My heart is pretty quiet right now, so I glance around the dining room, looking for a clue. *Come on? What should I do? Universe, I will take any sign you want to give me right now.*

I think about marriage. Think about being married to Roman. A smile grazes my lips at the thought.

Husband; Mr. Alex Giuliani.

Oh yeah, I like that a lot. Marriage... it all seems so ridiculous. *What is marriage?* The union of two people. Why do people get married? Because they love each other.

I snort at that.

Love.

I love Roman, sure. I love him deeply, madly, unbelievably. Too bad he doesn't feel that way.

Why would he want to marry me if...

Wait?

'I love you too, Alex.'

The thought slams into me like a car hitting a tree at sixty miles per hour. He told me he loves me. I jump from my seat, staring around the room once more.

Thank you, kismet.

Roman loves me.

I beam, throwing a fist up in the air like Rocky when he beat Apollo. I feel like I just won the biggest victory. Then all at once, the world comes crashing down once more because fuck; he told me he loved me and I shit all over his proposal. My heart drops at the realization.

Oh no... No no no!

I practically run from the dining room in search of him.

I have to find him. I have to fix this.

ALEX

Chapter Eighteen

I sit on the edge of our bed, anxiety taking over every nerve in my body. I can't find Roman anywhere. I've looked over every inch of the house but he's not here.

I grab my phone and shoot him a quick text hoping he will respond that way.

Me: Did you leave?

I stare at the screen willing him to open the message but it remains on sent.

Fuck.

I flop back onto the bed. I wonder where he went, what he is doing?

Who is he with?

I stop that train of thought before it turns into something it shouldn't. Roman would never cheat on me. I grab my phone and send him another text.

Me: I'm so sorry for what happened. I really want to talk to you. Please come home. I love you.

I hit the send button and toss the phone onto my nightstand. I sigh, and turn onto my side, burying my nose in Roman's pillow. The smell of him lulls me into a dreamless sleep.

A knock on the door rouses me. "Alex? It's Leta. Can I come in?"

I rush to the door, pulling it open, ushering her inside. "Is everything okay? Have you talked to Roman?" I ask quickly.

"I did." She nods her head before walking further into the room.

Ah, details, woman.

I wring my hands together in worry. "Well, what did he say? Is he home?"

She shakes her head, voice stern. "He was home but he left. We had a meaningful conversation, he needed to hear some things."

"So why did he leave? Is he still pissed off?" I ask, confusion and hurt evident in my tone.

"He's not mad, he's upset with himself about what happened. In fact, he sent me here to give you this." She smiles warmly, handing me a sealed envelope.

My heart pounds wildly in my chest when I take the card. I stare down the elegant scroll of my name on the outside before turning it over and opening it.

> *Alex,*
> *I cannot apologize enough for what happened this morning. Will you let me make it up to you? I'll have a car ready to pick you up at five.*
> *I can't wait to see you.*
> *Love, Roman*

I tuck the note away and glance up, just as Leta comes strolling back in holding a garment bag.

"Well, isn't this fancy?" I smirk, reading the Armani logo on the bag.

Wow.

"Go get ready." She shoos me in the direction of the bathroom. "You need to shower and get dressed. Time is wasting." She practically pushes me through the open door.

"Leta, can I at least get some underwear?

Several beats later she comes back into the bathroom, tossing some boxers on the sink. "There, now get ready." She shuts the door behind her.

Alright, feisty, little lady. Guess it's time to get ready.

An hour later, I am dressed in a cream-colored suit and black loafers. My hair is styled neatly, the longer strands falling slightly across my forehead.

Leta sits in the armchair by the bed beaming at me when I do a slow spin for her.

"What do you think?" I ask, adjusting my collar.

"You are perfect." The smile that lights up her face is breathtaking and I can't help but smile back.

"Thank you," I mutter shyly. "Now, can you tell me what I'm supposed to be doing in this suit?"

She gives my cheeks a squeeze before dropping her hands and tugging me in the direction of the door.

"Nope," she says with a mischievous glint in her eye. "But Randal is downstairs waiting for you. He will take you to where you need to go."

How freaking mysterious.

I poke my lip out. "That's just mean, you know."

"You will love it. Trust me."

I huff and head down the stairs. As expected, Randal is waiting outside with the car and I hop in.

"Randal? Any chance you can tell me where we are going?" I ask, buckling up my seat belt.

"Not likely."

"I figured you'd say that." I sigh and lean back against the seat listening to the lyrics of *Chains* by Nick Jonas as it thrums through the speakers.

My foot is bouncing, and I have to stop myself from gnawing on my fingernail.

I'm anxious.

I don't like surprises; they tend to bring on more nerves than excitement. I take a few calming breaths and focus on the music. We don't drive for too long, and we pull up to a small cottage.

I stare at it in confusion. "Who lives here?" I ask Randal when he opens the door for me. He doesn't answer, so I try again. "Well, what is this place?"

I scan the area and take in the big trees and blooming flowers surrounding the house. This place is stunning.

Randal clears his throat before pointing to a stone walkway. "Just follow that path."

I arch my eyebrow at him. "Will I finally see Roman?"

He just stares on before a smile breaks across his features. "Good luck."

Good luck?

I let out an exaggerated sigh and make my way over to the path where the large trees are surrounding it. It has a secret garden vibe and I adore it. It's so peaceful here. I take in the multicolored flowers, the scent of daffodils, and the sounds of chirping birds. A peaceful calm settles over me.

It's breathtaking.

I glance up through the opening of the trees and notice the sky is an array of purples and pinks as the sun sets.

Beautiful.

I make a slow circle, taking it all in before strolling the rest of the way down the path. Once I reach the end, I gasp at the sight awaiting me.

Roman.

Roman in a navy-blue suit, looking delicious.

Roman in the middle of a field with wildflowers. In a daze, I close the distance between us.

"Hi," I whisper once he's in touching distance.

"Hey, baby." He stares down at me with so much love showing behind those blue eyes. He presses a light kiss against my lips, then rests his forehead against mine. "I'm so sorry."

"Me too." I pull back to look deep into his eyes. "I wanted to find you almost as soon as you left. I shouldn't have reacted like I did."

"No." He shakes his head. "It was me. I should have gone about all of that differently. I just lose my mind when it comes to you. I want you so badly. I'm not used to feeling like this." He rubs his hand over his chest.

"I feel it too. With you. I feel it." A tear slides down my cheek and he wipes it away before cupping my face.

"Alex, I know we have a lot to talk about and I know we haven't been together long. But the way I feel about you..." He sighs, grasping my hands tightly. "I know that it's not going to change. I love you. I can't imagine not being with you. You broke me wide open and I need you in my life."

He stares down into my eyes, mask gone and so open and vulnerable.

"I want to give you the world. I want to grow old with you. Not only spend my life with you, but share it with you. I want to be everything you need. Let me show you how strong we are. How good we can be together." He pulls a box out of his pocket and drops down to one knee.

I gasp, hands cupping my mouth in surprise and sheer awe.

"Roman..." I whisper, heart slamming painfully against my ribs.

"Alexander, from the moment I laid eyes on you, you changed something inside of me. You give me something that I have never had before. I love you so much. Please, marry me. Be my husband." His face is flush and his expression is so open, so hopeful.

I stare into those big blue eyes that I love so much and smile. Happy tears well in my eyes and I eagerly nod. "Yes, Roman. I will marry you."

"Thank fuck," he whispers, a wide smile breaking across his face.

He stands, sliding the beautiful, diamond encrusted, white gold ring onto my finger before pressing his mouth against mine. The kiss is sweet and sensual, lighting up every nerve ending in my body. I groan into his mouth and his tongue peeks out, sliding against my closed lips. He wraps his arms around me pulling me closer, lifting me slightly so my feet are dangling. I wrap my arms around his neck, enjoying the feel of him.

I have no idea how long we kiss. How long we stand there, wrapped up in each other. I just know that, in this moment, I never want him to let me go.

We eventually separate and Roman whispers, "I love you," against my lips.

"I love you too."

I glance down to admire my ring just as my stomach rumbles, effectively ruining the moment.

"Are you hungry?" he asks with a chuckle.

"Starving."

"Let's go, I have dinner reservations." He slides his hand to the small of my back and guides me back towards the path.

"That sounds good." I glance around one last time at the field of flowers, soaking in the last bit of beauty this moment has to offer.

Dinner was on the rooftop of one of the hotels Roman owns. Our table was set up perfectly with rose petals and candles. It was beautiful and elegant and I adored the view of the strip.

I rub my hand over my full belly and stare out at the lights. "I love it up here. We should come here more often. If I had known this was an option, I'd have asked to have done this ages ago," I say with a hint of sarcasm.

"Then this time wouldn't have been as special." He grabs my hand and kisses my knuckles. "Do you want any dessert?"

I shake my head, groaning at my full stomach. "No way, I don't think I can eat anything else."

His face turns dark when he says, "Nothing?" Eyes scanning the expanse of my body.

Fuck me. Never too full for that, sir.

"Are you trying to seduce me, Mr. Giuliani?" I rasp out, voice suddenly husky.

"I sure am, Mr. soon-to-be Giuliani." My heart picks up at his words. "Oh, you like that, huh? Like knowing you'll have my last name soon?"

I nod, licking my lips, watching his eyes glaze over with lust. "Come on," he says, tugging me from the table to the doors.

We can barely keep our hands off of each other once we are in the elevator. Kissing, sucking, biting every inch of exposed flesh.

When the elevator dings, Roman barely stops kissing me to pull me down the hall to our room. After fumbling with the key card, he finally manages to get the door open. Once inside he's on me again, practically tearing my suit off of me.

"Hey, slow down. I like this suit," I manage to say around a whimper as he kisses down my jaw.

"I'll buy you another one," he rasps against my throat, causing shivers to erupt across my skin.

"Fuck, Roman. You make me so fucking hard."

He grins, stripping me of the rest of my clothes and pushing me back onto the bed. He makes quick work of his own clothes before joining me. Our teeth clash together when we kiss but it doesn't matter. It's rushed, we are eager and desperate to be together.

Roman uses the lube to get me ready before sliding inside of me and we both gasp at the sensations, staring into each other's eyes. He doesn't go fast now though. He slows down, moving leisurely inside of me. Sighing, he brushes his lips over mine softly.

"I love you, Alex."

"I love you too," I whisper back.

The sex is slow and gentle, nothing like we usually do and I love everything about it. I drink him in, memorizing the way he looks as he makes love to me. The way his shoulders flex under my hands, how the sweat rolls down his hairline to the base of his neck, the way his lips part as the pleasure consumes him.

This man is breathtaking, and making love to him like this is everything.

He grabs both of my hands, bringing them above my head and tangling our fingers together. I can feel his finger running over the band of my ring and a groan erupts from his throat as he stares into my eyes.

"Mine," he growls out.

It's not a question, and we both know it.

Because I am his, completely one-hundred percent owned by Roman Giuliani.

ROMAN

Chapter Nineteen

The sun shines through the curtains, highlighting the golden strands of Alex's hair. I can't believe he agreed to marry me last night.

After our fight, I sat in my car in the garage for almost an hour before finally calming down enough to go back inside. I immediately wanted to go to Alex, but Leta caught me before I had a chance to go upstairs.

To say I got my ass handed to me would be an understatement. Which is why I came to the conclusion that if I wanted Alex to say yes to my proposal, I needed to make a grand gesture.

Best decision ever.

I can't take all the credit because I didn't do it all on my own. Leta gave me the idea of what to do, and Sawyer asked his mother about letting me use her garden.

Thank fuck for them. Now, here we are, engaged. One step closer to the finale.

Mine.

My phone vibrates from the nightstand and I jump out of bed, grab it, and walk into the living area so I don't disturb Alex.

"Sawyer?" I say upon answering.

"Boss, I just wanted to let you know, I have confirmed your appointments for today."

"Excellent. Do you have Alex's documents and everything available for our trip?"

"I do." Amazing. I can't wait to surprise him with a honeymoon.

"Perfect. I will grab them from you shortly," I say before hanging up. The ending is so close I can practically taste it.

I turn to go back to bed but stop when I see Alex leaning against the doorframe.

"Good morning. How did you sleep?" I ask, smiling at his bed head.

"Really well. How about you?" he asks, walking over to me and wrapping his arms around my waist.

"Good." I lean down and kiss his head, nuzzling him.

"Are you hungry?"

"I am. Room service?" he asks, looking up at me with pleading eyes.

I chuckle, shaking my head. "I wanted to take you out for breakfast. I have a few plans for the day." He's silent for several beats. "What do I need documents for?" He eyes me with curiosity.

"Were you eavesdropping?" I ask, poking him on the nose.

He bats my hand away, releasing a light chuckle. "I heard my name and got curious."

"Right."

"Well, tell me," he urges, pushing me back to sit on the couch. I comply, pulling him with me.

"It's a surprise."

He sits back on my thighs, glaring at me.

"No, no more surprises. I'm all surprised out." He crosses his arms over his chest, his lip pursed in a pout. He is so adorable.

"Just a few more."

"Roman," he groans, and I lean forward to snag his lip between my teeth. I suck on it hard before releasing it with a pop.

"What can I say? I'm just full of surprises."

"What is it, Roman?"

"Do you really want to know?"

"Yes." He nods enthusiastically.

I sigh. "Fine. I want to get tattoos."

"A tattoo?" His face scrunches in confusion.

"Yes, I was thinking about getting your name written here." I tap my hand over my heart. "I thought maybe you would want to get something also?"

I phrase it like a question, but it's not one. I know he will get my name on him. My brand.

"I don't want your name on my chest."

"Well, you can get my name anywhere. It doesn't have to be on your chest."

"I don't know, Roman," he whispers, biting down on his bottom lip.

My sweet, pouty lip.

I push him to stand before following suit and smacking a kiss to his lips. "Trust me. It will be fine. Now, let's go get ready. We have a big day ahead of us and we need to get started."

He wants to argue. I can tell by his expression. He doesn't though. He releases a deep sigh and turns to head to the bathroom.

He's brushing his teeth when I follow him a few moments later, I lean against the doorframe watching him. He is in nothing but my crinkled, button up shirt from last night and I don't think I have ever been so hard in my life. He rinses and spits before turning back to me.

"So, big day? What all do you have planned?" I don't answer. I stalk towards him, grab him by the waist, and set him on the counter.

This isn't like last night.

This is primal.

I suck on his tongue and lick into his mouth with hungry strokes. He is right here. In my space, wearing my shirt, and wearing my ring. Soon enough, he will have my mark.

Fuck.

My only thoughts are to *claim.* "This is going to be hard and quick, baby. I need you too bad right now."

"Yes, Roman. Please," he begs.

Thank fuck.

I groan at the sight of him laid open and bare for more when he places his feet on the edge of the countertop and spreads his knees wide.

"Don't you move. Stay just like this." I crouch down and lean forward, licking a wet strip on his asshole, getting it nice and wet. There is no time for prep. I need to get inside of him more than I need my next breath. I stand back up and shove my boxers down before reaching past Alex to grab the lotion off the counter. I smother it all over my dick, then drag his legs over my elbows. Lining up against him, I push inside.

Heaven.

This will be the only heaven I ever know. I groan and look down, seeing the spot where we are joined together.

"You look so good stretched around my dick. Your hungry little hole is so full. I'm going to fuck you now, baby. Nice and hard. Just how you like it." I hook my arms around his thighs, splaying him even more open for me, then pull almost all the way out before slamming home again.

I will never understand how I lived so long without this feeling.

He groans loudly, and I watch his eyes close as his body starts to quake. He reaches forward to grab his dick, but I smack his hand away. "No! You come when I say you can." He whines, back arching, as his head falls back onto the mirror. He's folded practically in half on the counter, but he looks completely blissed out.

"Roman, please, please let me come."

"You want me to touch you, baby?" I ask, leaning forward and running my tongue down the valley of his chest.

"Yes! Please, PLEASE!" He gets louder with each thrust and I fight not to give in. Fuck, he begs so goddamn pretty.

My thrusts are picking up and I'm barely leaving his body now, pistoning in and out, my orgasm so close I can taste it. I reach out, grasping Alex's dick, pumping it twice before he groans and convulses, cum shooting from the tip, coating his stomach and chest. The sight and the sounds he's making, along with the death grip he has on my cock are enough to have me soaring.

I flood his body with my release, groaning loudly as the whole world shifts. And for that moment nothing else exists besides us. I sit still, blissed out, chest heaving from exertion. It's always just so good with him. I will never get enough.

I release his legs, sliding out of him, I help him readjust on the counter. He groans, stretching out his legs, leaning forward slightly to kiss me.

"I love you." I feel his whispered declaration against my lips and my monster sighs with contentment.

"I love you too."

"I cannot believe I let you talk me into this," Alex says through gritted teeth as the tattoo gun glides over his skin.

"It's not that bad." I just got mine done and am currently standing in front of the mirror admiring it.

The artist did a good job. Alexander is written in cursive, straight across my pec. I nod to the guy, letting him know that I approve; he cleans and covers it before I re-button my shirt.

Alex decided to get my name, as I knew he would, below his left collarbone. He also wanted something with more detail. I can tell he is strongly regretting that decision. "Almost done," the artist says.

"You're doing really well for your first time," I tell him, smirking at his scowl.

"Whatever, just know I'm never doing anything like this again," he practically growls at me.

It takes great effort but I manage to suppress the chuckle wanting to escape.

Fifteen minutes later, Alex is admiring his tattoo and I'm standing behind him, arms locked around his waist as we stare at it together. The tattoo is an infinity symbol and in the middle, connecting the two ends together is my name.

Seeing my name on him does things to me. I love seeing my mark on him in general, but knowing this is permanent and cannot be removed changes the game.

Like it snapped something inside of me; he is fucking *mine.*

Always mine.

"It looks really good," he says to the girl. "Thank you so much for doing it." He turns to her, offering a radiant smile. She cleans and wraps it for him, going over all the cleaning instructions.

Once we are outside I turn towards him, stomach heaving with nerves. "You want to see Elvis?"

"What, where?" He glances around, expecting to see him on the street, but I nod in the direction of the chapel on the corner. He follows my gaze and his eyebrows shoot up in confusion. "You want to go to a chapel?"

"Yes." I nod, reading his expression carefully.

"Why?"

"I thought that'd be obvious." It doesn't take long before realization hits.

"Roman, you cannot be serious right now."

"Oh, I'm serious. Seriously in love with you. Now put me out of my misery and marry me already."

I start, very badly, singing the lyrics to Elvis, *I want you, I need you, I love you,* all while holding Alex against me, and rocking him back and forth slightly.

He's giggling, playfully shoving me off, but I know he loves this. *He wants this. He wants me.*

"Come on, marry me! Become my husband right now, officially. Become Mr. Giuliani, please." I grab his hand, bringing it up to my lips, kissing his palm, and resting it over my heart where I just got his name tattooed. I look deep into his eyes, finding that connection, hooking him in the way I do so he won't tell me no.

So he can't tell me no.

"Fine. Yes, fine. Let's get married by Elvis."

I smile triumphantly, holding my hand out for him to grab. "Come on."

He stops suddenly, turning towards me with a serious face. "Roman, I don't have a ring for you."

"I have one. I bought ours together as a set. They match, my band is thicker than yours, though." I give him a wink.

He smiles and we walk the rest of the way to the chapel.

"So, is this why you needed my documents?"

"Yes."

"Well, you thought of everything, now didn't you." He chuckles, shaking his head in astonishment.

"What can I say? I wanted you to be mine."

Nothing has ever been truer than that.

"I now pronounce you Mr. and Mr. Giuliani, you may kiss the groom," Elvis tells us and I smash my lips to his. I fucking did it. I married him.

MINE.

My heart thrums in my chest as I look into his smiling face. Fuck, I love him so much. *No one will ever take him away from me.*

I'm grinning so hard, I can feel the tingle in my cheeks. This is everything I've been dreaming about. We sign our marriage certificate and Alex is giggling like a schoolgirl. I sigh happily. In this moment I don't feel like the big, bad, mafia motherfucker that I am.

I feel normal, happy. "Okay, last surprise. I promise," I say, pulling him to the car where Randal is waiting.

"Congratulations," he says, and we both nod enthusiastically, thanking him.

"No more surprises. You have done enough."

I chuckle, shaking my head. "I promise this is the last one."

He sighs loudly, giving me the evil eye. "Fine, husband."

Oh yeah. I like that.

"How about a honeymoon?" I ask, nipping at his chin.

"Are you serious?" he squeaks.

"How do you feel about skiing?"

"I could definitely ski."

"In Switzerland."

He squeals, launching himself at me. "I love you so much!"

He loves me. My husband loves me. And all is right in the world.

For now...

PART THREE

THE STRANGER I MARRIED

Chapter Twenty

"God, this is delicious. It has been too long since we ate here last," Lacey says, shoving another piece of sushi into her mouth.

"It hasn't been that long," I mutter around a mouthful.

She nods her head. "Think again, mister. It has been at least a month."

My face scrunches in confusion. "Has it really been that long?"

"Yes, my sweet baby, you have been so wrapped up in your honey dearest, you've been missing our date nights."

I hate that she's right. I have been so engrossed in my time with Roman. They call this the honeymoon phase for a reason after all.

"Hey, you still see me."

"Work doesn't count," she argues, poking me with her chopsticks.

"I see you more than that." I rub the sore spot left from her jab.

"Not lately." She sighs. "I miss you, Alex. I know you're all graduated and married now, but don't forget about us little people." Her voice holds humor, but I can see the sadness hidden behind her gaze.

I reach across the table, snagging her hand and lacing our fingers together.

"None of that. Forgetting about you is literally impossible. And I'm sorry, I haven't been the greatest friend lately, it's just Roman..." I sigh, trying to gather my words.

"What about Roman?"

How do I even begin to explain how he's been lately?

"I don't know, he has just been really off?" I groan and rub my hand over my forehead. "I can't explain it. The few weeks after our honeymoon were incredible. He was home a lot more. He seemed lighter somehow."

I bite down on my lip. Memories of hot tub sex and couch cuddles dancing behind my closed eyes.

"He went to work one night; said there was some sort of emergency that no one could handle but him." I run my finger over the expanse of the table. "When he got home it was almost like a different man took over his body. He's more frustrated, really short-tempered. I try to talk to him and he just brushes me off, saying it's work stuff. But I can't shake the feeling that something is really wrong. He also started acting like he's afraid of me going anywhere." I shrug. "I guess he's just being overprotective."

"I don't like the sound of that." She looks worried when she says, "Have you talked to your bodyguard?"

I shake my head, crossing my arms over my chest. I hate having a bodyguard. Not only is it pointless because I have literally no enemies, but I can't stand the lack of freedom I once knew.

"Please, as if they'd tell me anything. All of Roman's staff is a hundred percent devoted to him. Trying to get them to dish out any information is like pulling teeth. Believe me, I have tried."

"Right, so they are his minions and all that." She waves her hand, face scrunched up in thought. "Have you ever considered snooping?"

Now, there's a thought. I can't say that it hasn't crossed my mind, but I also feel like it's a breach of trust.

I sigh. "I don't need to snoop on Roman. I trust him, Lacey. I just want him to open up more and talk to me."

"You can trust him and still be curious."

"You know what they say about curiosity."

She sighs, waving me off. "Fine, whatever. I won't say anything else about it. I'll be Switzerland." She takes a swig of her wine. "Speaking of Switzerland, did you ever get those pictures printed from your honeymoon?"

Damn, I meant to bring those with me and I completely forgot.

"I did, and they came out so good. You need to come over and see them. I got a few blown up on canvases to hang around the mansion. Ah, the snowstorm one wa—"

"Alex, we have to go, right now."

I twist to look at Liam, my guard, in confusion. "But I'm not done eating." I gesture to the table of food.

"We need to go. Now," he states more firmly, pulling me from my chair.

"What do you mean? Is Roman okay?"

Panic takes over when I take in his slightly flushed appearance.

"We need to go," he says again with even more force.

I turn back to Lacey, but she's already shooing me off with a worried expression.

"Go. Just text me later and let me know you're okay."

I grab my wallet, pull out a few twenties, and toss them onto the table.

"Thanks, sorry about this. I will call you as soon as I can." I lean over, planting a kiss on her cheek before following Liam out of the restaurant.

Once we are through the double doors, Liam grabs my arm, practically yanking me down the sidewalk.

"Liam, what's going on?" I stumble, trying to keep up with his pace.

"Everything is being handled."

So why am I being dragged down the street?

"Okay, that's good, but what happen—" A loud screeching sound cuts me off and I turn just in time to see a black van pull up beside us.

Who is that?

Liam grabs me, shoving me behind him while simultaneously whipping out a gun from his holster.

What the fuck?

My heart pounds wildly in my chest and I look around frantically for help. Five masked men jump from the van with large weapons and I can feel the bile rise in my throat. I'm going to die.

"Alex, run."

I stand stock-still, frozen in place. A million scenarios playing in my head.

"What?" I sputter, pulse pounding in my ears.

"RUN! GO, ALEX, NOW!" Liam barks, pushing me towards the left.

I take off, my feet pounding on the asphalt as I run in the direction of the car. Yes, Randal, he can help.

My arms feel like noodles, and my thighs burn, but I don't slow down. I can't slow down.

I hear the gunshots behind me and turn to see Liam fall to the pavement.

Jesus, please be okay.

I can feel my eyes filling with tears and I blink several times to rid them.

So close.

Almost.

Thirty more feet...

You can do this.

Twenty more feet...

Just a little bit more.

Ten more feet...

I dive into the car, slamming the door shut behind me. "Randal, we have to go right now, and we have to call the police!" I exclaim, staring out the window.

"Now, now, little bird. No need for all of that."

A gasp tears from my throat and I whip around, coming face-to face with a man I've never seen before. Gray hair, crooked nose, and lips tilted in a sneer. He looks sickly and I can't help the shiver that racks my body when I notice the gun against Randal's temple.

"Who are you?" I whisper, back now firmly planted against the seat.

"I see my nephew didn't get around to telling you about me." He sighs and plasters a big smile on his face. "That's okay, you and I will have plenty of time to talk later." He waves noncommittally. I haven't grasped what is going on yet, and my thoughts are scrambled when I glance at the door handle. On instinct I reach out and grab it, wanting to get out of here and to safety as quickly as possible, only to have the sound of the gun cocking stop me in my tracks.

"I wouldn't do that if I were you. You wouldn't want me to put a bullet in Randal here, now would you?"

My lip trembles and I shake my head vehemently.

"What do you want?" My voice comes out shaky, and that causes him to smile. Suddenly, he brings the gun up and comes down hard, nailing Randal on the head with the end.

I shriek as Randal slumps forward, and I grab the door handle, prepared to jump out when he whips the gun in my direction.

"Let's not do anything rash, huh? He's just resting. He will be fine in about thirty minutes." He steps out of the car and comes around to open the door on my side.

Tears slide down my cheeks, and my voice quivers when I ask again, "Who are you, and what do you want?"

"Now, isn't that the question of the century? I want a lot of things, Alex. Unfortunately, that's not how the world works now is it?" He sighs, looking off into the distance for a second before pulling something out of his jacket.

A syringe.

HELL NO!

I shriek and slide across the back seat trying to get away from him, but he's faster. He grabs me by my ankle, pulling me back towards him. I try to struggle but halt instantly when I feel the cool metal of the gun press against my leg.

"What are you going to do with that needle?" I look up, expression pleading.

"Oh, nothing to fear, it'll be like taking a nap." He flashes me a smile that doesn't reach his eyes, "You will barely even feel the pinch."

I shake my head, trying to pull back. "No, please, don't."

My plea falls on deaf ears as he grabs my arm and yanks me out of the car.

"Don't worry, it'll all be over soon."

With those last words, he jabs the needle into my arm. I flinch and then immediately the world tilts.

"You, come here. Take him to my car."

I don't know who he is speaking to, but suddenly I'm shifting through the air. I feel my head getting fuzzy as my body relaxes. Darkness clouds my vision, and my eyes grow heavy, all thoughts go to Roman.

Roman, please find me.

"How much longer until we get there?" I ask, peering out the window of the plane. Excitement is bubbling up inside of me and I can barely sit still.

"The answer is the same as it was a minute ago when you asked," he grumbles playfully.

I fold my arms over my chest and turn to glare. "I'm excited," I mock pout.

"I know. I'm glad you are." He runs a single finger down the expanse of my throat.

"So, tell me?"

"About an hour," he says and I squeal, vibrating in my seat.

"I cannot wait to go skiing. Oh, can we go sightseeing? I want to eat freshly made Swiss cheese... Oooo and a real Swiss chocolate bar." He chuckles, wrapping his arm around my shoulder and pulling me into his side.

The position is awkward with the armrest digging into me, but I don't care. I cannot believe we are going to Switzerland. I never, in a million years, thought I would have the means to travel anywhere, let alone another country.

He chuckles warmly, peppering kisses across my neck. "Yes, whatever you want. I will buy you all the chocolate they have to offer."

A shiver racks my body as a chill sets in. I pull away from Roman to grab the blanket from the seat opposite mine.

"We must be almost there; it's getting really cold." *I shiver, my teeth clacking together, and turn to look out the window.*

Wait? Where are we?

We are no longer on a plane.

What?!

"Roman, I think something's wrong?" *I question, turning towards him, only to find that he is not here.*

He's gone.

I scan the empty space quickly and call out his name, hoping he will hear me. "Roman?" *I glance around the darkness but can barely see anything. Where am I? I rub my hands over my arms vigorously, trying to fight off the chill.*

This isn't right. The room is dark, I can't see anything now.

Blackness.

Cold

It's so cold.

My eyes snap open and I groan at the heavy feeling in my limbs. What the fuck happened? What is going on?

I blink several times, trying to clear the fogginess from my brain, but it doesn't help. I close my eyes and groan again. Why do I feel like this? My stomach hurts, as does my head and I feel really sloshy.

What the fuck did I do last night? Drink, drugs?

No, that's not right.

A yawn tears from my throat and I go to stretch but can't move my wrists. My eyes snap open again and realization hits me.

What the fuck? I was kidnapped.

I sit up quickly, instantly regretting it as my stomach rolls with nausea. I gag, lean over, and vomit the contents of my stomach onto the concrete floor.

"Well, isn't that just lovely?" a voice speaks and I stand shakily, stumbling several times before managing to lean against the wall for support, my arms handcuffed behind my back.

It's the man who took me.

"Who are you?" I say through chattering teeth. *Fuck, why am I so cold?*

"Oh, not this again." He sighs in exasperation, throwing his hands up in the air. "I thought we established that already. I am Roman's uncle, Giovanni Giuliani."

Wait? I didn't know Roman had an uncle.

"What do you want with me?"

He looks to the side and snaps his fingers at a man leaning against the doorframe. "Hey, you. Get him in a chair, would you? Can't have him falling over on me. We haven't even gotten to the good stuff yet." A sinister smile crosses his face.

What does he mean? I break out in a cold sweat and the goon drags me in the direction of the red-stained wooden chair.

Oh, is that blood? My stomach heaves at the thought and I gag once more.

"Oh, no more of that," Giovanni says, voice laced with annoyance.

The goon slams me down onto the seat, staying behind me, as Giovanni stalks in my direction.

"How much do you really know about your husband, I wonder?"

I can tell he's baiting me, but I answer anyway.

"I know everything about Roman." My tone lacks conviction and by the lift of his eyebrow, he noticed.

"Is that right?" He's mocking me now.

"Yes."

"So, you're aware that Roman fought in an underground boxing ring for over ten years."

He did what now? My mouth drops open in shock.

"I take it by your facial expression you didn't know that." He chuckles, shaking his head. "Oh, how fun this is going to be." He paces the length of the room before stopping in front of me once more. "Let's play a game, Alex."

I eye him suspiciously. "What kind of game?"

"I was hoping you'd ask." The sinister smile is back. "I'm going to say something about Roman, and each time, you get to guess if that statement is true or false. If you are right, nothing happens, but if you get it wrong I get to cut into your pretty flesh." He leans forward and runs a finger down the length of my throat.

"I don't understand. Why are you doing this?" I say, my voice barely recognizable.

"Because, Roman took something from me a long time ago, and now I want to take something from him."

"What do you mean? What did he take?"

"Oh, you are about to find out now aren't you? Are you ready to play?" he asks, looking at me expectantly.

I stare at him for several beats before finally nodding.

He rubs his hands together excitedly and says, "Goodie." He taps his chin. "One, Roman's mom died in a tragic accident the day he was born."

That I do know.

"Yes."

"Oh, good job. This one won't count against you. I am curious... Do you know how she died or why?"

"No."

"She was kidnapped and beaten within an inch of her life while Roman was still inside her womb."

An uncontrolled gasp slips from my throat before I can stop it. The image alone has my stomach rolling again, and the urge to gag is strong. What the fuck kind of person would do something like that to a pregnant woman?

Sick bastard.

"Yeah, it was a rough day. Maybe that is one of the many reasons Roman is so fucked up."

Those words piss me off and I speak before I even realize I'm doing it. "Roman is not fucked up!" I bite.

He erupts in manic laughter, talking through bits of broken chuckles. "Oh, you have no idea how wrong you are. Number two, Roman's first kill was when he was fourteen years old."

What?

"No." I don't even have to think about it.

"This is going to be fun." The goon produces a knife from I don't know where and hands it over to Giovanni. "This won't hurt... much," he says before making a shallow cut across my bicep. I yelp in pain, wincing as he pulls away.

"You're lying, Roman hasn't ever killed anyone," I spit through clenched teeth.

"Oh, you are a fool, and I pity you for your naivete. Three, Roman has a high body count, one being his own cousin."

This can't be true.

"No."

He stalks towards me and when the knife cuts across my cheek, I cannot help the sorrow that settles over me. I don't know what hurts worse right now, my heart or my body.

"When they were sixteen years old, Roman killed my son." For the first time, I notice true emotion through Giovanni's facade.

"I don't understand. Why would he do that?"

"It was a test to show strength."

"I don't understand." I shake my head in confusion.

"How blinded he has you." He tsks. "Roman has certain preferences that are frowned upon. Many people in our world believe homosexuality is a sign of weakness." He starts pacing, a faraway look in his eye. "Many wanted Roman to be dealt with for his perversions. So the three set up a match. Whoever dominated, wins all."

I'm so lost. What is he talking about? Who are the three? What kind of match? What do they win?

He starts again before I can voice my confusion.

"Roman being a fag cost my son his life."

"What?"

Okay, seriously this guy has to stop and explain better.

"He wanted to be with men, so he had to prove he was strong and not some pansy. Unfortunately, my son was one of Roman's many casualties."

"You say this as if being gay is a decision." I get the momentary urge to bust out with the lyrics of *Born This Way* by Lady Gaga but I refrain.

"Isn't it though? For years, sexuality was so black and white. Now you have boys with boys and girls with girls. Disgusting. It's wrong."

"It's called repression. It's bigoted opinions like yours that cause people like me to keep themselves hidden. Your view is what's wrong, not us."

I don't even see the smack coming until it's too late. His hand connects with my cheek and my head snaps to the side. I shut my eyes, fighting the wince. I don't want to give this son of a bitch the satisfaction of seeing my pain.

"You would be wise not to test me," he spits out, yanking my head back to meet his steely expression.

I nod, lips clamped together tightly. He releases me and takes a step back, rolling his head on his shoulders.

"Now, where were we? Ah, yes. Number four, Roman is an underboss for one of the three families in Vegas and a part of the Italian Mafia."

I suck in a sharp breath, surely that cannot be true.

"No." The words are a whisper from my lips. And just like that, the world I thought I knew crumbles around me.

The laughter that leaves his mouth is manic as he slices through my shirt, across my torso. I cry out in pain, my skin feeling like it's on fire.

"This is fun, I really like this game." He paces a few steps before turning back to me. "How does it feel knowing your entire life is a lie?"

My lip wobbles, but I don't let the tears fall.

"No, response? Pity. Okay, five, Roman loves you."

"Yes," I say with conviction. There was not a doubt in my mind that Roman loves me. I start to frown because my next thought tears me apart and doubt takes root in my mind... How can you lie to someone you love?

He sits back and stares at me, eyes pinging back and forth between mine. "You really believe that don't you?"

Before I can answer a knock sounds on the door. "Giovanni, we have a problem."

"I will be back soon, pet." He taps the top of my head before leaving with his goons.

Tears spill down my cheeks as I stare at the wall unseeing. Oh my God; I've married a monster.

ROMAN

Chapter Twenty-One

I knew I shouldn't have let him leave tonight.

As the days since Giovanni's disappearance have passed with no sign of him, I've become more and more disconcerted waiting for him to be found.

I had Alex on a very short leash, but was starting to feel like I was suffocating him. When he wanted to go out tonight with Lacey I allowed it, instead of fucking him into submission like I usually would. I have never regretted anything more in my life.

When Randal sent me a 9-1-1 text, I knew instantly something was wrong. When he didn't answer my calls, I called Liam and told him to bring Alex home immediately.

Sawyer and I jumped into action, tracking down Randal's car. When we got to the scene, cops littered the area. Detective Dominic Valentina told me my guard, Liam, was dead and Randal was incapacitated upon arrival. He assured me he was fine and that an ambulance had already taken him to a hospital.

It was all a big fucking mess and worse, Alex was no where to be found.

I have never been more grateful about having a cop on my payroll than I am at this moment. I have no doubt my ass would be sitting in an interrogation room right now had that not been the case. Instead, I'm currently standing in my office, pacing back and forth waiting for Sawyer and Dominic to map the route for getting Alex back.

Thankfully I had a tracker installed in his wedding band. I want to go in there, guns blazing, but I have no idea how many men they have or who all are involved. The only way to get in while maintaining the element of surprise is to find an alternative route.

When I get my hands on Giovanni, he is a dead man.

"How much longer?" I bark at Sawyer, my patience is long gone. I can feel my control slipping and my body is vibrating with unshed anger.

"We have the map now, Boss," Sawyer says, sending the details to my phone. "We need to enter through the west side tunnel underneath the Giuliani Hotel, from there it's about a twenty-minute walk."

Fuck! That's so much time.

I start towards the exit waving my hand behind me for them to follow. "Let's go, we need to be fast."

Giovanni you better pray that Alex is alive because if he's not...

There will be a reckoning.

Pop. Pop. Pop.

Blood splatters across the wall as I nail another guard between the eyes.

I expected a lot more out of Giovanni and am extremely disappointed by his lack of security. It all seemed a bit too easy if I'm honest, but I guess that's what happens when you don't have a lot of men under your thumb. Being a snake doesn't inspire many followers.

A gunshot rings out just as a bullet flies past me and embeds itself in the wall.

I turn to see a wide eyed Giovanni just as he turns to dart down the hallway. I sprint after him, bullets flying from the chamber of my gun. He shoots wildly over his shoulder and a bullet grazes my arm. But I barely feel it with the adrenaline coursing through my veins. I stop running and aim just as he's about to round a corner but he's too slow. The bullet slams through his middle, and he lets out an agonized roar before falling to the ground.

Chest heaving, I walk to him laughing as he slides away from my advance. Slithering like the snake he is.

"You sack of shit," I shout, aiming and pulling the trigger once more.

He howls, writhing on the floor. I pull the trigger two more times, careful not to hit any major body arteries, even though I want nothing more than to press my gun against his forehead and shoot him at point blank. I can tell by the blood loss that he won't be making it out of this one and I'm equally pissed about the quick death, as I'm relieved that I won't have to worry about him anymore.

Sawyer yells to me, telling me he found Alex in the back room and I nod before crouching down in front of Giovanni.

"It didn't have to be like this, you know."

"But it did, it was always going to end like this. I tried to tell your father, but he was just as weak as you. What kind of man would allow his son to be a cocksucker? It is a disgrace." He spits, disgust evident across his pain scrunched face.

"And yet, you're the one here bleeding out on the floor."

"You will get yours one day, Roman, and I hate that I won't be here to see it." He coughs, blood running down his parted lips.

"I'll see you in Hell, uncle," I mutter, standing.

I make it a foot away before he says, "Don't get too comfortable. They are still coming for Alex. This one was for me, but they have their own agenda and they won't stop until they have him."

My blood runs cold and I turn towards Giovanni once more.

"Who is coming for Alex?" I ask, but he doesn't answer, his breathing is coming in and out in shallow puffs. "Who is coming after Alex?" I scream, kicking him in the ribs.

It's pointless. He's gone; the son of a bitch.

I turn towards Sawyer. "I want twenty-four hour surveillance on the Morelli family. I want to know every fucking detail," I spit through clenched teeth.

Looks like my torture of Anthony may not have been enough of a warning.

"You got it, Boss."

"Have a doctor waiting at the house, I want someone ready to look at Alex. Then get the clean up crew down here. This needs to be taken care of as soon as possible."

"On it," he says, pulling out his phone.

I walk the rest of the way down the hall, opening the door and breathing easy for the first time in a few hours. There in the corner, huddled up shaking is my baby.

I rush toward him, falling to my knees in front of him. I want so badly to pull him into my arms, but I don't want to scare him. I rub his head gently as he lifts it to look at me. The expression on his face leaves me confused, it's like he's looking at me but not seeing me.

"Are you okay?"

He blinks, just staring through me.

"I want these handcuffs off." His tone is off and my eyes ping pong between his, searching. Is he in shock?

I gesture toward Dominic and have him remove the handcuffs.

Alex looks so lost. So, not right.

I go to pull him to me and he jumps like a startled cat. *Woah.*

I hold my hands up in a placating gesture. "Alex, it's me. I won't hurt you. I just wanted to check you over. You don't look good."

He shakes his head vigorously, face becoming ghostly pale and he loses his balance before collapsing. I scoop him up before his body crashes into the floor.

"We need to leave. Now!" I bark, turning and hurrying down the bloodied hall.

ALEX

Chapter Twenty-Two

I'm in a fog.

It's like the whole world is moving around me but I am sitting still.

I don't want to eat. I can barely sleep; the nightmares get worse as the days go on. I feel like there are spiders crawling on my skin. I feel dirty.

I feel *wrong*.

Roman tries to talk to me, but I don't talk back. I have nothing to say.

He wants to know what happened to me, what his uncle did, but I'm too lost in my own head to even tell him.

I'm angry.

So fucking angry at him. I cannot stand the thought of him touching me; I don't even want him anywhere near me.

My husband.

The one person who is supposed to be my go-to for everything and I can't even stomach being in the same room as him. I feel disgusted with him, and I'm even more disgusted with myself; I can't believe I ever let him touch me. I can't believe I ever *wanted* him to touch me.

Silent tears stream down my face but I don't bother to wipe them away. It doesn't matter anyway, there will just be more to come. I feel like I'm mourning the life I used to have. Mourning the life that will never be, my future looks bleak and I have never felt so lost.

It's been two weeks since the kidnapping, and I feel like I'm losing more and more of myself every day.

Leta brings me breakfast, setting the tray on the side table, but I don't look at her, I don't even speak. I feel betrayed by her too. They all knew what I was up against and no one tried to warn me, no one tried to help me. They willingly let me walk into the hands of a monster and now they are seeing what happens when someone is chewed up and swallowed.

I hope they are enjoying the show.

I stare out the window as Roman comes storming into the bedroom. He slams the door so hard I hear the frame rattle. He stalks over and sits down in front of me, but I don't look at him.

"Alex, this has to stop! Tell me what happened. Tell me what he did so I can help you."

"You can't help me," I whisper, my voice cracking from lack of use.

"I can, you just have to tell me," he says pleadingly.

We sit in silence for several moments and I continue to stare out the window. His temper flares and the next thing I know, he is grabbing me by my biceps and pulling me out of the chair.

He shakes me roughly. "Fucking look at me. Tell me what he did!"

And just like that the bottom falls out. All my days of sorrow and disgust, every bit of pain I was holding inside come barreling to the surface and I unleash it all.

"HE TOLD ME ABOUT YOU!" I spit, stepping out of his hold.

He goes deathly silent, eyes searching mine.

"He told you what about me?" His expression is closed off and I push.

I want a reaction. I want him to hurt like I've been.

"He told me about what you do! Who you are. How you kill people, about your mom. All of it. Every twisted, fucked up detail."

He lets out a curse before stepping back and grasping fistfuls of his hair. He turns towards me like a wounded animal and I want nothing more than to laugh. He's far from the victim here.

"I didn't want you to find out from anyone but me," he whispers, searching my expression, for what, I don't know.

"Well, it would seem you didn't want me to find out at all," I spit, arms wrapped protectively around myself.

He shakes his head, face serious. "I was going to tell you."

"When Roman? Because honestly the best time for you to have told me would have been before you fucking married me. You had so many opportunities but you never did."

"I was scared. I didn't want you to react like this. I knew you would freak out."

I can't help it, I laugh. It's not a happy one. It's laced with bitterness. "Freak out, of course I'd fucking freak out. This isn't a small thing, Roman. It's a big thing. Multiple big things. Huge things, life changing things! You're a fucking Mafia boss. You kill people! Why the fuck would you have ever thought I'd be okay with this?" I shout, throwing my hands up in frustration.

"I'm not going to stand over here and say I'm sorry, because I'm not, Alex. I fucking love you, love you with every single piece of who I am. I know if I would have told you, I would have lost you, and that just wasn't an option," he replies with so much conviction, it makes my stomach sink. The fucking audacity of this man.

"And you don't think you're going to lose me now?"

He huffs, shaking his head. "You are my husband; you won't leave me."

His tone of voice pisses me off. "The fuck I won't, I didn't sign up for this, Roman. I didn't sign up to be married to a mafia, murdering, monster." I don't see it coming until it's too late.

Roman's hand flies up, connecting with my cheek, my head snapping to the side from the momentum of the hit. I keep my head turned as the tears threaten to escape.

Fuck this and fuck him.

I lift my hand to cup my cheek when I feel a warm wet sensation against my skin. His ring must have caught me, because when I pull my hand back I notice the blood on my fingertips.

I look at his shocked expression, ready to detonate.

"Alex, I-"

I raise my hand, successfully cutting him off. "Get out."

"Alex," he tries again, but my patience is long gone.

"GET OUT!" I scream, pointing towards the door.

He looks at me for several beats, before walking away. Once he's through the door, my legs give out and my body slumps to the floor.

ROMAN

Chapter Twenty-Three

What did I just do?

I fucking hit Alex. I crossed a line. A line I'm not sure I will ever come back from.

I wish I could explain the feelings that are warring inside my body. I feel like I have a literal devil and angel sitting on my shoulders, both tugging me equally in each direction. On one hand, I want to go upstairs, fall to my knees and beg for Alex to forgive me. And on the other, I want to slam him back against the wall and make him see reason.

How can he not understand that I am the same man? The details may be a bit different but the man he married is the same. Just because he now knows the darkness I keep inside, doesn't change the fact that I've always been this.

Roman Giuliani, underboss, fighter, murderer.

I storm over to my desk sweeping everything off of it onto the floor. I need to calm down, but there is no calming down right now. This destruction doesn't even scratch the surface of my rage and I lash out. I'm too far gone. I'm losing control...

I come to several moments later, chest heaving and my office destroyed.

What the fuck?

I grab a handful of my hair and after righting it, sit down in my chair. My chest is heaving with exertion and I can feel my pulse pounding so hard it's making me light headed.

Fuck!

I need to hit something. I whip out my phone and call Sawyer, letting him know to be ready to leave in five minutes before calling Jimmy.

"Boss?" he answers almost immediately.

"I'm on my way," I bark over the line.

"Ring or basement?" Jimmy asks.

"Ring."

"Weapons, or no?"

"No, just fists tonight."

"You got it, Boss."

I hang up and walk to the car where Sawyer is already waiting on me. I need this.

I inhale deeply, the rage completely taking over my entire being. I slam my fists into his flesh quickly with rapid succession before taking a bouncing step back. I roll my head on my shoulders trying to calm my murderous rage.

I take a few breaths, channeling all my energy into this fight. He charges at me, but I side step him, throwing an elbow into his ribs before locking my arms around his neck from behind. He's struggling, trying to get out of my grip but I don't let him. I hang on like a snake, breathing deeply through my nose.

One. Two. Three. Four.

I count down in my head, waiting for the anger to subside and the endorphins to take over, but it just isn't happening. The rage I have inside is outweighing my usual release.

This was supposed to help. This was supposed to help me regain control, but it isn't. I'm too keyed up right now.

I let go of the man's neck, and he sputters, trying to catch his breath.

I shut my eyes briefly. Stupid though, because the second I do, the man charges me, knocking my body to the ground. He straddles me, pinning me to the mat, as his hands squeeze my throat. I'm thrown back to all those years ago, to a similar situation but with reversed roles. I think about all the people I have killed; I think about the lives lost in this very ring. I can imagine the amount of blood that has coated these walls.

Do I even deserve love after all of this?

No, no. I can't lose him.

Mine. Fucking mine.

I close my eyes attempting to let my mind settle, as my brain fights the lack of oxygen. He won't kill me. My men will stop him in time.

I can start to feel myself drift into a state of unconsciousness when my thoughts settle on Alex. I flash through our entire relationship like pictures on a slideshow. Seeing him for the first time, feeling his skin as we danced, tasting his lips, sliding inside his body, hearing him tell me he loves me, all of our nights wrapped together in warmth and happiness. A smile crosses my lips as the thoughts of Alex calm my tattered soul.

The calm doesn't last though as new images start flying behind my closed eyelids.

"He told me about you!"

I can hear Alex's disgust in just those few words alone. That was the moment my entire world started to crumble.

"He told me about what you do! Who you are. How you kill people, about your mom. All of it. Every twisted, fucked up detail."

My eyes snap open as his words wash over me.

"You kill people! Why the fuck would you have ever thought I'd be okay with this?"

I reach up, grabbing the hands from around my neck, and with all the strength I can muster, I roll, managing to knock the guy off of me and stagger to my feet. My throat burns from the sudden release and my head pounds as oxygen re-enters my system.

"You don't think you're going to lose me now?"

My faded anger is back tenfold and I growl, rushing forward and slamming my fist into my opponent's face.

FUCK!

I throw several more punches, blackness taking over my vision as Alex's words run through my brain like a freight train.

He thinks he can leave me? He thinks I would let him?

I don't know how it happened but we are now on the ground, rolling around fighting for dominance.

"I didn't sign up for this Roman."

"BUT YOU DID!" I scream out loud, causing the man's body to pause momentarily but it's enough for me to gain the upper hand, now I have him pinned to the mat.

He thinks he can make vows to me; all these promises to me and just break them. He thinks he can just walk away.

A laugh tears from my throat as I slam my fist into the man's face.

I can picture the day we got married, vividly. Alex's beaming smile as he looks up at me with so much love. I never knew true happiness until Alex. I never felt loved until him. I never knew what it was like to be happy. Happy until it was stolen from me.

Just like that, the images of our wedding turn to ash and are tainted. I can no longer look back on those moments with pride and warmth because all I see are lies. Lies and broken promises pouring from his sinful lips.

"I promise I will be there for you with each beat of my heart."

WHACK!

"I promise to be there for you in both dark and bright times."

WHACK!

"I promise to love you in good times and in bad."

WHACK!

"I promise to cherish you for better or for worse."

WHACK!

"As long as we both shall live."

My fist is slamming down over and over, blood pouring from his busted face, but I don't stop. I can't stop. I'm too far gone. My mind is racing, all of Alex's lies running through my head, destroying any good I thought I ever had inside me.

"I didn't sign up to be married to a mafia, murdering, monster."

A scream tears from my throat and I unleash every bit of anger I have.

WHACK. WHACK. WHACK.

"YOU WILL NEVER LEAVE ME, EVER!" I scream, red tinting my vision.

"ROMAN! ROMAN!" I can hear my name being called, but I can't focus on that. I'm drowning.

Hands wrap around my shoulders and drag me off the motionless body. I try to tear myself away, wanting to continue my onslaught, but Sawyer's words stop me in my tracks.

"He's dead, Roman, he's dead. Stop."

Dead?

I glance down at the corpse below me; his face is caved in from my assault.

"FUCK!" I scream, my legs giving out from underneath me as my body falls into Sawyer. I can feel my body wracking with unleashed sobs, as I try to calm my inner turmoil.

Giuliani men aren't weak.

I inhale deeply, letting the anger take over. I dig deep inside myself going back over my father's lessons from so long ago.

"Our world is very dangerous."

My blood runs hot, and I can feel myself start to lock up.

"You never know who could be lurking, what friend may be a foe."

He was right. I should have never let this happen. I should have never thought I could be something I'm not.

"So, I need you to be ready. I need you to always be ready."

My eyes snap open, as realization dawns on me and I know what I have to do. A triumphant smirk crosses my lips. Alex needs to be taught that Giuliani men aren't weak.

Considering he is a Giuliani, after all.

ALEX

Chapter Twenty-Four

I am sitting on the shower floor, legs drawn up to my chest, as the hot water splashes over me.

My mind at this point has shut all the way down. Numbness is my new best friend and I revel in the lack of feeling.

I have no idea how long I've been sitting here, I just know my skin is almost raw by the time I reach up and flick the water off. I stand on shaky legs and manage to wrap a towel around myself. I lean heavily against the bathroom counter, staring at myself in the mirror. I don't even recognize the man staring back at me. Has it really only been two weeks since my entire existence shattered around me?

My eyes are red and swollen from all the tears I've cried, with dark smudges underneath them due to my many sleepless nights. My one cheek is still healing from the knife cut left by Giovanni, and my other is newly bruised from my husband's hand. My lip quivers and I bite down on it to stop the sob from escaping.

What is happening to me? Who is this person?

I turn to head into the bedroom, teeth chattering so hard, as I pull on a sweatshirt and drawstring pajama pants. I don't usually wear socks to bed but I grab my fluffiest pair, shoving them on my feet, before crawling beneath the covers on my bed.

I need more comfort.

I'm freezing. My nerves are bad and I cannot seem to calm myself down. My body is shaking so hard, I can hear the headboard vibrating against the wall. I tunnel under the blankets and pull my legs up to my chest, wrapping myself into a ball. I'm basically just trying to create a cocoon of safety around myself. My skin feels too tight and yet, I need comfort in the worst way.

I just want to disappear. I want a rewind and to go back to a time when I was happy. I squeeze my eyes together tightly, leveling out my breathing, praying for sleep to find me.

"Open up and let me feed you," Roman says, dangling a strawberry in front of my lips. I do as he says and groan, eyes closing as the sweet juices coat my tongue.

"That is so good." I lean forward and snatch another strawberry off the tray and start feeding Roman this time.

He bites the fruit, licking his lips suggestively after he chews. "Very good indeed." His voice comes out like a purr and I grab a cheese cube and toss it at him. It bounces off his cheek and I burst out into a fit of giggles.

"You are a horn dog, we literally just had sex for the third time."

He chuckles, setting the tray on the nightstand then grabs me from beside him on the bed and sets me on his lap. His eyes are warm and he smiles, pushing a few strands of hair off my forehead. "I can't seem to get enough of you." He nuzzles my jaw and inhales deeply. "You smell like me."

"I smell gross, I need a shower." I unsuccessfully attempt to push his face away.

He growls, nipping at my neck. "You smell delicious, like sex and mine." He runs his fingers up my spine causing goosebumps to appear across my skin.

"Roman," I moan, and he licks the column of my throat.

"Yeah, baby, what do you need?"

"To shower," I say, and with one last smirk, I slide from his grasp and take off in a sprint to the bathroom.

"You little shit," I hear him mutter, as his footfalls sound behind me.

I laugh, making it to the bathroom and flip the water on, just as his arms wrap around me from behind.

"Shower with me?" I ask and he nods. We maneuver ourselves under the spray taking turns washing each other. After we rinse off, we stand under the water together, just enjoying the feel of each other's bodies. He rests his cheek against my head and I feel his puffs of breath against my damp hair.

"I love you, Alex," he whispers, squeezing me a little tighter.

"I love you too, Roman," I sigh, pushing back harder into his chest.

"Will you always love me?"

"Yes, of course I will."

"No matter what?"

I frown, turning towards him to get a better look at his face. I reach up and cradle his cheeks between my palms. "No matter what. I promise."

I don't know how long I was asleep or what time it is when I wake up. I just know that when I went to sleep it was dark outside and now the sun is streaming through the blinds.

I sit up stretching my arms over my head, blinking lazily around the room. It isn't until my eyes land on a figure sitting in a chair by the bed that my spine straightens and the memory of last night comes to mind.

Fuck, I told him about what his uncle told me. We got into a really big fight. He hit me.

Everything snaps into focus like a rubber band as I stare at him.

My eyes trail over him slowly, taking in his swollen knuckles, busted nose and lip. His clothes are dotted with blood. I can feel my anger subside and I frown taking in his battered appearance. He looks horrible. What happened to him?

My eyebrows scrunch together in wonder, as I take in the half empty bottle of bourbon next to a half full glass. When my gaze finally meets his I involuntarily flinch at his smoldering gaze. He looks pissed off.

What is going on?

I arch my eyebrow in confusion as we stare at one another. I can't read him, and that is completely unsettling to me. What is he thinking? What is he feeling? And more importantly why do I care?

I have no idea how long we sit like that, taking in each other before Roman finally says, "We need to talk." A shiver racks my body at his icy tone.

Uh-oh.

ALEX

Chapter Twenty-Five

I sit stock still, staring at Roman, waiting for him to speak. I'm thrown off completely by his demeanor and appearance, and for once have no idea what to say to him.

His stare intensifies as he looks at me, almost like he's trying to read my soul. He's searching for something, but I'm not sure what.

After what feels like forever, I tear my gaze away from his. "I don't know what to say here." I state, staring at my hands.

"You don't have to say anything. I just need you to listen."

I snap my head up at his tone. It's like nothing I've ever heard before. Roman's callous emotion is new to me and I'm stunned by this side of him. He takes a sip of his drink before continuing.

"I understand that you're upset I didn't tell you about myself, but can you honestly not see that none of that matters? I'm the same man, Alex. I am the man who met you on the dance floor of a club, the man who took you to Switzerland for our honeymoon, the man you make love to almost every night. That hasn't changed. The only difference now is that you know what my job is."

He cannot be serious. How can he not see how this is for me?

I shake my head. "It changes everything. I thought you were different, thought what we had was different. You have been lying to me for months. Hell, the whole time we have been together. Doing these horrible things to people and then coming home to me like nothing ever happened. How can you even try to justify this?"

His eyes narrow. "I'm not trying to justify anything. I just want you to see what's right in front of you! I am the same man I always was. You just know more about him now."

I sigh in exasperation, and throw my hands up in the air. "How are you not getting it? What you did was wrong, Roman. It was a total blindside for me and a big breach of trust." I sigh, rubbing my temples, before looking back up at him. "I wish this hadn't ever happened."

His spine snaps straight and his expression turns fierce. "What is that supposed to mean?"

"This, Roman. You, me, all of it." I'm angry, I really should calm down, because I can't seem to stop the words pouring from my lips.

"You can't mean that. You love me."

"I don't even know you!" I shout, hands balling into the bedspread.

He stands then. "You do! Stop saying shit like that. I am the same here." He slams his hand to his chest, over his heart.

"It is wrong, this is all wrong!" I stand, wanting to leave. I need to get away from him.

"No, it's not. The only thing that's wrong is your reaction to this. You promised that no matter what you would love me, that you would always be here. We said vows."

How dare he try to use that against me.

"Vows you have already broken with your mistrust and deceit," I spit out.

He releases a throaty chuckle turning to me with pained eyes. "Why can't you see that I did this because I love you, because the thought of losing you would literally kill me? I was dead inside before you. I had nothing that I cared about, nothing that mattered. I was a ticking time bomb, ready to go off at any given moment. Then, one night I was working in my club and this angel appeared, sucking me in. Literally opening up a part of heaven to me I never even knew existed."

My heart cracks at his words and I stifle the sob wanting to escape. "You can't guilt trip me on this, you should have told me!" I dash away a few fallen tears.

"I couldn't lose you."

God we are literally getting nowhere with this. It's like we are on a damn merry-go-round.

"You can't make me stay," I state, walking into the closet to grab a suitcase.

"Like fuck I can't," he shouts, snatching the case from me, as I exit the closet. "Do you really think after everything, you will just walk away from me?" He throws the bag to the side, before he grabs my biceps, lifting me up so my feet are dangling from the floor, and slamming my back into the wall. He brings my nose to meet his, looking deep into my eyes. "I'm sorry that I hurt you, I'm sorry you are having a hard time coming to terms with this. But make no mistake, I am not sorry for doing what I had to in order to make sure you wouldn't walk away from me."

I shake my head using all my strength to push him off of me. "You are being crazy, let me go."

"You make me crazy!" he growls, before setting me back onto the floor. "You don't understand now, but in time you will," he spits, turning to walk away.

He pauses momentarily at the threshold turning back to look at me once more. "I will give you as much time as you need to heal. No more lies and secrets between us. You will learn how my world works and I will teach you everything I can." His expression darkens as he stares at me. "Just remember that you are mine and leaving is never going to be an option."

I open and close my mouth several times as his words settle over me. The click of the lock is loud in the silent room. I rush to the door, heart slamming in my chest when I grab the door handle. I twist the knob but it doesn't budge. My stomach heaves when I realize there is no way to unlock the door from my side.

The son of a bitch locked me in.

I have no idea how long I stand there pounding my fists into the door, I just know once I finally call it quits my knuckles are raw and my voice is hoarse from screaming.

I still can't fathom how I got here. I was seemingly happy days ago and now I've been locked away by some fucking looney mafia boss and what makes it worse is that I am legally bound to him.

My chest feels tight and my lungs are deprived of oxygen. I stagger to the balcony doors and push them open with a little more force than necessary. I stumble to the chair and sink down. Panic grips me and I drop my head between my knees to try to slow my breathing.

Calm down. It's just a panic attack. Everything is fine.

I repeat the mantra in my head several times and the anxiety attack finally releases me from its clutches. Slowly, I stand and walk to the balcony edge and glance down at the ground below. I contemplate the three story drop before shaking my head and walking back into the bedroom. I don't want to break anything or freaking die.

I can't believe he locked me in. I can't believe this is happening!

I pace the expanse of the room trying to come up with a plan. I need to get out of here as soon as possible.

ALEX

Chapter Twenty-Six

Hours later, Roman returns with a tray of food and I force myself to eat. I don't want to, but I know I have to keep my strength up if I plan on getting out of here.

Once finished, he instructs me to get ready.

"Where are we going?" I ask, once done.

"You will see," he says, expression neutral.

I can feel the unease creeping in, but I try to push it down. It's Roman after all. He would never put me in danger.

Right?

I have no idea where we are. It looks like a boxing ring with rickety stadium seats. I turn towards Roman, confusion evident on my face. "What are we doing here?"

"I wanted to show you a piece of my world." His expression remains unchanged and that is so unsettling to me. He pulls me to sit and turns to me once more. "I was fourteen years old the first time my father put me in that ring."

I shake my head. "I don't understand."

"For generations, Giuliani men have been trained to fight early on. It's how it's always been. My training began when I was ten years old."

I shut my eyes tightly, not wanting to ask but needing to anyway. "What were you training for?"

"To survive."

Almost on cue, two men enter the ring and I shrink back further into my seat. I don't like this. My throat feels tight and I can't help the wave of nausea that rolls through me.

"Roman, what are they doing?" I ask, voice tight with tension.

He doesn't answer me.

A loud bell rings and both of the men start for one another. Everything happens in slow motion after that. Like a car crash you can't look away from. The men exchange blow after blow and the sickening crack of flesh meeting flesh reaches my ears with a residual finality.

My pulse is pounding, my palms are sweaty, and my lungs are aching from lack of air.

The one in blue shorts, staggers falling to the floor with a loud thwack. The man in yellow falls on top of him, locking him down to the mat.

"Roman," I squeak, voice barely audible. I ball my fists up so tight I can feel my fingernails biting into my skin.

Blue shorts face is red now from lack of oxygen as yellow shorts mashes his airway.

"Roman," I repeat, voice frantic. I turn to him when he doesn't answer me. Unsurprised to see he is locked onto the fight as well. I reach over tugging his arm trying to get his attention. "You have to stop this. He is going to kill him."

Roman turns towards me then, expression dark. "That's the game. This is what they signed up for."

I shake my head, eyes flying back towards the ring as blue shorts body begins to go limp. "This is not a game," I spit, disgust rolling off of me in waves. "That is barbaric. Stop this now."

"It's too late," he says, voice calm, and the bell sounds once more.

My gaze snaps to the stage just as the man in yellow shorts stands. My eyes zero in on the motionless man on the mat and I plead for him to get up. I beg the universe and every higher power I can think of to have this man get up, but he doesn't.

"Oh, God."

I fall back onto the seat, hands resting heavily on my bent knees, and silent sobs rack my body. I just watched a man get killed right in front of me and there was nothing I could do to stop it.

Roman's voice startles me from my wandering thoughts. "We start training young so we can survive. You say it's barbaric, but everyone who walks in here knows the risks before they sign their lives over."

I shake my head. "Why would anyone sign up to do something like that willingly?"

"There are so many reasons. Money, power, debt, greed. You see the world as black and white, but you miss all the shades of gray."

I feel his hand start to rub small circles on my back and I fight back the urge to flinch. This man is a fucking psychopath.

"You fight like that?"

He nods. "Not so much anymore, but for a long time I did." The memory of Giovanni's words slams into me and I gasp.

"You killed someone at fourteen years old?" I don't even recognize the sound of my own voice.

He nods. "Kill or be killed."

A whimper escapes me and my hand flies to my mouth in shock. "You kill teenagers?"

He shakes his head expression darkening. "I put a stop to anyone fighting under the age of eighteen once my grandfather passed. It's not something I have ever been able to get behind." He turns away from me, jaw tight.

There's a story there, but I can't even bring myself to ask about it. Not when I'm still reeling from his other confessions.

"How often did you have to do this?"

"More than I can count," he says, voice far away.

I try to come back with a response but I have none. I feel sad for the little boy who was forced to endure this kind of pain by people who were supposed to love him. But I also feel sickened by the man who still allows such disgusting rituals to take place.

He sighs and engulfs my hands with his. "I was raised to show strength in everything I do. You cannot afford to show weakness of any kind to anyone." He tips my chin up to meet his gaze. "And I never have. Until you."

I bite hard on my lip as his stare intensifies. I feel raw, sliced open by his words. I feel as if I've stepped into an alternate reality and I have no idea what life is anymore. I sigh, and lean back heavily into the seat.

"This is a lot to process." I rub my temples absently. "I really want to go home, Roman. I'm not feeling very well."

That's the understatement of the century.

"Of course," he says, face scrunched with concern. He stands, pulling me up on wobbly legs.

It's all a blur after that. My mind is unable to keep up anymore.

At some point later on, we end up in the bath with my back pressed against Roman's chest, as he runs the loofah down my chest. I sit there still, completely lost in my own head when I feel the rumble of his words against the skin on my neck, "I love you, Alex. You are mine, forever."

And just like that the world snaps back into focus with one fact abundantly clear.

I have to leave and I need to do it soon.

I glance at the clock, my heart pounding wildly in my chest.

Three-thirty in the morning.

I muster up every bit of courage I have and slide from the bed with caution, doing my best to not disturb a sleeping Roman. I grab my phone from my nightstand and put it in the pocket of my sweatpants.

Okay, you can do this.

With one last deep breath I take slow, measured steps until I reach the door of our room. I wipe my sweaty palms down my shirt before grasping the handle tightly. I do my best to turn it slowly, careful to not make any sounds when I do.

I glance over my shoulder to ensure Roman hasn't moved and pull the door open. When he doesn't stir, I sigh with momentary relief before tip-toeing out into the hall. I shut the door quietly and rest my forehead against it. Thankful to not hear any movement behind it. With one last mental pep talk, I make a silent trek down the stairs.

The house is quiet, but I swear I can hear the thuds of my pounding heart as if someone was beating on a drum. I feel flushed and a layer of sweat is coating my neck and forehead.

Almost there.

I have no idea what I'm going to do once I leave, but right now I could care less. Getting out of here is my number one priority, the rest will come later.

The alarm panel is bright like a beacon calling me and I quickly smash in the four digit code before the quiet beep informs me the alarms have been disengaged. I slide on a pair of flip-flops that are by the door and quickly unlock the deadbolt.

Freedom.

I pull the door open and inhale deeply as the fresh air assaults my senses. I could weep with sweet relief.

Now the gates. I just need to figure out how to get past the guards unseen. That's my last thought before an arm wraps around my middle and the rug is pulled out from underneath me once more.

I cry out in shock as the hold tightens almost painfully.

"Going somewhere?" Roman growls against my ear.

I flinch, grasping his arm tightly with my hands. "You're hurting me."

He says nothing, just keeps his hold firm as he drags me back into the house. I thrash and wiggle, trying desperately to break out of his hold, but it's no use. He has me in a vice grip. He drags me up the stairs and back to our room.

"Roman, stop. You're hurting me," I shout again, raking my fingernails across his arm.

"You hurt me first," he sneers, looking at me with pure hatred. "You were going to fucking leave me."

He walks me back to the bed and pushes me to sit down roughly.

"Don't move or your punishment will be more severe," he growls, eyes dark.

Punishment? What the fuck does that mean? I don't have time to think because Roman is back and snapping a handcuff to my wrist and the other side to the headboard.

"What the hell are you doing?" I screech, desperately pulling against the metal. The harsh material pinches my skin and I yelp at the surprise pain.

"You think you can just leave me? I thought if I showed you a piece of me, you would see. I thought you, of all people, would understand me." He shakes his head. "That wasn't the case though, was it? You were planning this the whole time. Get me to let my guard down so you could escape."

He grabs my ankle and I kick out furiously, screaming and flailing, trying to get him off of me. I nail him in the face and he lets out a loud curse, cupping his nose. It's only then that I notice the blood seeping down his chin.

Fuck.

He snarls at me, and grabs my chin harshly with his bloody hand. "That was your one. It would be wise to not test me on this."

I stifle the sob wanting to escape as my teeth cut into my cheek where he's squeezing, eyes widening.

"Do you understand me?" he spits, eyes filled with fury.

I lock my jaw tightly, glaring at him with equal hate and nod around his hold.

"Good."

He produces a piece of corded rope, binding my ankles together and ties them to the footboard.

"Roman, please don't do this. Just let me go," I try to reason with him.

He shakes his head and meets my gaze once more. "I didn't want it to be this way, but you leave me no choice," he snarls, walking towards the exit.

"Roman, where are you going?" I call, but he doesn't answer. "You can't leave me like this." He keeps walking.

"ROMAN!" I scream. "Please."

He doesn't listen. He doesn't stop. He just walks out of the bedroom, shutting the door behind him with a residual click. Leaving me trapped and locked up.

I release a loud wail, turning as best as I can into the pillow, seeking comfort.

This man who is supposed to be my loving husband, just turned me into his prisoner.

ALEX

Chapter Twenty-Seven

It's been two months since my life was turned upside down, and I have never felt so lost, so broken. The man I thought I loved is here no longer, and replaced by someone I can't even stomach to be near.

I think I'm turning into a zombie. I feel dead inside.

I spit my toothpaste into the sink, wiping my mouth with the back of my hand before staring at my reflection in the mirror. My eyes look vacant and I don't recognize the man staring back at me. I touch the black bruise on my right cheek, before running my finger across my busted lip.

The bathroom door opens and I flinch, putting my head down.

Please just go away.

He doesn't though. I can feel the heat radiating off of his body as he stops a mere inch from me. He wraps his arms around my middle, pulling me back into him before guiding his hand up my chest, so he can tilt my chin up to meet his gaze in the mirror.

When I look into his eyes, I can see the remorse written all over his features, the same look he always has after.

"I shouldn't have hit you," he says, running the pad of his thumb over my busted lip.

No, you shouldn't have. Not this time or any other time before.

I just nod, dropping my chin once more, not wanting to see his face.

If you had told me three months ago, this is where our relationship would be right now, I'd have laughed in your face. I mentally shake my head, trying to rid myself of those thoughts. I can't think back to that time, it breaks my heart to know the man I loved is gone. Disappeared without a trace. Like he never existed.

I guess he never really did.

Most days I still cannot believe this is our new reality. I no longer am *Roman Giuliani's husband*. I'm his prisoner, *his pet*, his punching bag.

"Let me take you to dinner. We can go to that Thai place you love so much," he murmurs against my hair.

My stomach heaves at the thought, but I nod my head anyways. It's easier to just give him what he wants.

He kisses my head and exits the bathroom. My lip wobbles but I suck back the sob before it escapes. I am so sick of crying. All I ever do is cry.

I bat my face angrily, dashing away a few fallen tears and ignore the throb in my cheek.

I hate this. I hate him. I hate what we have become.

God, how is this my life?

Dear Diary,
God how pathetic am I? I am writing in a diary,
like a preteen talking about her first crush. I
cannot even believe this is what my life has
come to. Being so completely isolated from
society, that I have to write my thoughts down

on paper just to get them out of my damn head.

I got the idea of writing in a journal from the movie, **Freedom Writers.** *It's basically about a teacher who gives her students each a journal to write in so they can express themselves. Get all of their emotional turmoil out.*

So that's what I'm going to try to do here.

I just can't keep this bottled up inside anymore. I literally feel like I am suffocating.

Roman has gone away on 'business' and won't be back for five days. That means I get five blissful days of peace. I know what you're thinking. Get your shit and get the hell out of there, and let me tell you, I wish it was that simple.

It has been two long, tiresome months since the world as I knew it dissolved into nothing. And in those two months I have learned the true meaning of fear.

I tried to leave Roman the day after he told me it wasn't an option. He was so angry he locked me in our bedroom for a week, only allowing me to leave for meals.

The second time I tried to leave was just days after that first punishment, this time I did it when Roman was preoccupied, thinking I would be able to sneak away unseen. Wrong, I was so wrong. One of the guards caught me before I exited the gate and dragged me back to Roman, kicking and screaming. That time Roman punched me so hard, I was knocked unconscious and woke up to find I had seven stitches across my eyebrow.

The third time I tried to escape, I thought I would wait until Roman left on one of his business trips. I managed to get away successfully for about three days, until Roman found me hidden in a seedy, cash only motel.

I still to this day have no idea how he found me.

I will never forget the fear of waking up, handcuffed to the bed with a pissed off Roman leering at me. I made him leave his trip early to come fetch me, which made my punishment more severe. Roman had delivered several jabs to my ribs, before whipping my naked torso with his belt, all while I laid there, defenseless.

Since then, Roman's anger has grown tenfold. Now it takes almost nothing to set him off. He can go from zero to sixty at a snap of a finger and literally flip on me before I know what is going on.

Like last week, we were having dinner and he asked me if I liked the seafood alfredo. I just nodded, not wanting to speak with a mouthful of food, but apparently that response was not good enough, since the next second Roman smacked my mouth before screaming at me for being disrespectful.

I tried to explain that it wasn't my intention, but that just fueled the fire and he flipped the table, sending our dinner with all the glassware to the floor.

This is how it has been for the last sixty something days. Random smacks, tons of bruises, broken dishes and household items.

Sixty days of crippling fear. Just waiting for the ball to drop.

My anxiety is horrible now because I have my guard up constantly. I just want to relax.

Which is why I'm so glad he is gone for the next several days. I feel like my lungs aren't as tight as they usually are. I can breathe just a little easier.

What has my life become?

I miss Lacey. I barely see her anymore,

especially now that Roman practically forced me to quit my job at Drought. When I do get to see Lacey, it's usually supervised by Roman and we act like the happy 'newlywed couple' we are supposed to be.

The couple we should be.

You're probably wondering why I haven't told Lacey about Roman. That answer is simple. When I tried to leave the first time, Roman took my phone from me and told me if I even considered telling Lacey about him, or asking her to help me escape him, he would kill her and make me watch.

Lacey is literally the only person in the world who means anything to me, so risking her life to save mine just wasn't an option. I will deal with this hell ten times over if it means my girl is safe.

To be honest, I don't ever want her to know anyway. It would crush her if she knew what was happening to me behind closed doors. It's better this way, better for all my secrets to be kept hidden away.

Hidden in the darkness where they can rot.

Like me.

Rotting away from the inside out.

I just... Hate this.

I hate everything.

I hate Roman most of all.

Yet, I miss him with equal measure. I miss the old him. I miss what we had. I miss my life.

Why did it have to come to this?

I wish I had a magic Genie. I would rub the fuck out of a lamp right now for just a chance to go back and change all this fucked upness that has become my life.

If only magic were real.

I guess for now I will just keep hoping for a miracle.

Miracles happen everyday, right?
Hmm. There's some food for thought. I guess
I will have to get back to you on that one
diary.
Until next time.
Alex

Chapter Twenty-Eight

I squeal in excitement, wrapping my arms around Lacey as she enters through the front door.

We haven't had a night together in so long. With everything going on with Roman, I've been keeping her at arm's length. It's for the best though. It's really hard to hide any marks or bruises from her and I can only use the 'I fell' excuse so many times.

"I missed you! I was considering filing a missing persons report. I mean come on, surely the honeymoon phase is starting to wear off." I smile, holding in the sense of dread her words bring. If only she knew.

"What can I say? Married life is wonderful." I try to manage a sincere smile.

"Well, I guess I will just have to take your word for it now, won't I?" She runs her fingers through my overly long hair. "I cannot wait to trim this mess. Why on earth have you waited so long? It's dreadful," she quips. Poking me in the forehead before dropping her hand.

"Hey, I haven't seen you in weeks and this is how you treat me?" I mock pout.

"Oh, my sweet little baby, suck in that lip and let's go to your ginormous bathroom. I have all my supplies right here." She gestures to the rolling bag by the door, an excited smile crossing her face.

I point towards the kitchen. "Oh, wait, we need drinks."

She beams, pumping a fist in the air. "Please tell me you have champagne. We need mimosas!" She exclaims, doing a little jump in place.

I can't help but chuckle, "I have no idea, but I'm sure we can find something."

I grab her arm and pull her to the kitchen.

Roman is still out of town for a couple more nights and I am going to bask in every moment of this best friend time.

Two hours and one pitcher of mimosas later, I am feeling good, and my hair looks fabulous. Lacey not only cut it for me, but added in an array of blond highlights giving my hair a bit more of a honey glow.

I run my fingers through the strands laying over my forehead, admiring the new do. I love it, it makes me feel like the old Alex, which is a rare commodity these days.

"Now, get dressed. We are going out!" Lacey shouts, leaving the bathroom.

"What? Out? Where?" I question, following behind her.

"We need to go dancing. We haven't had a night together in so long. We had to cancel the last one because you had that Roman emergency, so this one is very overdo."

"I can't go out."

"You can, and you will."

"Lacey," I sound almost frantic.

"Alex, I am not taking no for an answer, go march your cute tushy to your closet, pick out your sassiest outfit and let's go out."

"But I-"

"No, buts. I am going to my car to grab my clothes, and I will be right back. You better have your outfit picked out by the time I get back," she states, blowing me a kiss, before heading out my bedroom door.

Fuck, Roman will be pissed if I go out. I already had to beg him to let Lacey come over.

With a sigh, I pull out my phone and text him.

Alex: Hey, do you mind if I go out to one of your clubs with Lacey tonight? She really wants to go out and spend some time together. We haven't been able to in a while and I feel like I need this time with her.

I hit send, staring at the screen, waiting anxiously for Roman to reply. It doesn't take long before my phone comes to life in my hand.

Roman calling.

I hit the answer button quickly, heart pounding wildly in my chest. "Hey, sorry to bother you while you're working, you didn't have to call if you were busy."

"It's fine, I had a free moment. I really don't like the idea of you going to a club without me there," he states, and I know before he says anything that this is about to be a fight. "But I think you do deserve some time with your friend."

Wait what? He's letting me go. I barely stifle the gasp before it escapes.

"Really? You don't care if I go?" I ask hesitantly.

Why does this feel like some kind of trap?

"No, but we need to have a few rules because I'm not there to ensure you are safe. You need to take your security with you, I want one of them near you at all times. All this stuff with Giovanni seems to have blown over for now, but I still want you to be careful. I can't join you tonight, so be smart about what decisions you make." The warning in his voice is clear.

"Okay, I will."

"Don't be out past midnight and don't get drunk, Alex. I need you to be aware of your surroundings, just in case."

I roll my eyes and mentally sigh. At least he still cares. That's something, I guess.

"I will. Thank you."

"You're welcome. I love you, Alex."

I wish you didn't.

"I love you too, Roman."
I wish I didn't either.

"Damn, little baby, you look like a treat," Lacey states, before motioning for me to do a twirl. I comply easily, laughing at her antics.

"You lie, I pale in comparison to you." Lacey looks beautiful. She has on a red romper with gold pumps and matching accessories. Her blonde hair is down in big waves and her makeup is perfect as always.

I am wearing a white button-down shirt, sleeves rolled up, collar open, a black pair of skinny jeans, and black vans. In all honesty, my outfit is pretty basic.

"Alright, Milady. Let's go," I say, holding my arm out for her to grab. We walk out to the car where Randal is waiting to take us to the club with my security in tow.

The club is slammed by the time we get there. No surprise though, it is Roman's business after all. Once inside, we are ushered upstairs to the reserved section and have our own personal waitress seeing to our drink needs. I guess being married to Roman comes with a few perks, in public at least.

We order Martinis and down them instantly before making our way to the dance floor. The music is vibrating through the speakers and I get lost easily in the lyrics. Lacey has her arms wrapped around my neck and we are doing a salsa kind of dirty grind together to *Despacito* by Luis Fonsi, the remix version with Justin Bieber.

"I wish I knew Spanish," I shout over the speakers.

"It's never too late to learn," she shouts back and I nod, grasping her hand and spinning her out from me. She lets go and we laugh as the song changes.

"God, I missed you so much. Why in the world have we waited so long to do this? It should be illegal for us to not spend time together. What's that expression? We go together like celery and carrots?" she asks, lips pursed in thought.

I laugh, shaking my head. "I believe you are looking for peas and carrots, and how terrible of you to ruin that *Forrest Gump* reference. You should be ashamed."

Her face lights up with humor. "Whatever, I was close enough. You knew what I was talking about." She points an accusing finger at me.

"Only because we have seen that movie together at least ten times."

"Well yeah, it's a classic," she says, poking me in the ribs.

"A classic you can't even remember the words to?" I question, eyebrows drawn up in wonderment.

"Don't judge me!"

"Never." I hold my hand over my heart in mock horror, earning an eye roll from her.

The night passes in a blur of drinks and music and before I know it it's almost time to leave.

"We need to be heading out in about twenty minutes," I yell into her ear just as *Pillow Talk* by Zayn starts.

She pouts, glancing at the time on her phone. "Already? It's not even midnight."

"I know, but I'm getting tired. Plus, I think I drank too much. I'm not feeling too great." I fake a yawn to prove a point. That's a lie. I barely have a buzz, but I can't tell her that. I need a believable reason to go.

"Okay fine. We can leave soon. But for now, we dance." She smiles, pulling me to her once more.

We laugh and sway in time with the beat of the music. The chorus hits and I feel strong arms wrap around my waist. My whole-body freezes and I jerk out of the person's hold. I whirl around to motion for my bodyguard, when I come face to face with a smirking Roman.

"Fuck, you scared me." I hold my hand over my rapidly beating heart. "I thought I was about to have to call for help."

He wraps his arms around my middle, pulling me to him.

"What are you doing here? I thought you would be gone for two more days," I ask, staring up into his smoldering gaze.

"I was already on my way home when we talked. I figured I would just surprise you," he says, grinding his hips against mine.

I gasp, my cock responding to him instantly. "Well, I'm definitely surprised."

He smirks, lacing our fingers together. "Dance with me," he rasps, voice husky.

He spins me around, pulling my back to his front as we grind together to the song. It's been so long since we did this. Since I felt like this. Roman grips my chin, tilting my face back towards him as he claims my lips in a needy kiss.

My senses are completely overtaken by him. I turn, plastering our fronts together as I delve into his mouth with my tongue. I need this. I need to feel good, even if it's just for a little while.

"I want you," I murmur, voice laced with desire. He groans into my mouth, and pulls back tugging me off the dance floor. "Wait, Lacey."

"Sawyer has her," he punches out, not slowing down. Expression dark with hunger.

Well, okay then.

Randal is waiting for us outside once we exit the club.

The ride back home passes quickly, as we are unable to keep our hands off of each other. We stumble out of the car, laughing as we stagger up the steps. Roman lifts me as soon as we cross the threshold, practically sprinting up the stairs to our bedroom.

It's been so long since we had this kind of intimacy between us. Don't get me wrong, we've had sex; but sex for need and sex for desire are two very different things.

He drops my legs once we enter our room, quickly unbuttoning and discarding my shirt. I kick off my shoes and shed my jeans, before starting on his shirt. After we are void of all clothes, Roman slams his mouth back on mine, kissing me with raw desperation. I don't think either of us have ever been so hungry for one another. He walks me back several steps and we fall onto the bed once we reach it.

Roman's kisses are scorching and I cannot get enough. He pulls away to grab the lube from the nightstand and I whine, tugging him back to me. I need him... Need this. I need to forget the last few months.

I am so desperate. Desperate to feel anything other than pain and devastation.

His lips roam over my neck and collarbone as I feel the slide of his lubed fingers at my entrance.

"Yes, yes, yes. Now, fuck me now," I beg, pushing my ass down onto his digits.

"Fuck you are killing me," he growls, working me over with skilled precision.

"Need you inside of me. Want to feel you," I gasp, writhing around on the bed.

He doesn't wait or hesitate before removing his hand and applying lube to his cock. We sit there, eyes locked as he slowly pumps his dick. I bite down on my bottom lip and the dam breaks. The head of him nudges against my hole and I bare down, allowing him to slide in easily. His groan is so loud I can feel the vibrations on my skin. I wrap my legs around his waist, pulling him on top of me, so we are completely mashed together. Not even an inch of space between us.

"You feel so good. I love how it feels inside of you." His voice comes out desperate as he settles over me.

Roman looks deep into my eyes as he rocks his hips. We are both so gone for one another in this moment. Pulling and pressing trying to get as close as possible. Each just as desperate for that connection we once knew.

He slides his arms under my back grabbing onto my shoulders for leverage, as he pumps in and out of my needy body. Our groans and ragged breathing fill the air as we chase our release.

"I love you." He breathes the words over my lips as he stares deeply into my eyes.

It's been so long since I felt like he actually meant those words. My eyes fill with tears and I whisper back, "I love you, too," before kissing those lips I crave like water.

He shifts his hips, rubbing against my prostate with perfect strokes and it's not long before my orgasm explodes, coating our stomachs with cum.

"Fuck! Oh, fuck," Roman cries, hips stuttering as he empties inside of me, never breaking our eye contact.

We are lost in each other. He kisses me, sloppy and lazily, but I don't care. I have never felt so sated in my life.

When he pulls away, we don't even bother to clean up. He just rolls over, pulling me on top of him and I rest my head on his chest. He runs his fingers through my hair and I am lulled to sleep by the beating of his heart.

Praying to never wake up from this dream.

ALEX

Chapter Twenty-Nine

I wake up with a smile on my face, thinking about how wonderful last night was. I roll over and reach for Roman, but my hand meets cold sheets.

I sit up and glance around the room. No Roman in sight. *Maybe he went to get breakfast?*

I slide out of bed and stretch, recoiling at the feel of dried cum on my stomach. I head straight for the shower, adjusting the temperature before sliding underneath the spray. The warm water glides over my skin and I soak in the warmth that it provides. I feel good, lighter.

I wash my body quickly, ready to get out and go in search of my husband. We had a good night last night. It was almost like I was looking at the man I thought was lost. Maybe just maybe there is some chance of saving us after all?

I step out of the shower, wrap a towel around my waist and head into the closet to get dressed. The smell of French toast and coffee reaches my nostrils and I inhale greedily, causing my stomach to growl.

Once dressed, I walk into our bedroom, smiling when I notice Roman. He is standing with his back to me, and I make my way over to the table. I glance around him at the spread on the tray.

"Thanks for bringing me breakfast. That was thoughtful." When he doesn't respond I glance towards him only to stop when I see what he is holding. Roman has my journal, not only holding it, but reading it. I look at his face, noting the hard set of his jaw and the murderous expression in his eyes.

Fuck! Why didn't I put that away? I have a few days' worth of entries in there now. Nothing good and I am dreading him knowing what is going on inside my head. I take a small step back and the movement causes Roman's head to snap in my direction.

My heart pounds rapidly as I stare into his dark expression.

"What the fuck is this shit?" he snarls, tossing my journal at me. I don't try to catch it, I just let it smack to the floor with a thud.

"Roman, I can explain." I take another step back as he takes a step towards me.

"Explain? How can you explain that? You hate me." His face morphs into sadness and he turns away from me.

I shake my head. "I don't hate you. It's not like that at all. It's just been really difficult lately-"

He cuts me off before I can finish. "Whose fault is that? Huh? You could have accepted me for who I was, but no. The second things got rough, you wanted to run out that door. So forgive me for being a little hard on you." He turns back to me then, face stricken.

"Hard on me? Roman, you beat the shit out of me. You speak to me like I'm nothing. You are literally tearing me apart. That's not just being hard on me. It is abuse," I whisper the last words, voice tight with tension.

He scoffs, shaking his head. "It's tough love."

He cannot be serious. How can he not see how wrong this all is? Every single moment of the last two months has been hell for me. The constant fear and worry for my general safety and to him it was some kind of lesson?

"Love isn't supposed to hurt like this, Roman."

"How do you think this is for me? You don't think I'm hurting?" He motions to the notebook thrown haphazardly on the floor. "Or am I really only a monster to you now?" His expression looks somber as his eyes search mine.

I don't answer him. I don't know how to. I open and close my mouth several times before finally just offering a small shrug.

"Answer me!" he shouts, taking another step towards me.

Hopeless. This is hopeless.

"I don't know," I say, backing up until I hit the wall.

"Liar," he shouts, hand coming up and connecting with my cheek.

The cracking sound reverberates off the wall as my head snaps to the side. I feel the warm blood trickle down my cheek but don't make a move to catch it. I stay as still as possible with my head turned to the wall and my eyes smashed tightly closed.

He makes an animalistic roar then I hear the crashing of glass and other objects hitting the floor.

He's mad. And it's my fault.

Again.

I take very shallow breaths, my body leaning heavily into the wall. Maybe if I'm completely still he won't see me. Maybe this once he will forget that I'm here.

Wishful thinking.

I hear his heavy footfalls as he approaches me slowly. I haven't moved, my whole body stiff with tension. Prepared. Waiting for him to finish what he already started.

"Fuck," he curses, bringing his hands up to oh so carefully cup my bruised face. "Oh, baby. I am so sorry. I just lost it. I shouldn't have done that." He gently tilts my face, leaning his forehead against mine. "I really am just a monster."

My heart cracks a little more with his words. It feels like I'm drowning all over again.

His fingers now so soft, contradicting the earlier assault, as he lovingly caresses my nape and neck. "I know this is hard on you. I know I haven't been a good husband to you. Fuck. I keep screwing up." He rubs my neck slowly, drawing circles around my shoulder. "Please forgive me baby. I promise it won't happen again. I love you. You know I do. I swear, I'll change. I will do whatever you need me to do."

His lips, light as a feather, start at my forehead, graze my eyelids, nose, and whisper over my battered cheek.

"Forgive me." He nuzzles my jaw. "I won't ever do it again. I promise." His lips brush over mine. Once. Twice. Three times. "I love you. I love you so much, Alex. Please. I'm sorry." Four. Five times. "Please say you forgive me." My chest heaves as sobs rack my body.

"I know, I love you too." I rub his back soothingly because what else can I do?

"You forgive me?" His hands glide down the front of my shirt.

"I forgive you." The button to my jeans comes next.

"I'm going to make you feel so good. I promise. Only good from now on." My clothes are gone too quickly and when he lifts me, my legs automatically snake around his waist for support.

I feel the slick slide of lube. I have no idea where he got it. Not that it matters, I don't care; I just want the pain gone. Don't want to feel like this anymore.

He slides inside of me slowly, lovingly. Whispering sweet nothings into my ear. Telling me how good I feel, how much I mean to him, how much he will love me forever.

All these empty promises.

I zone out, away from him and focus on the sensations and just...feel. My world is set ablaze when he shifts his hips, nailing my prostate and pinning my dick between our abs, causing just the right amount of friction.

Endorphins are a beautiful thing and I let my head fall back against the wall as my orgasm barrels through my body. I groan as pure pleasure takes over.

Twenty seconds. The smallest amount of bliss in this fucked up mess.

It's ecstasy.

"Promise me you won't ever leave me." He's still moving inside me, hips pumping, chasing his own release. His eyes meet mine. That sky blue that I love so much. His brow furrows in concentration as he takes in my face.

I can see it now; the remorse. I know he regrets it. He wishes he was different, that things were different. He wished he hadn't done it.

That's the problem though. He did do it. He keeps doing it. And he will do it again; he can't help himself.

As much as he loves me, and I love him...it isn't enough. There is no stopping it.

I stare into those eyes, so full of pain and love for me and I lie. "I promise, I will never leave you."

He slams his eyes closed on a guttural moan as he comes. His features relaxing as contentment takes over.

I lean forward and rest my head on his shoulder, holding his quaking body against mine. Soaking in a few minutes of solace.

I have to get out now while I still can, because if I don't, his love is going to kill me.

PART FOUR

ESCAPE

ALEX

Chapter Thirty

One month later

GO. GO. GO.
My feet pound on the asphalt as I hurry into the truck stop bathroom. I slam the door behind me closed and click the lock. I have one hour. One hour to change and get the fuck out of here.

I hop onto the counter with shaking legs and remove the ceiling tile above the sink, before reaching inside pulling down the duffle stowed there. My hands are shaking so bad, I have a hard time grasping the handle.

Breathe.

I jump down and dump the contents from the bag onto the floor. A letter, a set of clothes, a phone, hair dye, and other items clatter to the tile floor. I grab the letter first.

> *Mr. Giuliani,*
> *If you are reading this it means you made it through phase one as discussed. Inside this bag you will find all the contents needed to change your appearance. Please move quickly as your window is now less than one hour. There is a black Honda parked behind the*

rusted fence, inside the glove box you will find an envelope with your new identity as well as directions to your destination. There is a burner phone in the bag. Only call out to the programmed number if you run into any problems.
-S

I toss the card on the counter and get to work; it's time to get rid of Alex.

Make him disappear...for good.

I pull my hat down over my now midnight black dyed hair, taking one last look at myself in the mirror. I don't even recognize the man staring back at me. My once sandy blond hair is gone and my eyes, sea foam green, are now covered with brown contacts. My designer clothes are replaced with some off brand I've never heard of before.

I slide the dark sunglasses over my eyes and grab the burner phone, stuffing it into my back pocket. I take one last look around, validating I have all of my things, and that nothing is left behind.

Disappear. No traces left behind.

I snatch up the bag and exit the bathroom with twenty-five minutes to spare.

Thank you, God.

My nerves are shot to shit and my heart is pounding so hard I'm surprised it hasn't cracked through my rib cage. My throat is so dry it almost hurts to swallow, but I don't stop. I keep on moving; walking fast to get to the car. I glance around the desolate parking lot, visions of *Saw* and *Texas Chainsaw* flashing through my mind.

I quicken my steps when I see the rusted fence, freedom so close I can practically taste it. I jump into the car and toss the bag onto the passenger seat. The key is dangling in the ignition and I hastily crank the engine. I grab the envelope from the glove box, as instructed previously, and begin reading the note on the outside.

> *Mr. Smith,*
> *If you are reading this it means we are onto phase three. Inside you will find your new passport, money, and directions to your final destination. Please do not stray from the route provided. This is for your safety. If you have any issues along your way, use the burner provided. Otherwise, good luck to you.*
> *-S*

I retrieve the directions from the envelope, hands shaking so badly I almost drop them.

Breathe.

I squeeze my eyes shut and take several calming breaths.

You can do this, you *have* to do this.

Freedom. A new beginning.

It's time to go. I shift the car into drive and pull out onto the main road. I glance down at the map one last time, head east and follow the highway into the sunset.

Literally.

I kiss my fingertips and place them on my rear-view mirror, sending a final goodbye to Roman.

It's time to leave the past behind me.

Arizona

I just crossed the border into Arizona and that realization alone is surreal. It has been two hours since I left that truck stop bathroom and I can't help but wonder if Roman has realized I'm gone yet.

Who am I kidding? He knows. He always knows.

I wonder if he was worried, frantically looking for me. Or is he pissed that I managed to slip under his thumb without being caught, and coming up with ways to punish me once he does.

I let out a tantalizing laugh at the thought. I can practically see him vibrating with anger as he barks for Sawyer to find me. Little does he know, it's a lost cause.

Sawyer won't help. That's just a part of my master plan.

I turn up the radio and try to not anxiously chew on my thumb nail. Glancing at the clock and watching the minutes and miles pass me by, I coast through the valleys of desert and desolation.

New Mexico

The stop to refuel at a gas station in New Mexico was the most nerve-wracking experience of my life. I rushed inside quickly grabbing some supplies to hold me over until my next stop. The clerk probably thought I was tweaked out from my jumpiness and bouncing eyes.

No sir, just running across the country from my Underboss husband, trying not to die.

I laugh out loud at my inner turmoil, earning an unamused look from the clerk. Great. Now, he is watching me with even more suspicion.

I throw the water, chips, beef jerky, and snack cakes onto the counter and pay quickly before going out to pump my gas. I try to stay hidden behind my car as I do. "Come on, come on," I chant, as my tank fills.

I am about seven hours away from Roman, but I still don't feel safe.

Texas

Not long after I crossed into Texas, I pull into the parking lot of the motel marked on the map. My stomach heaves as I park and I have to squeeze my jaw tight to keep my teeth from chattering. I am buzzing with nervous energy. It's been hours and yet I keep expecting for Roman to just pop up and ask me what the hell I think I am doing.

I check in with my fake name, and pay with cash before retiring to the assigned room. I pace back and forth across the expanse of the space, nervously checking the lock over and over. I need to shower, I need to sleep, but fuck I'm so anxious. I rub my temples with my fingers, trying to talk myself down from my impending panic attack.

Roman is in Vegas. Miles away, Sawyer has him looking in all the wrong places.

You had a deal, remember. Sawyer has too much to lose.

I repeat the mantra in my head over and over and finally manage to calm myself down enough to shower. The bathroom is distasteful and I put a towel down inside the yellow stained tub to prevent my feet from touching it.

The water pressure is terrible and I barely have the soap off, but I cannot express the feelings of liberation that come over me while standing under the spray.

I'm really doing this. After a ton of planning, I can see the end in sight. So close I can almost taste it.

I dress quickly and fall into bed, letting sleep pull me under.

I jump out of bed a few hours later and collect all my things before heading back to my car. I got about five hours of sleep and even though I can stay longer, my anxiety just won't allow it. I need to get out of here. I need to move. I won't feel safe until I am stopped indefinitely.

I never realized how incredibly long Texas was. That sounds stupid, Texas is the second biggest state in the United States I know, but knowing how big it is and actually seeing it are two totally different things.

With that being said, Texas is beautiful. There was so much to look at, and I bet even more to do. I stopped at a really awesome convenient store; it put every other gas station to shame. I bought a pulled pork sandwich that was delicious, and a souvenir beaver. I couldn't help myself. He was just so cute.

I wished I had more time to stop, but I can't. Maybe in a few years, I can come back through and do some exploring, I think absentmindedly, as I increase the volume to *It'll Be Okay* by Shawn Mendes.

Louisiana

I fly through Louisiana, not seeing much as it's too dark now anyway and mostly just interstate at this point. I munch on my beef jerky, while my stomach growls for a real meal.

I've been having a hard time eating with how bad my nerves have been.

Hell, that's been months. I can't even tell you when the last time I had a whole meal was. Ever since I decided I needed to leave Roman and then started moving to make it happen, my stomach hasn't been able to handle much. I have a naturally sensitive stomach anyway, throw in my anxiety and boom insta-sickness.

For now, I will just nibble on this beef jerky, sip some water and think about my first real meal as *John*.

Alabama

I pass the 'Now Leaving Mississippi' sign and soon cross over the line into Alabama.

Alabama; I am almost there, the safe house.

Spring Haven, Alabama. Even the name sounds fresh and safe.

A safe space.

I start counting the miles down in my head, trying to remember to breathe as the time ticks on.

Ten miles- I am practically shaking.

Seven miles- I can barely breathe.

Five miles- My body feels hot.

Two miles- Freedom.

Destination.

Pulling into the driveway I park, admiring the little white and yellow lake house. I climb out of the car on shaking legs, and hesitantly make my way up the stairs. My vision feels black around the edges as I trudge up the steps to the porch. I use the key on my keyring, open the door and walk inside. There is soft music playing and the smell of spices wafting around the living space.

Tears are pouring down my face as I walk in the direction of the smells. I stumble over my feet as I try to contain my emotions. When I cross the threshold into the kitchen I stop and all the air leaves my lungs in a harsh woosh. There, standing in my kitchen is the most beautiful woman I've ever seen. She looks familiar but a little different with her once blonde hair now dyed a dark brown.

My throat feels raw as I open my mouth to speak, but I only manage to squeak out a name. The name of my constant. The name of my person. The name of the greatest friend I have ever known. "Lacey."

She whips around to look at me and we both just stand there staring at each other for several moments. My lip wobbles as I take in her messy bun, and overalls. "I missed you," I choke, just as the sobs begin.

In a flash, she is in front of me, wrapping me in her arms. My legs give out and I pull us both to the floor. I don't know how long we sit like that; crying, and rocking. I just know that in this moment I feel the first sense of calm I've had in entirely too long.

Chapter Thirty-One

"We are a pair of snotty, sticky messes," Lacey mutters around hiccups.

I'm sure we both look like the hot mess express just rolled through.

"Your hair," she cries, running her fingers through the dark locks.

"I know, it's not very fitting."

"Everything is fitting on you; we just need to cut and style it." She grabs my cheeks, giving them a little squeeze. "My sweet little baby. I cannot believe how strong you are. I wish you had told me. I would have done something sooner," she says, tears slipping down her cheeks.

"I couldn't tell you. I wanted to, so many times. Roman threatened you and I couldn't risk it."

"Roman is a sack of shit and if I ever see him again, I may just kill him myself," she spits, her voice laced with venom.

I shake my head. "We won't ever see him again, so no need to worry over that."

She looks at me, lip wobbling. "I still cannot believe it. I feel like the worst best friend in the world. How could I have not known? In the last week, I've been going through every detail of the last several months and there were so many signs. So many things that I should have questioned."

I shake my head, cupping her cheeks. "No, don't do that. There was nothing you could have done, and I didn't want that anyway. You have to believe me when I say that everything happened the way it was supposed to. You being in the dark was one of the only ways I was able to make this work."

"How did Sawyer get involved? Did you go to him? Did he come to you? Did he plan this? How long have you been planning this?" she says all in one breath.

"It's such a long story. I don't even know where to begin. What did Sawyer tell you?"

"He didn't say much. He came to my apartment last week, told me I had to leave right away, and gave me this folder with all this new identity stuff inside. Freaked me out honestly; thought he was a part of the CIA or something. He told me what busses to take, where to hide from cameras on my way out of the city, and where my hidden car was..."

She bites her lip, eyes pinging back and forth between mine, eyes filled with sadness. "When I asked what was going on, and why I was doing this, he just said it was to keep me safe. He wasn't going to tell me anything more, but I pushed. You know me. You can't just say jump and I will; I needed to know why the hell my whole life was being flipped upside down. It took a lot of cuss words, but he finally told me that Roman wasn't a good man and he had been hurting and threatening you. I didn't want to leave you, but he literally gave me no choice. He said it was life and death, and that you would be here by midnight tonight. He even gave me a number to call in case you didn't make it here by then."

I sigh, staring at her, exhaustion weighing heavy on my mind. "I know I owe you a lot and we have so much to talk about, but honestly I am so mentally and emotionally exhausted. Do you think we can pick this up tomorrow? I swear we will talk about everything over breakfast." A yawn tears from my throat just as I finish speaking.

She nods her head, standing up, then pulls me from the floor. "I have one condition though."

"What's that?"

She squeezes my sides affectionately. "I want to sleep with you tonight. I need a bestie snuggle cuddle session."

I laugh, pulling her to me for a hug. "That I can do."
Honestly, nothing has ever sounded better.

I wake up to the sound of birds chirping outside my window. I blink several times, confused at first before realization settles over me.

I did it. I really did it.

"Well, good morning sleepy head. I was starting to wonder if you were ever going to wake up," Lacey says from beside me.

I smile and roll over to face her. "Good morning."

She reaches up and runs her finger down the length of my face. "I love you. You know that right?"

"I know. I love you too," I murmur back.

"I'm sorry he hurt you," she whispers, tears pooling in her eyes.

"Me too." I lock our hands together and we lay like that looking at each other for long minutes.

"Okay, why don't we go get dressed and head into town and grab breakfast? I don't have much in here for food, but maybe we can stop by the grocery store after we eat," she says, sitting up.

"That sounds good. We also need to find a clothing store or something. I couldn't exactly bring any clothes with me. I had a small bag Sawyer packed but that was it."

She squeals, bouncing on the bed. "Oh, yes. Shopping, we definitely need to do that. Some retail therapy will do you some good. Come on! Get up! I want to go now," she gushes, earning a chuckle from me.

"Okay, crazy lady. Let me at least get dressed first." I hold my hands up in a praying gesture.

She jumps out of bed and practically sprints out of the room. "You better not take too long. We got some shopping to do!" she shouts over her shoulder.

I smile at her retreating form.

I really did miss this.

We walk into this little burger joint called *Auntie Jo's*. It's a fifties style diner with white and black tiled floors, pink and white booths, and a jukebox in the corner.

"Look, how cute. It's so charming," I coo, glancing around at the vintage decor lining the walls.

"I just love it here. I am ashamed to say I've eaten here almost every day this past week." Lacey grabs my hand and pulls me to a corner booth. We slide inside and I grab the menu from the caddy.

"What do you usually get?" I ask, scanning the menu items.

"So, I have only come for breakfast once, but I got the grits and egg special. I usually get a burger, but it's too early for that," she says, glancing at the menu.

"I have never had grits before. Did you like them?"

"They were delicious. Mabel recommended I add butter and hot sauce to them. It was a hit."

I blanch at that because that sounds gross.

"Who is Mabel?"

"That'd be me, Sugar." I look up to a woman with red curly hair, and the biggest smile I have ever seen. "Hey Sidney, you are back again I see, and you brought a friend."

Sidney?

I smile at her, raising my hand in a small wave. "Hi, I'm John."

"John. Nice to meet you. Welcome to our little town."

"Thanks." I grin back. She has one of those contagious smiles.

"Did you know what you both wanted to order?"

"We both want waters and I want the grits and eggs again, please," Lacey says.

"Uh. Can you make a bacon and egg sandwich?" I ask, before glancing back down at the menu.

"You got it Sugar. Do you want to add cheese?"

"No thank you," I say, smiling once more before setting my menu back in the holder.

"You are missing out. Cheese goes on everything."

A memory snaps to my forefront, so quick I almost get whiplash from the intrusion.

"I was hoping you'd show me what's so special about your grilled cheese."

Leta.

My mind wanders and I think about the time I taught her how to make a famous Alex grilled cheese. I wonder if she misses me. A sadness settles over me. Regardless of everything, Leta was one good thing that came from being with Roman.

Fingers snap in front of my face pulling me from my thoughts.

"I'm so sorry. What?" I glance between them quickly.

"Are you okay?" Lacey asks, concern written all over her face.

I wave her off. "Fine, sorry. I was just in the zone."

"It's alright. I was just asking if you were staying for good or just visiting?"

"Staying with La-Sidney for now." Damn it, this name business is really going to mess me up.

"Oh, that's nice. We love having new people. It doesn't happen much around here. Where are you from?"

A cold sweat breaks across my body and my brain cycles through what to say.

Fuck, I hadn't even thought of that. Why didn't I think about this? Fuck I'm screwing up this new life already.

I open my mouth to answer, having no idea what to say when Lacey cuts in, "Mabel, I think that guy over there needs you." She points somewhere behind me.

"Oh, right. duty calls. I will have your food out shortly, okay," she says, before turning and walking away.

I sigh, body slumping forward. "That went about as well as a root canal."

Lacey looks at me guiltily. "I should have given you the run down before we even left the house. I'm sorry about that."

I wave her off. "It's fine. I choked up. Thanks for the save. I would have blown my cover had you not stepped in."

Just then Mabel brings our waters over. "Food will be up in a few minutes."

We thank her and she walks off.

I inhale deeply, meeting Lacey's gaze. "Okay, so what's our story?" I ask, before taking a sip of water.

She smirks. "My name is Sidney Jones. I'm from Landing, Kansas. No family to speak of. I decided it was time for a change, so I got in my car and drove until I stumbled upon this little town, fell in love and just couldn't leave."

A laugh tears from my throat before I can stop it. "You're kidding?"

"Listen, Sawyer gave me the identity but didn't give me the story. I had to wing it, okay."

We both burst out laughing at that.

"Well, better than me, I was about to blurt out a penguin farmer from Alaska," I say between chuckles.

"Shut up, you were not," she gasps, laughing so hard tears are streaming down her face.

"No, I wasn't. But fuck, it would have been close to that."

We both continue to laugh and it's...nice.

"I missed this," she says once we have calmed down.

"Me too," I say, reaching across the table and locking our hands together.

"So, are you going to tell me about it?" she whispers, and my whole body tenses at her words.

I sigh, "I will, soon. I promise. I just need to decompress a little bit first."

She nods in understanding. "I get it. Just remember I'm here, okay? When you're ready."

I just nod, before glancing down at the table top once more.

I don't know if I will ever be ready.

The clothing store we decided on was actually a second-hand shop. I freaking loved it. Not only were the prices awesome but I look really good in flannels.

Lacey bought a cowboy hat. Why? I don't know, because I doubt she will ever wear it; but it did look cute on her in the store.

"So, that was fun," I say as we head into the grocery store.

She hums in agreement, "Yeah, it was and I cannot get over the prices. You got six pants and like twelve shirts for not even a hundred bucks. We would never find a deal like that in Vegas," she says, grabbing a cart as we head into the store to buy groceries.

"I know. I wish they had some pajamas though, and I need to find a department store or something because I need some more boxers."

"I mean, I'd offer to let you borrow some of mine but..." she trails off.

My eyebrows draw up in wonder. "Yes, because that's not weird at all."

She shrugs, a devious smile crossing her lips. "What's a little panty sharing between friends?"

My gaze snaps to the side as I hear a gasp.

Jesus Christ.

I meet the horrified gaze of an elderly woman. I shake my head vehemently. "I'm sorry ma'am, just ignore her." I practically rip Lacey's arm out of the socket, as I pull her to a different aisle. "For fucks sake."

Lacey laughs, smacking at my hand that's gripping on her.

"Hey, I wanted some cookies." She mock pouts.

"Too fucking bad. No cookies for you." I waggle my finger at her.

"Fine, but I'm getting cereal and that's just not optional."

The smile drops from my face as the memory washes over me.

"Okay. Marshmallow Stars or Berry Crunch?"

Fuck. No. No. No. No. Get out of my head!

"Hey. Are you okay?" Lacey asks, face scrunched up with concern.

"Yeah, sorry. Just lost in thought," I say, shaking away the memory. "Um, can we just grab a few things and head home? I'm not feeling so great all of a sudden."

"Of course. No problem. Are you sure you're okay?"

"Yeah. Fine. I think I just need to rest. It's been a long few days."

"It has been. Let's just grab some snacks and sandwich stuff for now. We can always come back another time."

I nod and follow behind her, lost in my own head.

Praying for a time when the thought of Roman doesn't gut me completely.

Chapter Thirty-Two

"Oh God. Look at all the snow," I squeal, looking out our cabin window, giddy with excitement.

"It came down good last night," Roman says, wrapping his arms around me.

"I wish it snowed more in Vegas. I want to go out there and play."

"Let me warm you up first," he murmurs against my skin.

"No way, mister." I bat his hands away, sliding from his grasp. "We were at it for hours last night, aren't you tired yet?"

"Never tired of you." He flashes me a devilish smile.

"You are a sex addict." I point an accusing finger at him.

"I'm an Alex addict, now let me get my fill." He reaches out to grab me once more, but I dodge him.

"No, later. I want to build a snowman."

He sighs, shaking his head. "Please don't start singing that ridiculous song."

I almost laugh at that.

"You know about Frozen?" I arch my eyebrow in wonder.

"I may be a busy man, but I don't live under a rock." He shrugs, and I can't help but smile at his expression.

"Oh, you like it," I tease. "Admit it, you like Disney movies." I jab a finger into his chest.

He rolls his eyes, and reaches out to snatch my hand before I can pull away. "I'm not that gay."

"Hey," I smack his chest playfully, "I take offense to that." I mock pout, and he laughs, pulling me flush against his body.

"I'm so sorry." He leans in and kisses my lips softly. "Let me make it up to you." He continues to kiss my lips in little nibbling pecks.

"You're distracting me," I say, voice filled with desire. He pulls back to look at my face, fire dancing behind his eyes.

"Good."

"What do you think about the Blue Marlin?" My attention snaps to Lacey.

"What?" I ask, trying to push the memory away.

She turns to me, eyebrows raised in confusion. "Blue Marlin? To put in an application?" She gestures to the newspaper laid out in front of her.

Fuck when had we switched topics?

"Oh, um. No, I think I'm going to stay away from bars and restaurants."

She arches her eyebrow in surprise. "Really?"

"I'm just feeling something different? Maybe doing something else will help make this feel like a real fresh start, you know." I shrug noncommittally and stand up. "Do you want a drink?"

"I get that, and no, I'm good."

"Be right back." I walk into the kitchen and lean against the counter, covering my face with my hands.

It's been like this since I left. Getting lost in memories of Roman as time passes around me. I know it's only been a few days but for fucks sake, I'm ready for it to stop. Roman has no place here, in this new life that I'm trying to create for myself. I need to get it together.

I straighten and grab a water bottle from the fridge before heading back into the living room.

"So, do you have any ideas?" Lacey asks, when I settle back onto the couch.

"Not really. I was thinking about asking Mabel if she knew of any places hiring."

She purses her lips in thought. "Oh, that's smart. I should've thought of that."

"What about you?"

"Haven't found anything yet, but I'll keep looking. Something has to pop up soon, right?" She shrugs, turning back to the hiring section in the paper.

"Want to go for a walk down to the beach with me?" Our house is off the shore of the Gulf of Mexico, we haven't done much exploring together yet, and I'm eager to do so.

"Yes, let's. I need a break anyway. All this reading is giving me a headache." She stands, stretching her limbs. "We can go see Mabel for dinner. I'm craving one of those chili cheeseburgers."

"You and all those damn burgers, I swear you have been eating them every day." I slide on my shoes.

"I can't help it. They are just so good. I can practically smell them from here." She smiles dreamily.

"If you say so." I lean forward, smacking a kiss to her cheek. "Let's go."

The walk on the beach was more relaxing than I anticipated. We collected several colorful shells and I even found a shark tooth. Now we're sitting in a booth, sipping on chocolate milkshakes, waiting on our food to come out.

"I guess I will swing by the drug store and see if they still need a cashier?"

"Is that a question?"

She shrugs, rolling her eyes. "I mean, I don't really want to work as a cashier, but the other options weren't really anything I was wanting to do either. I could apply at the seafood place, but the thought alone makes me nauseous. Can you imagine working around tuna all day? Gross."

I nod at that. "Yeah, hard pass for me. I don't know. She said the grocery store was looking for someone to stock the shelves at night. Might not be such a bad idea. I mean I don't really feel like dealing with people right now anyway, so that might be just up my alley."

"You can always try it and if you don't like it find something else."

"That's true. It just seems like there aren't a lot of jobs to come by around here."

"Got to love a small town," Mabel says, dropping off our meals.

"You always show up at the right time." I smile at her warmly.

"I'm like a cat. I know everything, see everything, a little feisty and I'm super sneaky." She winks, throwing her hand up and striking the air.

I shake my head, a chuckle leaving my lips, "Good to know. I'll keep that in mind."

Lacey laughs, "Oh yeah. We will."

"Alright Sugar, y'all need anything else?"

"I think we're good."

"Just holler if you need me."

Lacey is already half way through her burger by the time Mabel walks away.

"Damn, is it good?" I ask, cutting into my meatloaf.

"The best," she mumbles around a mouthful.

"I don't know how you aren't tired of it yet."

"It's so flavorful. Do you want a bite?" She leans forward dangling the chili cheeseburger in front of my face.

I eye it with displeasure. "No thank you. I will stick to this. Maybe next time." We both know I'm not eating that, ever. I don't like chili. Who wants to eat something that looks like chewed up dog food?

"Well, I want a bite of yours. I haven't had it yet." She opens her mouth wide waiting for me to deposit a mouthful.

"How charming," I state blandly, before shoving my fork between her parted lips.

"Mmm, that's good. Maybe next time I will get that." She looks away as if in thought.

"I seriously doubt it."

"Yeah, me too." I just shake my head before finishing the rest of my meal.

Holy shit. My body is sore.

I punched my card, ending my first shift at the grocery store and let me tell you, that shit is for the birds. I had no idea how heavy a case of cans could be. Or that stocking shelves involved carrying the boxes from the back to do so. I mean I was expecting some kind of rolling cart or something, but nope. They don't have one.

I guess being the new guy means I'm stuck doing all the grunt work. The guy I worked with tonight, Toby, had me fetching all the cases and he was putting them up. That sounded good in theory until I lifted my fifteenth case and thought my back was going to give out. Luckily he was nice enough to let me switch and he took over the lifting as I started stocking.

I cannot wait to get into my bed.

The drive home is quick and I stumble out of my car, before heading inside. The lights are on when I open the door, which surprises me because Lacey should be asleep right now, considering it's four-thirty in the morning. I walk into the front door, setting my keys down on the end table by the door before heading down the hall. I find Lacey pacing back and forth along the expanse of the living room.

"Hey, why are you up?" She stops, turning towards me with tears streaming down her cheeks. I rush over to her. "What's going on? Are you okay?"

She sobs harder, burying her face into my chest. "I don't know what to do."

"About what?" She just shakes her head, clutching my shirt tightly, tears soaking through the material. "Lacey, talk to me. You're scaring me here."

I walk her backwards to the couch, sitting us both down, then reach over to the end table and grab a tissue before handing it over to her.

"Breathe, in and out. Copy me, okay."

She does, inhaling and exhaling, sobs slowly coming to a stop.

I sit there assessing her, taking in her swollen eyes and red flushed cheeks. "Are you okay?"

She shakes her head, lip trembling. "I fucked up." She looks at me with so much sadness.

"How?"

She sighs and gets up leaving the room, then comes back a minute later. She sits down again, biting her lip before holding up the white stick in her hand. I blink at it for several minutes trying to understand what I'm seeing, before realization dawns on me.

"You're pregnant?" I squeak, and she nods, tears once again rolling down her face. "How? Who?" She hasn't been seeing anyone that I know of.

"Ah, don't hate me." She looks at me with a guilty expression.

"I could never."

She inhales deeply before exhaling slowly. "Sawyer."

"What now?" I shake my head in confusion. "I thought you said it didn't work out after your first date."

"We didn't, not really. He was really nice and respectable, but honestly not my type. Then one night we met up again and we had too many drinks..." She trails off and I can put the rest together.

"When was this?" I question, still confused as to when this all could happen.

"About six months ago."

I glance down at her flat belly, eyebrows shooting up to my hairline. "Oh, so it was more than once."

She bites her lip, looking away from me. "It was a lot of times, Alex. We didn't stop sleeping together after that first time. I can't explain it. It's like he flipped this switch inside of me. I started to like him. A lot. Please don't be mad." She bats away a few tears.

"I'm not mad. Why would I be mad?" I shake my head in confusion.

"Because I didn't tell you," she whispers, eyes searching mine.

"Pot meet kettle," I say, pointing between the two of us, earning a smile from her. "Does he know?"

"Hell, no. And he isn't going to. The night he told me I had to leave because of Roman, that was the night he told me about what he does. Can you imagine raising a child in that type of environment? I wouldn't subject an innocent baby to that. Sawyer's life is violent." She starts crying again. I pull her to me, rub her back and tell her that it's all going to be okay.

"How can you say that? This isn't okay. None of this is okay."

"Look at me." She raises her tear glazed expression to mine and I cup her cheeks. "It's going to be okay because you have me, always. I will be there for you both every step of the way. You are not alone in this. I promise." Her lip wobbles and she wraps her arms around me tightly.

"I love you," she murmurs into my shirt.

"I love you, too." We hug, speaking quietly for long minutes before I pull back and look at her.

"What?"

"I'm going to be a Guncle!" I shriek, jumping from the couch, pumping my fist in the air. Thankful when her joyous laughter reaches my ears.

ALEX

Chapter Thirty-Three

The days fly by like pages flipping in a book on a windy day.

I don't really have a sense of time anymore. I just know today is Wednesday. If it wasn't for Lacey, I doubt I'd even know that.

I stare at the expanse of the ocean from my spot on the sandy beach. The water's crystal clear and the sun shines brightly. I remember being little and doing this same thing with my mom. We would sit for hours, watching the water splash against the shore, and admiring the sky change to oranges and pinks as the sun sets.

That was a good time, a simpler time.

I remember looking out and thinking of the edge of the water, wondering where it ended and what was on the other side. My ten-year-old brain didn't understand that the ocean was a body of never ending water. I just assumed everything had an end.

I used to think about pirates, how they'd ship out to sea for months at a time and I'd wonder about what would happen to them if they drove their ships over the ocean side. Was there a lip on the end, keeping all the water in so no one can just fall over? Or would they fall into an abyss of nothingness? And if they fell, would they ever be able to come back?

That's how I feel right now. Like a lost soul, floating around the edge of the water, waiting to fall into the abyss of nothing. And honestly, I don't know if I'd want to come back.

I don't understand what's happening to me. I don't feel better yet, aren't I supposed to be feeling better?

Freedom was all I ever wanted. Living a life that I chose for myself. So why, now that I finally have it, do I feel like my lungs cannot fully fill with air? I smile for Lacey because I don't want her to know how broken I really am. She would try to save me and at this point I'm not sure there is anything left to save.

I stand, grab a shell from the sand and walk to the shoreline. I rear back and toss the shell; I meant for it to skip, but it doesn't, it just plops into the water, sinking down to the very bottom.

Like I long to do; just dive in and not come back up.

The water is supposed to be like baptism, right? Soul cleansing.

I need that.

Roman is a monster. The living devil and I let him into my head and into my heart. I need some purity to wash away my sins; I need to get the bad out.

I don't even realize I'm moving until I'm waist deep in the ocean.

"Forgive me father, for I have sinned." I whisper to the waves.

I submerge my body into the water, sinking down to the ocean floor, releasing all the air from my lungs as I sit there. I open my eyes and the salt burns as I stare into the open abyss. It's peaceful down here.

I think about my mom and about that summer on the beach. I think about her flushed pink skin from the too hot sun. I think about her whimsical laugh as we tossed bread to the birds. I think about her encouraging words as I ran back and forth with buckets of water, as I tried to fill the moat around my sandcastle.

My lungs are past the point of burning but I don't come up for air. I just sit there, lost in memories of those days with my mom. I miss her.

I close my eyes, getting lost in bliss as a hand settles on my bicep, roughly pulling me to the surface. As my head pops above the water, I gasp, letting air fill my aching lungs.

"What the fuck were you thinking?" Lacey shouts, face pinched in anger.

"I was just swimming."

She shakes her head. "That was not swimming. Do you have any idea how long you were down there for? I was walking down from the house when I saw you go under."

"It was nothing."

She looks at me with worry marrying her features, and she grabs my hand, pulling me from the water. It's only then that I realize I'm still wearing my shoes and jeans.

Fuck, I'm losing my mind.

"It's freezing," Lacey says through chattering teeth.

Damn it, she's soaked now too.

"Come on, we need to get dry," I say, pulling her in the direction of the house.

She points an accusing finger at me. "We are talking tonight, I know you don't want to, but this cannot keep happening. I'm worried sick over you."

Her words are like knives stabbing into my heart. I never wanted to hurt her.

"I'm sorry," I say, as we head back towards the house.

She clings tighter to me. "Don't be sorry. Just let me help you. Give me some of your burden. That's what I'm here for."

I don't know what to say, so I just nod.

"Go take a warm shower. I'm going to change," she says and pushes me in the direction of the bathroom.

I do as she says, stripping and climbing into the shower. I hate this. These broken feelings I have inside. He did this to me.

Roman.

I shiver at the thought of him.

He plagues my dreams and every free moment, and yet he is still my every fantasy and the keeper of my heart.

I think about his eyes, so clear and blue as he stares at me. The way his lips dip before he kisses me. Kisses, sloppily wet, and needy. Desire, I think of his desire for me. His bulky frame dominating me into submission.

I slide my hand over my aching erection, pumping a few times to relieve the pressure. I think about Roman's dirty words, the way he smells all covered in sweat as he pounds into my pliant body.

Fuck.

My orgasm explodes through me like a bullet from the chamber. I groan loudly, leaning against the tiled wall for support as I come down. There is something seriously wrong with me.

I slide down to the tub floor, as sobs wrack my body. I need to talk to Lacey, I need help.

I lean back against the couch. My eyes swollen from all the crying. Lacey looks about the same, clutching my hand like it's her lifeline.

I just told her the entire story and it was brutal. I had to stop several times when the crying became too much to talk through.

"I want to kill him," she spits, anger contorting her features. "I cannot believe you've been dealing with this by yourself all this time."

I shrug. "He wouldn't let me tell you, and I didn't want you to know anyway," I say, wrapping the blanket tighter around myself.

Tears slide down her cheeks and she bats them away angrily. "But why? I would have helped you."

"You couldn't have, and I couldn't risk you getting hurt." I reach out, squeezing her hand in comfort.

"I want to kill him, then bring him back from the dead and kill him again," she grits out, teeth snapping together tightly.

"You're so cute when you're angry." I run a finger down her cheek.

Her face scrunches in disgust. "I'm serious."

"I know, and I love you for it." I bring her hand to my lips and kiss her knuckles.

We sit in silence, staring at the muted television.

"I feel like I've ruined our lives," I say, voice cracking.

Lacey, whips around to look at me, eyebrows scrunched in confusion. "What?"

"I mean if you weren't my friend, you wouldn't even be in this situation." Her face falls at my words and she scoots across the couch, wrapping her arms around me.

"No, don't do that. I don't ever want to hear you say that again," she whispers, rubbing circles on my back.

"But it's true," I bite out in frustration. "You should be cutting hair in a salon, not half way across the country with another identity, working at a drugstore. You had plans, plans that are now long gone."

She sighs, "Oh, my sweet little baby. We both had plans, but that's just life. Things happen, and you have no control over it. Maybe I didn't plan on being in Alabama as Sidney, but it's been an experience."

"But then you met Sawyer-"

She cuts me off, shaking her head. "And I'm getting a beautiful little baby out of the deal." She puts my hand on her slightly protruding belly. "Plus, you're forgetting another important thing."

I sniffle, grabbing a tissue and wiping my nose. "What's that?"

She looks deep into my eyes, cupping my cheeks before saying, "I wouldn't have you."

I lean into her, holding her like she's the only thing keeping me to the ground. And honestly, she is.

"I just want to feel better," I mutter, exhaustion taking over.

"And you will, but it's going to take time."

I nod, squeezing her to me more tightly, inhaling the comforting smell of her vanilla body spray.

"Just breathe," she whispers.

So, I do. I just breathe.

One step at a time.

Chapter Thirty-Four

I hate waiting.

I feel like the wait at a doctor's office is always the longest. Seriously, what is the point of making an appointment if you end up waiting for thirty plus minutes after said appointment anyway?

Lacey flips through a magazine, foot bouncing as she anxiously pops her gum. "You okay?" I wonder aloud.

"Fine, just nervous."

"Don't be, everything is going to be okay," I say, squeezing her hand.

She goes to respond just as her name is being called. We both jump up and head to the waiting nurse. She leads us back to a side room, where she checks all of Lacey's vitals, and weight, before taking us to a room.

Ugh, more waiting.

Luckily, it's not as long this time, and the doctor comes in shortly after.

"How are you feeling today, Sidney?" she asks, walking over to where Lacey is sitting on the examination table.

"Fine. Just nervous, ready to see the baby."

"No complications or issues?"

"None." She shakes her head, biting her lip anxiously.

"Perfect. Alright, dear, lean back and lift your shirt and we'll get started." Lacey complies easily as the doctor grabs a container of gel. "This may be a little cold," she says, pouring a glob onto her belly.

"It's not too bad. I've been having hot flashes like crazy lately," she says, zeroing in on the screen.

"Oh, that's normal, so don't worry. It happens because your hormones are changing."

Lacey nods at that.

We both stare at the screen in anticipation as the doctor rubs the probe over Lacey's belly. My heart beats wildly as I stare at the little life on the screen. My sweet little niece or nephew.

"There is your baby," she says, pointing out all the body parts to us as she passes them with the probe. "Do you want to know the gender?"

Oh my God, really? I glance down at Lacey, her eyes wide with wonder.

"Yes." Lacey beams, squeezing my hand tightly.

"It's a girl," the doctor says with a smile and I shriek, pumping my fists up in the air.

"A princess. We're having a princess." I look down at Lacey to see tears streaming down her cheeks, I'm concerned until I see her beaming smile. My whole heart melts at that.

"A girl," she whispers, looking at me in pure excitement.

"Our girl." I lean down and kiss her forehead. "Ah, she is going to be spoiled rotten. We have so much to do, so much stuff to buy. And oh my god, we have to come up with a name."

Lacey giggles at my enthusiasm and the doctor hands us the ultrasound pictures.

"Congratulations, you two."

We both smile and leave, traveling the twenty miles out of Mobile, back to Spring Haven.

"Are you hungry?" I ask, as we get closer.

"No, not yet. Do you want to go shopping? I was thinking we could go ahead and get a crib and some baby stuff now that we know it's a girl."

I nod my head, in excitement. "Absolutely, that's what I was planning on anyways."

"I cannot believe it's a girl. I was really expecting it to be a boy."

"I never doubted, I knew my princess was in there." I beam, reaching over to rub her belly lovingly.

"We're halfway there. Time just flies doesn't it?"

I blanch at that.

Everything is passing me by as I sit in purgatory.

"Don't lie to me."

"I'm not. Roman, please listen."

"Enough. I told you what would happen if you lied."

"Roman, please don't do this."

"You should have thought of that before."

A scream tears from my throat as I bolt up from the bed. I run into the bathroom, barely making it to the toilet in time. My stomach heaves as it empties and sweat coats my brow as the nightmare fades away.

I feel hands on my back, rubbing in soothing circles. "You're okay. Get it out," Lacey coos, setting a damp rag on my neck.

"Thank you," I mutter, after my stomach settles. "Sorry I woke you," I say, sitting down on the tiled floor.

"I was up already. Getting harder to sleep now," she says, rubbing her rounding stomach.

I smile at that; she's going to be such an amazing mom. "How is our girl?"

"Getting big, and living on my bladder." She pouts.

"I cannot wait to hold her."

"Well, get ready mister, because once she is out, she is yours." She pokes her tongue out at me playfully.

I rub the grooves in the tile on the floor, trying to push away the last remnants of the nightmare.

"Another nightmare?" she asks, pulling me from my wandering thoughts.

"Yeah," I sigh, rubbing my eyes.

"They are getting worse" she muses, running her fingers through my damp hair.

"I know."

"I really think you should talk to someone. I know you don't like the idea of talking to strangers about what happened, but there are support groups, therapists, people who can help you move on."

"I don't know if I can," I mutter, pulling my knees up so I can rest my forehead against my knees. I want to curl up into a little ball and disappear.

"You have to. You can't keep all this bottled up inside. It's eating away at you day by day. Sooner or later it's all going to rise to the surface and you're going to explode," she says, voice riddled with concern.

"I can't talk about this."

"Why not? Why can't you talk about it?"

"Because I'm fucking humiliated," I bite out through clenched teeth.

She sighs, "Baby, why? It's not your fault."

I look up. "No, it's not. I know that." I shake my head in frustration.

"Then why?"

"I don't want people to see how fucked up I am."

She rears back as if I slapped her. "You are not." She points at me.

"I am!" I say with conviction, smacking my hand to my chest.

"Why do you think that?"

"Because I miss him." The words tear from my throat before I've even registered that I'd said them. "And if I think about what happened, if I let go of it, then that means letting go of Roman and I just... I can't. Do. It." I rub at the tears streaming down my cheeks. I stare into Lacey's sorrow filled expression. "I know it doesn't make sense, but I can't just let it go... I can't let *him* go."

I want to rip my hair out; I want to scream. I want to be anyone else but me right now.

"I love him, Lacey. I love him, even after everything and I'm mad! Fucking angry that he could hurt me like he did. Angry he could look me in my face and lie so easily. Angry that I wasn't enough for him to want to be better. But mostly, I'm fucking hurt. I'm in agony, over the loss of what we had. Agony of the life we missed out on. Agony because I miss him." Lacey cups my face between her palms.

"Oh, Alex. Of course, you miss him. There's nothing wrong with that. I would be more worried if you didn't miss him. You married him, you planned a future with him. You cannot beat yourself up over that. It's normal. But healing doesn't mean you forget, it just means you're moving forward with your life."

I shake my head, rubbing the spot over my heart. "I feel like I need him. Like I'm suffocating without him, this can't be normal."

She looks at me, shaking her head. "You are so strong."

I shake my head vigorously. "I'm not."

"You are, and one day you're going to look back on this and realize just how much. You have been through something most people can't even fathom and look at you. You are here, and you are living. You picked up your entire life and moved across the country to start over. In a place you don't know, with people you don't know, just to get your life back. If that doesn't scream strength, I don't know what does," she says, voice warm and proud.

I wish I could believe her; I want more than anything to. But it's hard to believe in your strength, when you feel weak.

"I will talk to someone," I finally manage to say.

Her fingers squeeze me tighter. "It will all be okay. I promise."

I really hope she's right.

Chapter Thirty-Five

The diner looks even more pink than usual. Streamers hanging from the ceiling, big pink balloons, pink table cloth, little pink tiaras, pink cake, pink baby games...

Pink. Pink. Everywhere.

Lacey is having her baby shower today and Mabel helped me pull it all together for her. We have slowly been making friends and meeting people around town, so I wasn't too surprised by the turn out at Lacey's shower. I have a feeling that it had something to do with Mabel. She has been extremely supportive of Lacey and I since we came to Spring Haven.

Thank goodness for her.

"What do you think? Too much?" she asks, looking over the decked out room.

I shake my head. "Nah, I think it's perfect. Besides, nothing is too much for a princess," I say, sliding one of the pink tiaras on my head before handing one over to Mabel.

"That was my thought exactly."

Baby showers are fun, but oh are they exhausting. We did several party games and now everyone is oohing and ahhing over all the baby items. Did I mention pink? Ah, and glitter. Don't forget the glitter. Pink tutu's, bows, bottles, blankets, clothes.

I love it, don't get me wrong but damn it looks like a unicorn threw up in here.

I smile watching Lacey as she looks over all the items she got for the baby. I can't wait to see her become a mom. Lacey has such a natural instinct to love and nurture. I have no doubt this baby will be the most loved one on the planet.

I grab a trash can and walk around to start cleaning up the mess as people are starting to leave.

"John, will you unlock your car? I want to start putting all of the baby's stuff in there." I turn towards Lacey, eyebrows arched.

"You really think I'm going to let you load the car?"

"I'm pregnant, not incapable." She pouts, folding her arms over her chest.

"Not happening, you can sit your cute, little butt down, and I will start."

"I guess I'll just start picking up where you left off then." She motions for me to slide the trash can over to her. I sigh in exasperation, but do it anyway, it's not a fair fight, and she knows it.

I smack a kiss to her cheek and grab some of the gifts.

Several trips later, and with Mabel helping me stuff my car to capacity, all the gifts are in there. It's going to be really fun putting all of these away.

I slam the trunk just as a chill runs down my spine. I can't help but get the eerie feeling I'm being watched. I look around but don't see anyone. I frown at that.

"You okay?" Mabel asks.

"Yes, sorry. I think we're done."

"Let's hope so, otherwise Sidney is going to be carrying items on her lap."

We walk back inside, and I glance over my shoulder once more. I don't know why, but for some reason I cannot help the uneasy feeling that has settled over me.

The nursery is done.

I'm sitting cross legged on the floor, looking up at Lacey as she hangs the last picture on the wall. I smile at the little Dumbo painting. She wanted to do elephants for the theme, so the room is painted in a soft gray with pink fixtures.

"It looks so good." I turn towards the rest of the room, admiring it.

She taps her chin. "It's missing one thing. Stay here, I'll be right back," she says, before walking out of the room.

I stand just as she comes back in. She's holding some kind of sign.

"What's that?" I step closer, prepared to take it from her.

"It's her name. I got it made. It just came in the mail yesterday." She flips it around so I can see.

Tears instantly spring to my eyes as I look it over.

"Alexia Michelle," I read aloud. "You're naming her after me?" My lip wobbles as tears stream down my cheeks.

Lacey sets the sign down. "I couldn't think of a stronger name."

I rush forward, wrapping her in a hug. "I love you. I am so honored."

"I love you, too."

"Thank you for being here for me. For always being there for me. You pulled me out of the depression years after my mom died and now everything with Roman," I trail off, shaking my head, eyes radiating with love. "There are no words to express the amount of gratitude I hold for you. You are the kindest, and most thoughtful person I have ever known. I can't even imagine a life without you in it."

She rubs her eyes, smacking me on the chest. "Stop, now you're making me cry. I feel the same. I love you so much. You're the greatest friend I have ever had."

We sway back and forth, locked in a tight hug.

When I finally pull away from her I grab the sign. "Should we hang this up?" I ask, voice full of pride.

She nods. "Yes, we absolutely should."

I make quick work of hanging the picture before taking a step back and admiring the finished nursery. I don't know how but we've managed to take an entirely fucked up situation and turn it into something so beautiful.

I just need to remember. It's not a bad life. Just a bad day.

ROMAN

Chapter Thirty-Six

June
Day 1

Sweat. Blood. Urine.

They are all the same. These gangster wannabes think that they know the game.

They don't.

Then, to top it off, they're juvenile. What kind of man walks into the lion's den with nothing more than a loaded gun? I'll tell you what kind; a dumb ass.

Crack. Thud. Smack.

I roll my eyes, bored with this already as Jimmy takes another swing, brass knuckles cracking across the man's jaw. I watch the teeth and blood shoot from his mouth before landing on the ground near my shoes.

I glance down at my watch, then signal for Jimmy to stop.

"Send him back to his trivial little gang, and make sure they understand the message. No more selling on Giuliani territory, and if they do, I won't be so understanding next time." I nod to one of the guards, who grabs the guy and drags him out of the ring.

"I don't know if I should be worried about these kids lack of fear, or laugh at how stupid they are becoming," Jimmy says, wiping his bloody hands on a towel.

"I'm going with the latter," Sawyer chimes in.

I shake my head, and pull out my phone, frowning when I notice Alex still hasn't responded to my earlier text message.

"Jimmy, make sure you have the lineup for Saturday's fighters to me by midnight. I need to see who is going up against Valentino. The big bastard needs a top contender for it to even be a fair fight."

"You got it, boss."

I fire off instructions for my men to get the area cleaned up, then turn to Sawyer. "Have you heard from Alex's security?"

"Not lately, why? Is everything okay?" Sawyer pulls out his phone, I assume to call and check in, but I stop him.

"No, don't. He's probably doing something. I'll talk to him once I'm home."

You know the expression, there is a thin line between love and hate? Well, that is the perfect tagline to how our relationship has been for months. I'm a terrible husband, but I already knew that.

I follow Sawyer out to the car, thinking over the months in my head. After he found out about my uncle, he shut down completely. We hit a really low spot then, and haven't managed to come back up from it.

He just needs to see reason, eventually he will. Maybe with a little more time, we can get back what we had before all of this shit happened. I sigh, leaning back heavily against the seat in the car. I shake my head, trying to rid my wandering thoughts as we pull into the driveway of my home. I nod towards Sawyer, before getting out of the car.

I wonder if Alex will be happy to see me today?

Sometimes it's there, that look of admiration he once held for me, and I long to have those looks again. I long to have his sweet, unguarded touch. His passionate affections that he used to show so freely. If I could go back in time and unkill Giovanni, I would. The piece of shit got off too easily. He took the one good thing I thought I had and ruined it.

"Good evening." I turn towards Leta, who is standing at the stove, stirring.

"Leta, it smells wonderful in here." I walk over admiring the pot of food, before meeting her worried expression.

"What's wrong?"

"He hasn't come out of bed today," she murmurs, face scrunched in frustration.

"Is he sick?"

She scoffs, looking at me, shaking her head. "We both know that's not what's wrong here, Roman."

"Leta." My tone holds warning she knows better than to cross. So, I'm surprised by her stern expression as she glares at me.

"You need to do better. You cannot keep on like this. I don't know what all you do to that boy, but from what I do know..." she trails off, shaking her head at me.

"You don't worry about, Alex," I say, jaw clenched tight, before storming off.

I don't need anyone to preach to me about Alex. I know what's going on better than anyone. I storm through the house, anger coursing through my veins. Fuck, why did she have to do this? I was fine until she opened her mouth.

At the door to our bedroom, I lean my head against the wood, trying to control my flared temper. I don't need to go in there guns blazing, ready to rip him a new one. Being hard on him hasn't worked out like I thought it would, to my utter dismay, I cannot understand why not. My father's punishments were way harder than anything I could ever bestow upon Alex, so why is he acting like I'm the villain?

I just want him to understand me. I just need him to see me. The man he loves is inside.

I groan, turn the door handle and walk into our room.

To my surprise, the bed is made. I arch my eyebrows in confusion as I scan the expanse of the room. No Alex.

"Alex," I call out, walking into the bathroom. The light's off, but I still check, before moving on to the closet.

I frown, pulling out my phone to check his tracker. The red dot on the screen blinks rapidly, indicating he is home.

Where is he?

I turn to go check the rest of the house, when something on the dresser catches my attention.

I walk over to it, my heart pounding an uneven staccato as I pick up the envelope. On the outside *Roman* is written in neat cursive and I flip it around to open it, pulling the letter out that is tucked inside.

> *Roman,*
> *As you've probably realized by now, I'm gone.*
> *I'm done, Roman.*
> *Done and tired.*
> *Tired of being hurt the way I am, tired of watching every move I make, in the likely event I say the wrong thing to set you off. Tired of watching the man I once knew, turn into a man I no longer know.*
> *When I met you, I never realized how much I craved to have somebody. You gave me everything I never even knew I wanted. I was happy.*
> *We were happy.*
> *Until we weren't. You took everything I thought we had and shattered it. I watched it break and burn right in front of my eyes.*
> *I don't even recognize the man I call my husband anymore.*
> *This person, this man is not my husband. The Roman I knew who fed me strawberries on our honeymoon, the one who kissed me on the hotel rooftop, and the one who held me like I was the most precious thing in the world. He would have never hurt me the way you have.*
> *All we've become is pain and hate and I cannot live like that anymore.*
> *I won't live like that anymore.*

I love you, with everything I have inside me, but it's not enough. I'm sorry it had to end this way, but I guess fate had it wrong this time. Please take care and get some help.
You deserve more than this life. Try to do something with this chance.
Find Redemption. I know you didn't choose this; you were born into it, but you can choose your future.

All my love,
Alex

I don't even realize I'm crying until I see a teardrop fall onto the paper. The letter floats to the ground and I lift my hands, raking my shaking fingers through my hair. I then notice something gleaming on the dresser.

Alex's wedding band.

My knees give out from underneath me and before I even register what's happening my whole body crashes to the floor. My chest rises and falls in rapid succession as I try to catch my breath.

I can't breathe.

I rip open my shirt collar, tearing the buttons in the process, but I don't care. My lungs feel constricted, and I feel myself hyperventilating.

I pull my phone out of my pocket, hitting Sawyer, before shakily bringing the phone to my ear.

"Boss." Sawyer's voice rings out through the line, but I cannot speak, my heart pounds in my chest so rapidly, I think I'm going to pass out. "Boss?"

I shake my head, opening and closing my mouth like a fish. No words escaping. I feel the flush of warmth spread throughout my body, and I break out in a cold sweat.

I can hear Sawyer shout something, before I hear the sound of several feet pounding up the stairs. The room door bursts open and my men flood inside, shock and confusion clear across their expressions.

"Boss?" someone says, but I don't know who.

A jolt of pain hits me in the chest and I clutch my hand over the spot. My breathing is erratic and I am sucking in lungfuls of air, but it's almost like I cannot get oxygen.

Sawyer comes barging through the door then, taking in my state and glancing around the room.

"Roman?" That's the last thing I hear before the world around me goes dark.

ROMAN

Chapter Thirty-Seven

July
Day 35

"How can there be nothing?" I bark at Detective Dominic Valentina.

"I'm telling you, Roman, I have him on cameras just past the strip, after that nothing. It's the craziest magic act I've ever seen. I've run every camera in a thirty mile radius. No Alex."

"A man doesn't just disappear," I spit through clenched teeth.

"I know that, more than anyone. But I'm telling you, Roman, he's gone."

His words are clear, but the message isn't delivered.

"Keep looking." I smash the end call button before he can say anything else.

I slam my phone down onto my desk. My monster is warring with me to be unleashed. I grab the crystal tumbler and throw it against the wall with all my strength. It shatters, sending shards of glass across the expanse of my office.

FUCK!

I rake my fingers through my hair, anger coursing through my veins. How can he just be gone? Worse, he took Lacey with him, so I can't question her.

It doesn't make sense; how can one man disappear without a trace?

I have found people hidden away under witness protection, yet my husband vanishes like he never even existed.

He had to have had help, but who? Not one of my men would dare, or would they?

"You never know who could be lurking, what friend may be a foe."

My father's words ring through my head. Heaven help the person who took Alex away from me.

August
Day 72

Eleven weeks.

I feel every minute of those eleven weeks.

I can't sleep, I can't eat, I feel like the world is imploding.

He's gone; I will never accept this.

Dominic has yet to find any leads and I am desperate for not only answers but for a resolution.

Most days I'm in the ring, laying my anger out on some unsuspecting bastard. Trying to channel my aggression into something other than drugs and alcohol. I wince as Sawyer tilts my head to the side, assessing the bruise now forming on my left cheek.

"It could have been worse," he says, causing me to snort.

"Yeah, I could be dead."

His eyebrows arch. "There is that."

"I feel dead."

His eyes meet mine and I see a flicker of something pass in his expression but it quickly disappears. Before I can ask about it, the door to the ring bursts open and Jimmy comes barreling inside.

"Boss, we have a problem."

"What now?" I sigh in exasperation.

"We caught another one." I shake my head at that. These little street fucks have been becoming more ballsy lately. The guards follow behind Jimmy, dragging someone in with them.

They slam the guy into a chair, and he immediately goes to get up. But Sawyer pulls his gun, stopping the kid in his tracks. Yeah, a kid.

He can't be over eighteen.

I sigh, rubbing my forehead. "What's your name?"

"Fuck you." I laugh at that; this kid has more balls than half the men who have sat on the end of my punishments.

"I can see why you were chosen," I say, earning a glare from him. "Listen, kid-"

"I'm not a kid," he spits out.

"How old are you?"

"Nineteen." I arch my brow, crouching down to his level, meeting his fierce glare with my stern one.

"Want to try that again?"

He crosses his arms over his chest, looking down at the ground before muttering, "Sixteen."

"I thought so," I sigh, standing. "I don't hurt kids, not my style. They call me a lot of things but a child murderer is not one of them. Don't make me go against my own moral code, it's already practically nonexistent as it is." I pace the expanse of the room, stopping when I'm back in front of him again. "Tell me what I want to know and you can go."

He shoots me a confused look. "What's the catch?"

"No catch. I need information, you have it. I don't kill kids, you're a kid. It's simple."

He sighs, shaking his head and folding his arms over his chest. "You may as well kill me, if I go back known as a snitch, I'll have signed my own death sentence anyway."

He has a point.

I purse my lips in thought. "What if I make you another deal? You tell me what I want to know and I'll make sure no one finds out."

"Yeah, right. They always know. The second I walk out of here untouched; they'll know."

I nod to my left. "I'll let Jimmy here rough you up a little, does that help?"

He eyes me with suspicion. "Why would you do that? What do you gain from all of this?"

I sit there for a few seconds before settling on saying, "Information and a clear conscience."

After several minutes, he nods.

September
Day 94

I'm sitting in my father's office with Lorenzo Morelli and my father. Lorenzo is staring at me with so much hate I almost laugh. Way to show your cards, Morelli.

Apparently he isn't happy with the way I go about settling a score. First his Capo, now his soldiers are getting picked off one by one.

"You should have come to me," he spits, leaning forward resting his elbows on his knees. "This isn't how we handle things."

I scoff, "Like you handled Anthony for having my husband followed?"

"I can assure you that was all a misunderstanding," Lorenzo says, eyes narrowed, face scrunched in anger.

"Are you trying to tell me you were unaware of your Capo's involvement with Giovanni?" I arch my brow, waiting to hear his excuse.

"If I had known, I would have put a stop to that. What could I gain by causing a war after peace for so long?"

What indeed?

"And as for your soldiers, what can you expect? They were crossing into our territory, selling drugs and stealing profits. That goes against all of the rules," I state, matching him stare for stare.

He sighs, rubbing his forehead. "I never gave that order."

I don't believe that for a fucking second and if by some stretch it is true, he's lost his touch and shouldn't be in charge anymore.

"So, we are in understanding. A punishment was due," my father, Roberto, presses from his spot behind his desk.

Lorenzo's face is red and flushed as he spits his words through clenched teeth, "My punishment," he taps his chest angrily, "to handle as I see fit."

I cross my arms over my chest. "I disagree, my land, my punishment." We are in a stare off, neither backing down. I hope he can see the knowledge behind my stare, and has realized I'm not buying the bullshit he's trying to sell.

My father coughs and I turn towards him, waiting to see what he has to say.

He nods his head in an almost placating manor. "I understand where you are coming from Lorenzo, we like to handle our men when they step out of line as well."

Lorenzo turns to me then, a cocky grin stretched across his face. It drops almost instantly when my father continues, "But I also know a Capo won't overstep their Boss and soldiers certainly do not step out unless ordered to do so."

His face flushes and he spits through clenched teeth. "Are you calling me a liar?"

"I'm merely stating the truth. Now, I have work to do, Lorenzo. Can we agree that Roman's punishment was justified and move on?" Roberto asks.

He scoffs, "Move on? My capo is dead as well as several of my men."

"Technically Anthony isn't dead," I cut in and Lorenzo shoots me a withering glare.

He scoffs, "He's in a coma. With no brain activity."

"Semantics." I shrug uncaring, because fuck him and fuck all of them. They are getting what they deserve.

"Be that as it may, we have been dealing with these thug kids, crossing into our territory for months, selling their drugs to our regulars, stealing profits from our pockets, and the order was from your line of command. If that isn't a death sentence, I don't know what is."

Lorenzo stares at my father for several beats, before standing and heading to the door. "This isn't over Roberto, not by a long shot."

My father smirks, waving him off. "I expect nothing less. Good day, Lorenzo."

After several beats, my father turns to me. "Are you trying to start a war?"

I stand then, grabbing my suit jacket. "It won't come to that," I state, pulling my jacket on.

"I guess we will see."

I turn to leave, a smile crossing my face. "We shall."

October
Day 138

Still no Alex.

Dominic says we are no closer to finding him.

I miss him.

I heard once, you don't know what you have until it's gone.

I deserve this.

The pain of knowing my love is gone. The pain of knowing I may never see him again. The pain of realizing my chance for redemption was with him and I fucked it all up; that is my cross to bear.

I am in Hell because I destroyed an angel.

November
Day 161

The rain falls down in sheets as the casket lowers into the muddy earth.

How fitting for it to rain on this day; the day I buried my father.

It was a heart attack. I can't help but find the irony in that statement. How does one with no heart die from heart failure?

If I could, I would laugh. A death like this was too easy. Too gracious.

He should have been tortured, beaten, gutted like he had done to so many others. If it wasn't for the surrounding audience I'd probably spit on his grave. Hell, I'd tap dance on it.

As the service comes to an end, and I get my last goodbye handshakes, I turn towards the soon to be filled hole in the ground.

"See you in Hell, Father."

I turn walking back to the car, where Sawyer awaits, a smirk playing on my lips. For the first time in my thirty-two years, I finally feel a sense of freedom.

December
Day 193

Merry Christmas, Alex.

I tilt my tumbler to the moon, hoping that wherever he is in the world he's looking up and thinking of me too.

I take a long sip of whiskey before setting the glass down and lighting up a cigar. The air is chilled but I don't have it in me to go inside; not when the absence of him is colder than the night breeze.

A tear runs down my cheek and for once, I don't move to catch it. I just let it fall.

I close my eyes remembering a better time.

"Are you ready?"

"Come on. Stop asking already. Let's do this." I laugh at Alex's pouty expression, his left hand cocked back as he waits for my go ahead to toss the snowball.

"Are you sure?"

He doesn't say anything else, he just tosses the snowball, nailing me in the face and catching me by surprise.

I wipe my forehead, knocking off the bit of snow that stuck.

"Oh, it's on now." I lean down scooping up a handful of snow before throwing it back at him. We are both laughing and dodging one another.

He goes to run around a tree, but I see him before he hides and cut him off. He squeals, and turns to outrun me but it's too late. I snatch him up, and pin him to the tree.

I take in his pale features, flushed red cheeks, and his lively green eyes. He has a little snow flake stuck to his eyelash and his lips are slightly chapped, but he's never looked more beautiful than he does right now.

"I love you." The foreign words leave my lips only to whisper across his slightly parted ones.

"I love you, too."

My heart thuds wildly in my chest at his words and I shut my eyes, leaning my forehead against his. Just soaking in this moment. Soaking in the feeling of him.

I brush my lips against his once, twice, three times before pulling back. His eyes now flooded with heat, look at me with so much intensity. I keep him wrapped around me as I walk back towards the cabin.

This man is the greatest thing I have ever done. I am so glad I get to call him mine.

A ringing pulls me from my thoughts and I grab my phone. "What?" I bark, irritation flooding my system; I was almost to the good part.

"Roman, Merry Christmas. You are in a good mood, I see?" Dominic sing-songs through the line.

"The fuck do you want? I was in the middle of something," I sigh, leaning forward to rub my tired eyes.

"I was calling to give you a present." I can hear the smirk in his voice.

"Oh, stop with the mind games and tell me what I want to know."

"I found him."

With those words the entire world snaps back into focus.

PART FIVE

FOUND

ALEX

Chapter Thirty-Eight

I shiver, pulling the sweater more tightly around my body. I thought the south was supposed to be warmish in the winter?

I stifle a yawn and finish putting the last of the cans on the shelf. My shift is almost over and then I am off for the next two days. I have never been more ready for sleep in my life. We've been getting ready for the baby, so all my time off has been wrapped up in helping Lacey. Don't get me wrong. I love every second of it. I just can't wait to sleep some.

I yawn again, rubbing my tired eyes. "Why don't you go ahead and get out of here?" My coworker, Toby, says.

I stretch my arms over my head, yawning once more. "Are you sure? I don't want to leave you hanging."

"I'm almost done anyways. I just have to do some sweeping and recycle some boxes."

"Thank you. I appreciate it. I haven't been getting a lot of sleep lately."

"I get it. When my wife and I had our first child I didn't know if I was coming or going."

"Well, that's something to look forward to," I mutter to myself.

He laughs, "It's worth it though. I wouldn't trade my rugrats for the world." He smiles to himself lost in thought before turning back to me. "Anyways, get out of here."

I nod, pulling off my apron and walking to the back of the store. "Thanks, Toby. I'll see you Thursday."

He gives me a two fingered salute. "See you then."

I hang the apron on a hook in the back room and slide on my coat. A shiver racks my spine as I fish my keys out of my pocket. Fuck it's freezing, and I'm not even outside yet.

I zip my coat up all the way and hit the back door making a run for my car. The wind smacks my face but the quicker I get into the car the quicker I will be out of this cold. I slide the key into the door and unlock it before practically diving inside. I shove the key into the ignition and crank the engine.

Fuck I should have preheated my car.

I bring my hands up cupping them in front of my mouth and blow my hot breath into them trying to stay warm. I pull them back and rub them together vigorously. With chattering teeth, I shift gears and pull out of my spot. It's not until I'm almost home that my heater finally kicks on. I really need a new car, I think absentmindedly as I pull into the driveway.

The lights are on, and I'm thrown back to a time months ago when I came home to find Lacey pacing the expanse of the living room. I smile at the memory as I climb out of the car. I wonder why she is up now?

Probably cravings. I caught her eating a pickle and peanut butter sandwich the other morning. Gross. What is it about pregnancy that gives women such horrible cravings?

I walk into the front door and slide off my jacket. "Lacey," I call and set my keys down on the table by the door. I frown when I don't get a response.

"Lace?" I call again, as I round the corner into the living room. Lacey is sitting on the couch, head bowed as she stares down at her hands in her lap.

"Hey, what's going on?" I sit down next to her tilting her chin up to meet my gaze. Her lip wobbles as she looks at me. "Lacey?"

She turns from me, looking towards the side of the room and I follow her gaze in confusion. A gasp tears from my throat as I take in the heated gazes of not one but two men.

My gaze roams over Sawyer's clenched jaw and murderous expression, but he's not looking at me. He's looking at her.

Fuck.

I reach out grabbing her hand, not wanting to look at the other man in the room. Not wanting to see the same murderous expression I expect is there. I gulp, anxiety settling in my gut.

How did he find me? Did Sawyer tell him? Surely not. Sawyer had more to lose. Well, maybe not, since he didn't know about the baby before.

Oh the baby. They are going to kill us.

My gaze snaps up meeting the man I call my husband for the first time in months. All the air whooshes from my lungs, as I stare into those blue eyes I never expected to see again. His gaze holds a sort of sadness I wasn't expecting and that causes my lip to tremble.

He looks different but the same, if that even makes sense. His eyes are still the same blue, yet they hold a watery look I've never seen before and he has dark circles under them from lack of sleep. His face is thinner, more defined than it was months ago. The biggest surprise of all is his expression. His face holds a sort of wonder, like a kid seeing his favorite cartoon character in real life.

Like he almost cannot believe I'm here.

I sit there, half expecting him to charge across the room and drag me by my hair out of there. Yet, he doesn't. He stays exactly where he is. Hands opening and closing at his sides, like he wants to grab me.

A shiver involuntarily racks my body and I tear my gaze away looking over at Lacey once more. She is once again looking down, and I can feel the tension radiating off of her in waves.

I clear my throat, "Lacey, are you okay?" She doesn't answer, just shakes her head, still not meeting my gaze. "Hey, can you look at me please?" She does, hesitantly, and I can't help but frown at her action.

I reach up, tucking a strand of hair behind her ear. "What's wrong?"

Her lip wobbles. "I should have warned you. I should have called you, but by the time I realized they were here I couldn't get to my phone and I-"

"No." I shake my head adamantly. "Don't do that. This is not your fault and if you think for one second that I'd have taken off without you, you need a mental check. I would never leave you."

I hear a loud exhale, "But you could leave me so easily?"

My head snaps in Roman's direction, fury bypassing fear as I spit, "That was different. You abused me for months. Made me feel worthless, like I had no other choice. So no, to answer your question, leaving you wasn't easy for me. It was just my only option." He looks down, shaking his head.

"I know I have a lot to make up for."

I snort at his omission, shaking my head. "You don't get it, there is nothing to make up for."

His somber expression is so convincing, it's almost hard to believe this is the man who abused me for months.

"But there is. I fucked up really badly. I know I did, but I want to make it right. I want to fix it." He takes a small step in my direction, but I hold my hand up stopping him.

"Like I haven't heard that before." I shake my head, folding my arms around myself.

"Come home, let's talk. We can fix this."

"Once again you don't listen, there is nothing to fix. We are done."

He shakes his head. "I don't accept that."

"That's your problem not mine."

"I can't let you go," he whispers, voice broken.

"You have to."

"Please." The words are whispered so softly...so convincingly that my heart and body ached for me to give in. Tears burn my eyes, but I blink rapidly trying to hold them at bay.

"No." I have to be strong.

"Well, she isn't staying here," Sawyer interjects, pointing towards Lacey.

Lacey jumps from the couch, a mask of anger covering her expression. "The fuck I can't, Sawyer you don't get to control my life." She charges in his direction, poking him the chest.

"You are carrying my baby," he growls, grabbing her hand and pulling her towards him. "If you think for one second I won't be in my child's life, you are sorely mistaken."

Her eyes soften momentarily before she masks it. "You can be in her life and still let me stay here."

"I will not leave you here unprotected."

"But it was okay for Alex and I?"

Roman breaks eye contact with me at that his head turns towards Sawyer, his face a mix of anger and betrayal.

"The fuck did she just say?" Roman spits, taking a menacing step towards Sawyer. "Did you know they were here?" His voice is so deadly calm.

Sawyer doesn't waiver though. "I did."

Roman rears back, slamming his fist into Sawyer's face. It happens so fast, no one saw it coming.

The next second Sawyer is grabbing Roman slamming him back into the wall. "We don't have time for this," Sawyer spits, hands tightening around Roman's throat. "We have to get them and go home. Lorenzo is going to burn the city down before we get back." He lets go of Roman and steps back, while Roman stands, straightening up, glaring at Sawyer.

"This isn't over, not by a long shot," Roman spits through clenched teeth.

Sawyer grabs a tissue from the end table dabbing the blood from his busted lip.

"You both seem to have missed the part where we said we weren't going," Lacey sneers, crossing her arms over her chest.

Sawyer shakes his head, gesturing behind Lacey to the hall. "Get dressed. We are leaving in ten minutes."

"Like fuck we are," she seethes.

"So help me god, if you are not ready to go in ten minutes, Lacey I will wrap you in a blanket and carry you out of here myself. Do. You. Understand?" Sawyer growls, taking a step towards her.

I stand there stunned as she glares, before flipping him off and storming down the hall to her room, with a pissed off Sawyer in tow.

I fold my arms over my chest, turning back to Roman. "I'm not going."

God, I feel like a child. He's treating me like one.

"That just isn't up for discussion. You want to discuss terms, fine. This one is off the table."

"I can't just leave. I have a life here. People who will worry if I just disappear." Something dark crosses his features as he takes a menacing step towards me.

"You weren't worried about me when you disappeared so easily. You better still be mine," he growls, reaching forward to grip my chin. Not hard, but just enough to warn me. Like he always used to do.

I flinch, waiting for the pain to explode across my cheek. The bite of the smack as his hand meets skin. The feel of his fist as he unleashes the wrath he's been dying to since the moment I walked out on him. I sit here, eyes mashed together tightly but nothing happens. He loosens his grip, running his finger over my lips before dropping his hand. A shudder runs through me and I step out of reach, turning my head away from him.

"Please, just let me go," I breathe out.

"I can't."

A tear runs down my cheek and I bat it away just as Lacey and Sawyer come back into the room. Lacey is dressed but her face still holds that pissed off expression. Sawyer looks smug and I want nothing more than to knock the look off his face.

I look back at Roman but his face is masked in an unreadable expression.

Sawyer leads Lacey through the house, pausing at the front door for her to put on her shoes.

I watch them go and turn back to Roman with pleading eyes. "Don't do this, please."

He offers me a sad smile. "I have to."

ROMAN

Chapter Thirty-Nine

Alex sits next to Lacey holding her hand and staring out the window as the plane hits the runway.

The flight back home to Vegas went by a lot faster than I anticipated. I wanted to talk to him. Wanted to explain so many things to him, but he is guarded and I don't blame him.

It took every bit of willpower I possessed to not slam my lips onto his and claim him in that living room. I couldn't do that though. I knew that I had to tread lightly with him at first. He doesn't know the man I am now. I have had months to get my monster under control, months to fight and rid myself of the anger I had boiling just under the surface. I had a moment today when I could feel my anger rise, when he mentioned being missed by people. I immediately thought of other men loving my Alex, touching him, and I saw red. The difference from before though is that I was in control the whole time and the moment I saw him flinch away, like he was waiting for my strike, a piece of me died inside.

I did that to him. I made him scared of me and that was one thing I never wanted to do. I know how that sounds after everything I put him through, believe me.

I was beyond recognizable after everything with Giovanni. I thought I had to harden myself up so Alex wouldn't change me, little did I know I was already changed because of him. Then I thought maybe if I'm hard on him he will see that this is for his benefit. The way my father always did to me. He could learn my ways and come to accept that just because a man comes from violence doesn't mean he is incapable of love, but I went about that the wrong way too.

I went about it all the wrong way.

I sigh, pushing back harder into the seat. Now, here we are. On a plane after a huge separation, seemingly further apart than we were twelve hours ago. I don't know how to reach him or if I even can. I just am going to hope that maybe he can forgive me enough to try.

I wasn't kidding though when I said we could discuss terms. If Alex really wants to leave me, as much as it would kill me to let him go, I would. If that is what he really wants. I just couldn't leave him in that home in Alabama. If he wants to leave me, I will set him up in a secure location with private protection.

The reason I didn't do that initially was because Alex doesn't understand the threat he is under, and until I'm able to forge a truce in the war that is brewing, he is going to have to be under lock and key. I have to keep him safe. It may have taken months for Dominic to find him, but that means that anyone else could have been right on his tail especially with the price on my head so high right now.

My father dying opened a door for Lorenzo. He is gunning to take me down once and for all, and I have no doubt someone is out there looking for Alex so they can use him as the perfect bargaining chip. Giovanni was right, I played my hand and showed my weakness and everyone knows that comes in the form of Alexander Giuliani.

My husband, the absolute love of my life. My entire reason for living. The reason for my fight towards redemption no matter how futile that may seem.

So, for now, I will do my best to keep him safe and pray that he will let me work towards earning his love back; because the thought of him never wanting me again makes me physically sick. I rub my hand absently over the center of my chest, trying to rid the ache that has long since settled.

I need to earn my husband's love back. I need to win him back full stop.

He deserves far more than I will ever be able to give him.

But I'll be damned if I don't at least try.

Alex

I don't know what I did in a past life to piss somebody off so bad, but I want more than anything to scream out my apologies to the universe.

Life currently feels like a bad omen.

I still cannot fathom how he found me. He managed to track me down after all this time and now here I am, after finally starting to feel a sense of normalcy, being dragged back to the pit of despair. I feel like a murderer walking on death row to the electric chair.

We just arrived back at Roman's house and Sawyer took Lacey somewhere so they could talk. I wanted to stay with her but I know they have a long overdue conversation coming. They have a baby coming in just a few more months.

Roman grabs my hand pulling me in the direction of the stairs.

"ALEX!" I hear my name being called and turn just in time to catch Leta as she slams into me. I wrap my arms around her tightly, inhaling her raspberry and thyme scent.

So unique. So Leta.

"Sweet boy." She pulls me back away from her slightly, peppering my face in kisses then resting her palms on my shoulders. "Let me look at you." She runs her gaze up my body, nodding in approval at what she sees. "I love the dark hair." She cups my cheeks affectionately, tears shining in her eyes.

I smile, wishing I could share her enthusiasm and if it were just us, I might. But right here with Roman so close, I can't help but feel nothing except dread.

"How are you, Leta?" I ask, smiling at her warmly.

"Better now that you are home."

Home...the word is like a smack to the face and I visibly flinch at the impact it caused. The smile drops from her face as her worried eyes ping pong back and forth between mine. "Are you okay?"

"Fine Leta, just tired. I haven't slept yet and I work at night now." *Worked* nights, as in not any more.

I can feel the tears burning my eyes but I blink rapidly to get rid of them. They are not welcome here. I have cried enough because of this man.

"Leta, I'm going to take Alex to bed. Can you make him lunch when he wakes up?" Roman interjects.

"Of course, I will. I have been practicing making a famous Alex grilled cheese just for when you came home." I smile at that.

"I didn't think a grilled cheese counted as a meal," I say sarcastically.

"Well, I guess there is an exception to every rule." She pats my cheek and I lean in to hug her one more time before turning with Roman as he guides me to our old room.

Once inside, exhaustion like I've never known settles over me. Not only mentally but physically.

Roman stands a few feet in front of me, watching me with a hawk-like expression. Almost like he is expecting me to take off at any second. He clears his throat, "I know we need to talk and there are so many things I want to discuss with you, things I need to explain. But right now you look like you are going to fall over at any given moment and I want you to be all ears for that conversation."

I look down at the floor nodding because what else can I say to that?

He leans in as if to kiss me but I flinch back taking a step away from him. I look up to see his almost pleading expression. He sighs, sadness crossing his features, before turning and heading towards the door.

He pauses at the threshold, turning back to me momentarily. "Alex." I turn to him, eyebrows arched in question. "I know it isn't worth much right now, but I need you to know that I really am sorry I hurt you."

A tear glides down my cheek and I nod. "I know you are."

He holds my gaze for a moment, before nodding and exiting the room, shutting the door behind him. I sit down heavily on the bed, leaning forward and resting my head in my hands.

He loves me too much; too deeply. He is emotionally blinded by his obsession with me. I cannot do this again.

I *won't* do this again.

I stand up from the bed, in need of a shower; I need to think. I walk over to the dresser, not at all surprised to see all of my things still tucked away inside. I grab a pair of sleep shorts and an oversized shirt, then walk to the bathroom. I flip the handles, adjust the temperature of the water and strip off my clothes.

The warm spray cascades onto me, causing me to sigh. Damn, I missed this shower. With my arms against the shower wall, and my head bowed down, I try to think but my brain is too tired to come up with any plan or alternatives to get out of the situation I'm currently in.

I wash and rinse quickly, needing to get out so I can sleep. Maybe a few hours of shut-eye will bring me some clarity. I step out of the shower and dry off, pulling on the clothes I laid out.

A yawn erupts from my mouth so hard my jaw cracks. I rub my tired eyes exiting the bathroom and flip the light off in the bedroom before heading over to the bed. I barely manage to pull the covers down before I crawl between the sheets.

My head hits the pillow and I sigh, body relaxing almost instantly.

I'm asleep before I even realize it.

A hand pressing to my mouth wakes me from my dreamless sleep and I blink slowly taking in the scene in front of me.

Three men stand around me all holding me down.

I let out a startled yelp but the hand on my mouth only presses down harder. My eyes widen when he produces a knife, jabbing it against the base of my throat.

"Now you are going to be quiet," he whispers, leaning down over me, his dark eyes, staring into mine. "You so much as think about screaming and you are dead, understood?"

I blink rapidly taking in his words. I could take on one man, maybe, but three. Not a chance. So, I nod slightly, a sick feeling resonating in my stomach.

He slams a piece of duct tape over my mouth.

"Good, now that we have an understanding." He wraps a rope tightly around my wrist securing them together and his partner does the same with my ankles. "We are just going to take a little ride. I need you to cooperate for the time being, as soon as I have Roman to where I need him, you will be free to leave."

Wait! What?

I shake my head trying to get him to elaborate, but he doesn't get my memo. He just taps my cheek lightly before sliding a bag over my head. Next, I'm thrown over his shoulder and he walks towards what I am assuming is the balcony.

How did they even get in here? Roman keeps this place locked up tighter than a mental prison.

He sets me down and I panic when I realize it's the balconies railing.

No!

I can't see through the sack but I can definitely hear the humor in his tone. "Relax." He pushes me.

I let out a shriek as I tumble down from the balcony. I stiffen, expecting to slam into the ground, but am surprised when I hit something springy.

Oh, thank fuck.

I bounce several times confused as to what just caught me when I feel two sets of hands haul me forward. I inhale the best I can through my nose, adrenaline coursing through my veins.

Who the fuck are these people?

One of the guys tosses me over his shoulder, and I can feel him running towards where I think the gate is. *What the fuck is happening right now?* I don't understand, where are the guards?

I start to struggle when I hear a car pull up near the curb. I fling my body around but it does nothing to slow the masked man.

"Quit moving before I shove my gun down your throat and pull the fucking trigger," he barks, causing me to stop instantly.

The sound of the trunk popping open kicks my body into gear and my fight or flight takes over, consequences be damned. I start screaming as much as I can around the duct tape. Scrunching my body up like an inchworm, I flail my restrained limbs the best I can, thinking if I can get him to drop me, I have some type of chance to get away.

"Shut him the fuck up and stop moving," someone yells.

The guy grunts when I knee him in the stomach, momentarily losing his footing, dropping me to the ground.

"Someone stick him."

No. No. No.

I flail harder, inching across the ground, trying to get leverage in some way to hoist myself up. I scream as loud as I can this time, hoping like hell it can be heard through my covered lips.

I feel multiple sets of hands on me, pinning me down, before a pinch. My heart slows and my body feels sluggish. I stop struggling and blink drowsily several times. *No, stay awake. You can't sleep Alex.* But the thought is futile. I'm already going under. I try to flip over, try to do something but it's no use. I blink slowly one last time before I fade away into darkness.

ROMAN

Chapter Forty

I sit staring at the glow of embers slowly dying in the fireplace. The whiskey stays untouched in its bottle on my desk. The urge to drink is strong, the desire to numb the ache I feel deep inside my chest.

Everything I want is so close and yet so far away. I reach for the bottle for probably the hundredth time, but stop once more. I have to be clear headed when I talk to Alex. I refuse to hurt him in any way again.

Sawyer comes storming into my office then, pulling me from my self pity. I arch my brow at him. "Tough night?"

He groans, sitting down heavily in the seat across from me. "That woman is going to be the death of me."

He reaches forward and snatches the whiskey, uncapping it and taking a few gulps.

"That bad, huh?"

"She just has a way of getting so far under my skin, that I can't get her out, even if I took a blade to my flesh. Hell, I don't know if I want to strangle her or worship her most days. But this," he growls, glaring at the door behind him, as if she was standing there. "She was going to keep my fucking child from me. I have a daughter due with in a matter of months and I wouldn't have even known had it not been for-"

He cuts himself off, eyes flying to mine in sympathy.

"Me finding out where you hid Alex," I finish for him.

We stare at each other in silence. He's waiting for me to freak out. Waiting for the wrath of Roman to jump out and seek revenge for all the pain and suffering these months of grief have caused.

And here's the thing. I could kill him. I should have killed him. In a normal situation, on any other day, I'd have pulled my gun the second I found out about his betrayal. His brains would have been splattered across that shit house in Alabama and I would feel vindicated for my actions.

But, I won't. I just need to know. "Why?" I ask, as my eyes search his.

He exhales sharply, gaze holding mine. "Will it matter what I have to say?"

"I need to know," I manage, hands steepled in front of my face.

"You were changing into a man I didn't recognize. I've known you since we were kids, and I have stood by your side for a long time. I've seen you do things that most men have nightmares over. Then you met Alex and I saw another side of you. One I never knew you were capable of. You were kind, gentle, happy even. It was nice to see you get to have that. You deserve happiness after the bullshit from our pasts."

He trails off, looking away with a resigned expression. "Everything that happened with Giovanni flipped a switch and you went off the deep end, Roman. I couldn't sit by and watch you hurt that boy anymore. You were unimaginable." He shakes his head, disgust radiating off of him in waves. "We don't hurt innocent people or kids; when you threatened Lacey, that was the last straw for me. I knew you were too far gone."

He turns back to me then. "The night Alex came to me, crying, bruised, and broken, it snapped something inside of me. I knew I had to get him away from you."

I clench my jaw tightly, pain lacing my heart. "You could have talked to me."

He scoffs, "And said what? There was no talking to you, and you know it."

I don't know how to respond to that because I know he's right. Fuck if I want to admit that to him though.

"So Lacey?" I finally ask after several moments of silence.

He smirks. "I can honestly say I never saw her coming."

I chuckle, nodding my head in understanding. "I get it."

My phone chooses that moment to ring, breaking the moment and I retrieve it from my pocket, grimacing when I note the name.

"Lorenzo," I bite into the phone.

"Hello, Roman. I wasn't sure you'd answer."

"What do you want?"

"We have things we need to discuss."

"Last I checked we had nothing to talk about."

I can hear him tsk through the line. "Now, that's just not true. I think you'll find we have some very urgent matters to attend to."

"I don't have time for this." I go to hang up but his next words stop me in my tracks.

"Have you seen Alex lately?"

My heart picks up and a cold sweat breaks out across my body as his words register. I jump from my chair and take off up the stairs, barely registering the sound of Sawyer's footfalls behind me. I make it to the bedroom and burst inside, only to stop dead when I take in the rumpled sheets and the opened balcony doors. I check the closet and bathroom already knowing he won't be there.

This brings me back to realizing Alex was gone and I have to take a few breaths to calm the panic washing over me. How the fuck did anyone get in here? How the fuck did anyone get out? Where are my guards? So many fucking questions that will have to be dealt with later. Right now my only concern is Alex.

I bring my phone back to my ear, fury taking over. "Where the fuck is he?" I bark through the line.

"Oh, do I have your attention now?" he asks, voice riddled with humor.

"Lorenzo, if you so much as harm one hair on his head, so help me-"

"For someone with no leg to stand on, you sure are making a lot of threats."

He's taunting me.

My jaw pops from how hard I have it clenched. "Don't hurt him."

"I won't have to, if you do what I ask."

"What do you want?"

"A trade," he says, voice coated in arrogance.

"What kind of trade?"

"You in exchange for Alex. A life for a life."

"Done," I say without hesitation. He can do whatever he wants to me as long as Alex is okay.

"You will come alone. No weapons."

"I will bring Sawyer with me to take Alex away with him. I don't trust you to let Alex go once you have me."

"I won't need him once I have you."

"So we agree? We meet, you let Sawyer take Alex and I will come with you."

He hums his agreement through the line and I shut my eyes, phone smashed tightly against my ear.

"Tell me the time and the place."

His sinister chuckle meets my ears, "Excellent."

Alex

I have no idea how I managed to get myself into this situation once again.

I roll over onto my side, tucking my legs closer to my chest. I have no idea how long I've been here, or where *here* even is. As if on cue, the door at the top of the stairs opens and three masked men appear. I involuntarily shudder and scoot back, in an effort to make myself one with the wall. I rest my head on my knees, wrapping my arms around myself, trying to become as small as possible.

I feel a slight kick to my leg before someone says, "Let's go."

I glance up to see the larger of the three standing over me.

"Where are we going?" I ask, voice shaky.

"Don't worry, you behave and everything will be fine." He reaches out to pull me from the floor.

It's probably stupid to believe that, after all, I've seen almost every horror movie known to man. I know that escaping a kidnapping once is extremely rare, but two times? Yeah, right. That'd be like winning the lottery twice. Shit like that doesn't ever happen. And yet here I am, following behind him like a lamb to the slaughter.

I take a few wobbly steps, the shit they injected me with still messing with my system. With help from the large guy, I managed to make it up the rickety steps. My stomach turns when I notice the second man stepping towards me with a sack.

"What is that for?"

"Just need to keep you blind. Can't have you giving away our location can we?" Goon two says, before sliding the bag over my head.

I feel hands wrap around my arms as I'm guided to an awaiting car. I get pushed into the back seat and feel the weight of two people settle on both my sides. No way to escape.

My hands are still zip tied, or else I would have already ripped this suffocating bag from my head. I can feel the rapid movements of my chest as my lungs try unsuccessfully to get fresh air.

Calm down, it's just a panic attack. I tell myself as nerves eat away at me.

I try to play through the action movies I've seen, maybe I can think of a way to get myself out of this situation. Okay in movies they always count their turns and stuff right? After the third maybe right turn I give up. For anyone wondering, in the movies they lie. That shit is not as easy as you think it is.

Before long we pull to a stop and my body is thrumming with nervous energy.

"Where are we?" I ask as the doors open.

A voice to my left says, "Remember what I said? Listen and you will get out of here untouched."

Great, because that answered my question.

"Can we remove this bag yet?"

"Do as you're told," a voice I recognize but can't place, says before pulling me from the car.

Who is that?

I open my mouth to ask, but am caught off guard by the other voice I hear.

"Let me see his face. I want to verify he's okay."

Roman, he came for me.

"He is fine, we had a deal."

I have no idea who that is speaking.

"No funny business. One wrong move and your husband here will die."

Jesus Christ. Are they really talking about me as if I'm not right here?

"Touch him and you all die," Roman growls.

A chorus of laughter reaches my ears just before the bag is ripped from my head. The bright light assaults my eyes and I shut them involuntarily, blinking several times trying to adjust to the brightness.

"See, he's fine. I keep my word, you keep yours."

I turn towards the voice taking in the older man. I have no idea who he is, but man, he has to have seen better days. He reminds me of the Crypt Keeper from the comic book, *Tales of the Crypt.*

"He leaves with Sawyer and I come with you." My gaze snaps to Roman.

Wait, what now?

I glance around trying to place where we are, but I'm clueless. It looks like some type of shipping yard, maybe. I don't know. The ties are cut from my wrists and I'm shoved in Roman's direction. What's happening now?

"Alright, he can go to Sawyer and you will come with me. Don't try to play the hero today, Roman. I have men on every corner ready to take Alex out if I give the signal."

My gaze flies to Crypt Keeper before jumping to Roman. His face holds something that looks a lot like sadness when he says, "Come here, baby."

I run the thirty feet, slamming into his hard body with a thud. He wraps his arms around me, burying his face into the crook of my neck, inhaling deeply. Like he cannot get enough of my scent. I can't believe he's here right now.

He pulls away too quickly and I hold onto him, refusing to let him go. He offers me a sad smile, running the pads of his fingers across my cheek.

"I don't have all day, Roman," Crypt calls from behind us.

He leans down, resting his forehead against mine. "There are so many things I want to say to you. So many things I need to apologize for and I wish we had more time, because I would spend the rest of my life proving to you just how sorry I am."

He pulls back, looking deep into my eyes. "I love you. I think I've loved you since the moment I saw you dancing in my club. You wrecked me in the best possible way. You broke me open and showed me what life could be like. What life should be like." He leans down, placing a feather light kiss across my lips. "You, Alexander Giuliani saved my life. Now it's my turn to save yours."

Two men come up behind him, pulling him away from me. I shake my head. "Wait, no. What are you doing?"

I step forward reaching my hand out to grab him, but he shakes his head at me.

"You are free.. I want you to go live your life. The life we talked about so many times. Go see if the water is really as clear as they say it is in Fiji, and have a margarita in Cancun. Go dance under the stars on a beach in Hawaii. Be whoever you want to be."

He can't do this.

Don't give up.

Tears are sliding down my cheeks as the men flanking Roman start pulling him away from me. I take a step to follow just as strong arms wrap around me from behind.

"Go with Sawyer. He has everything you need. I set you up, baby. You will be fine. I promise."

"No Roman, please don't do this."

The two men start dragging him roughly back towards the Crypt Keeper. I become frantic, pulling away from Sawyer trying to get to Roman.

"NO! Roman. Stop. You cannot give up. You have to fight."

He stops walking, staring at me. A sad smile resting across his handsome face.

"I love you," I say, throat thick with unshed tears. I can barely see him through my watering eyes.

He shuts his eyes as if those words are the best ones he's ever heard. When he opens his eyes a new expression takes over just as he says, "Sawyer, get him out of here."

Wait, no.

Sawyer tries to pull me away once more, but I fight him, trying to break his grasp.

"No, I'm not leaving." He picks me up and tosses me over his shoulder and I start pounding on his back instantly. "Stop it. Wait, no! We have to help Roman. We cannot leave him!"

I look up to see the two goons knock Roman to the ground and begin kicking him.

Screams and agonizing shrills leave my lips as I get further and further away. "Roman! Roman!" I scream over and over, voice getting hoarse but I can't stop.

"Sawyer, you have to go help him. They are going to kill him."

Sawyer sighs heavily, setting me down onto my feet as we reach the car. Where two of Roman's guards are waiting.

I go to run past him, but he catches me, pinning me against the vehicle.

"You have to stop and listen to me. This is important." I shake my head, trying to push past him once more. "This is about Lacey too."

I stop fighting, as he knew I would.

"Here." He slides me a note and opens the car door pushing me inside. "Lacey is waiting for you at the airport. She has everything you both will need for phase two. Just like last time, do you remember?"

Remember? Yes, no evidence left behind.

I nod my head absently. "Just like last time."

Everything happens in slow motion after that. The sounds of bullets fill the air, and Sawyer slams the door effectively locking me in before taking off and running in the other direction with several men trailing behind him.

What the fuck?

The two men jump in the car before speeding out of the lot, I can hear the sounds of more gunshots going off and I fumble with the door handle trying to get out.

Roman. Roman. Roman!

The door doesn't budge and I start slamming my hands against the window. I'm frantic.

He can't die. He just can't. As bad as things were between us, I can't imagine living in a world he's not a part of.

"Sorry about this," is the last thing I hear before a cloth is placed over my nose and mouth and the whole world goes black.

When I come to hours later, I'm on Roman's private plane. Lacey is sitting next to me, clutching my hand tightly as she stares out the window.

"Hey," I croak, voice hoarse, "Do we have any water? My throat hurts."

"I have some juice."

She hands me a small container of apple juice and I suck it down greedily. I wipe the back of my mouth with my hand and set the bottle down.

"Where are we going? Where are Roman and Sawyer? What happened?"

It's then I notice her tear streaked cheeks.

"Alex," she starts, grabbing my hands and holding them tightly.

"What?"

"Sawyer is going to meet us in Fiji."

My heart begins to pound rapidly in my chest, "What about Roman?"

Her lip wobbles, and her expression is filled with so much sadness. My entire body locks with tension.

I shake my head. "No, don't say it."

"Alex."

"No." I drop her hands, standing from my seat quickly.

"Sawyer said he did everything he could."

"Don't say it Lacey, please just don't."

Lacey stands, cupping my cheeks gently, but making me look at her. "I am so sorry."

No. No. No. No.

It's not real. He can't be dead. He can't be. I can't accept this.

I run to the back of the plane barely making it to the toilet in time to expel the apple juice from my system.

Lacey is behind me in an instant, rubbing soothing circles on my back. "I'm sorry," she repeats over and over.

I stand after a while and rinse my face off in the sink before gazing at myself for long minutes in the mirror. My eyes are bloodshot, my face is red and splotchy, and my nose is stuffed up from all the crying.

When we settle back into our seats, I rest my head against her shoulder trying to stifle the silent sobs.

"It will all be okay, I have you. I'm here," Lacey says, rocking me.

If only that felt true.

PART SIX

NEW BEGINNINGS

ALEX

Chapter Forty-One

One Year Later

"We haven't been out in ages," Lacey says, sliding me over a coconut filled mixed drink. The sun just crested over the horizon and the sky is lit up with an array of colors.

It's Friday night and we're at the Tiki Bar on the beach for their *Summer Nights Bash*. Sawyer is keeping the baby, so we can have a much needed friend night out. I take a sip of the tropical goodness, groaning when the flavors hit my tongue.

"This is delicious."

She hums her approval. "Now hurry up and drink. I'm ready to dance."

She sways her hips provocatively, already earning a few glances from the men around.

"Keep that up and Sawyer is going to show and kill every man within a twenty mile radius."

She laughs, shaking her head. "They can look, as long as they don't touch."

"Yeah, for some reason I feel like he won't much agree with that."

"Probably not, but I am a big girl. I can handle Sawyer." She waggles her eyebrows at me.

I groan, shaking my head. "Too much information."

As soon as I finish my drink, Lacey is pulling me into the throng of people. The music is thrumming and the energy around us electric, it's easy to get lost in the beats. I'm approached by several people wanting to dance, but decline every time. I haven't wanted anyone since him.

I motion to Lacey that I'm going to grab a drink and she throws me a thumbs up. I head to the bar and order a Corona before plopping down on the seat. My mind begins to wander and I think about him.

I haven't brought myself to say his name; to even talk about him much. It honestly is just too painful.

What we had was so raw and all consuming, no one will ever be able to hold a candle to that. I will never condone violence or what he did to me, and I still stand by my leaving him. It was the best option at the time for the situation.

But I won't ever forget what he did for me. He literally sacrificed himself for me. That, to me, deserves my forgiveness.

I sigh, standing from the bar as the bartender slides the Corona over to me. I slide him some cash before nodding, and turning to head back to Lacey.

My foot catches on something in the sand and I trip, falling forward into another person.

Fuck.

The beer slides from my grasp, successfully flipping back and soaking the front of my body on its descent to the ground.

Damn it; I am drenched, and smell like beer now.

I sigh, muttering a quick apology to the person I ran into and side step them to head back to the bar to grab some napkins.

"It's no problem. I've been hoping you'd run into me all night."

I stop dead in my tracks. I know that voice. That is the voice of my every fantasy.

Roman.

I turned so fast I almost gave myself whiplash. My breath freezes in my lungs as I stare into those blue eyes I know almost as well as my own.

He looks different yet the same, if that even makes sense. Hair the same dark brown, eyes so blue like the ocean. He has a beard now, which I find to be extremely sexy.

Fucking lumberjacks.

Tears well in my eyes and I blink rapidly, figuring my mind is just playing tricks on me and my brain just hasn't caught up yet. After several moments, when he hasn't moved, I take a cautious step in his direction.

"Roman?" The words are whispered from my lips.

"Hi baby," he says, and I lose it.

Tears come to my eyes and I rush forward wrapping my arms around his neck and he picks me up. My legs wind around his waist and I cling to him.

"Are you real?" I mutter into his neck.

He releases a chuckle, "Yeah, I'm real."

I pull back to look into his eyes.

"How? You died? I don't understand," I manage to say around broken sobs.

He shakes his head, leaning forward to rest his forehead against mine.

"Later. Right now I just want to feel you. I missed you so much."

I can't help but nod, leaning into him more. He turns to walk me away, when my senses finally come back.

"Wait, Lacey," I say, hooking my thumb over my shoulder in her direction.

"Sawyer has her."

That just gave me the biggest sense of deja vu. I glance back, only to see that she is indeed with Sawyer.

He must have found another babysitter.

I meet Roman's heated gaze once more. "Let's go."

We stumble into the door of my apartment, lips urgent and hands eager.

I haven't been with anyone since him and my body is thrumming with delicious anticipation.

I pull him in the direction of my bedroom, as we strip our clothes off on the way.

Shoes, pants, shirts, and underwear are all thrown haphazardly around the living room in our haste to get naked as quickly as possible. We are all over each other, bumping into walls and furniture as we move down the hall towards my room, but the desire is turned up too high for either one of us to care.

He lifts me when we walk into my room, carrying me the last several feet to my bed. He doesn't drop me down like I'm expecting. He spins and lays down, dragging my body over his. Our cocks rub together and I gasp at the sensation.

Fuck yes!

I kiss along his jaw, running my tongue down the expanse of his neck. His groans meet my ears, like the best played music and I relish in the pleasure I'm giving to him. I kiss down the length of his chest, nipping and sucking along his abs.

Yes, I missed this so much.

His dick is sticking straight up, red and swollen with need. Precum pools at the tip and I run my tongue over it eagerly.

"Fuck, yes. Oh my god, just like that," he growls, rocking his hips forward, trying to get his cock between my slightly parted lips.

I open my mouth wide accepting his girth, swallowing and humming around him as he hits the back of my throat. It's been so long that I gag and sputter a few times before finding my rhythm. Roman pulls from my mouth with a groan, squeezing the base of his dick to stave off his orgasm.

"It's been too long. Not going to last, with you touching me like this."

I bite my lip, avoiding eye contact. "How long has it been?"

He leans forward, tipping my chin up to meet his gaze. "Baby, I haven't been with anyone since my last time with you."

I don't know why that surprises me as much as it does, but I can't help the joyous feeling that the words bring.

"Really?"

He runs his fingers across my cheek, smiling softly at me. "Anyone else would pale in comparison to you."

I lean forward, brushing my lips over his again, before reaching over and grabbing the lube from the nightstand.

"You're going to have to get me ready. I haven't been with anyone else since you either."

He releases a sound like a half gasp half sigh, before rolling me over onto my back and settling over me. The snap of a cap reaches my ears, and I feel the slick slide of lube as he works me over with a finger. I groan, shutting my eyes as sensations wash over me.

My cock is rock hard, leaking against my abs as I roll my hips down on his probing finger. One finger turns to two then three, and before long I'm thrashing on the bed, fucking his fingers.

"Please, I need you so badly," I manage around groans.

He pulls back, applying more lube to his dick before lining his cock up to my ass.

"Are you still mine?" he rasps, voice laced with desire, eyes lit up with so much hope.

I stare up at him, memorizing every inch of this man all over again.

"Always."

He slides inside of me slowly, like he's savoring every inch of me. I gasp when he brushes my prostate, before settling fully inside of me. I run my palms up his back, enjoying the feel of his muscles flexing beneath my palms. It feels so normal; so right.

Like coming home again.

He pulls out slowly and thrusts back in, letting me adjust to the intrusion.

"You feel so good," he breathes, running his lips across my jaw, then sucking gently on the pulse point of my neck. "I missed you so much."

His hips rock forward as he moves in and out, his dick rubbing me perfectly.

"I missed you, too."

His eyes glaze over as we stare at one another and I rake my fingers through his hair, before pulling him down so his lips can meet mine for a hungry kiss.

He starts rocking faster, pistoning in and out of me with more urgency. He grabs my hands, slamming them down onto the mattress interlocking our fingers together.

Fuck, nothing has ever felt so good as Roman being inside of me.

All of the old feelings surface and mix with all the new ones. It's pure pleasure and ecstasy. I want to drown in it. My back bows off the bed, and I arch into him more, rocking my hips to meet his thrusts. The desire to come, is overwhelming.

"Fuck, baby. Not going to last," he growls, sucking what I'm sure will be a mark onto my shoulder.

"Yes, so good. Jack my dick," I groan out.

He releases my hands, sitting up, dragging my ass onto his lap, and I fold my legs down to rest on each side of his hips.

"God you look so good taking my dick," he growls, spitting into his hand and grasping me firmly.

I groan loudly, rocking forward trying to fuck his fist.

"So damn good. Always so good," I mutter, eyes screwing shut as I feel the telltale signs of my orgasm start to resonate. He pumps me once, twice, and I unleash.

A loud groan tears from my throat as spurt after spurt of cum covers my torso. "Fuck, yes, yes!" I cry, as he milks me dry.

"Baby, fuck," Roman lets out a guttural groan, and his hips stutter as he comes inside of me. He rocks lazily, giving me every last bit of what he has to offer.

We lay there, chests heaving, trying to catch our breath, looking at one another with expressions of bliss and wonder. Both of us equally satisfied.

He pulls me up and rolls onto his back, settling me on top of him. Not wanting to break our connection just yet. I rest my head against his chest, nuzzling into him as he runs calming fingers over my back.

I release a sigh, and shut my eyes, just enjoying the feel of his hands on me. I quickly fall asleep to the feel of his gentle caress and the sound of his very much beating heart.

Chapter Forty-Two

I sigh, rolling onto my back, enjoying the feel of the warm breeze brushing against my skin. I feel the rustling of sheets and an arm wraps around my middle. I cannot remember the last time I felt so completely sated and happy.

I blink awake, and turn my head to gaze at Roman's sleeping profile. He is so handsome. I shift onto my side, and run a finger across his forehead, down his nose, before stroking his full beard. Jesus this is so sexy. I bite my lip as I tug slightly. Imagining how it would feel rubbing against my skin as he ate out my ass.

"See something you like?"

My eyes fly up to his and I can feel my face flush with embarrassment.

"I might," I mumble, dropping my hand and rolling onto my back once more.

"I'm glad you like it. I was worried it'd be too much of a change."

"No, it's very sexy."

He arches an eyebrow, a smirk playing across his lips. "Yeah?"

"Look at you, fishing for compliments." I smirk back, poking him in the chest.

He laughs, rolling on top of me and kissing my lips softly.

"I really missed you."

"I missed you, too."

We lay around, kissing lazily, just simply enjoying each other, until my stomach grumbles and my bladder protests.

"I need food," I mutter, sliding from the bed and snagging a pair of boxers from my dresser.

I pad into the bathroom and take care of business before walking into the kitchen. Roman is standing in front of the refrigerator, scanning the contents, when I come up behind him, wrapping my arms around his waist.

He too is only wearing his boxers and I can't help but chuckle at the thought. He turns towards me, eyebrows raised in question.

"What's so funny?"

"I was just thinking about how Leta would have had a fit if she caught you in nothing but your boxers in her kitchen."

He laughs as well, and the sound is like music to my ears. *I missed his laugh.*

"She would never let me hear the end of it."

"How is she?" I ask, smiling at the thought of her making an Alex grilled cheese.

"Retired. I set her up. She will be able to live out the rest of her life and take care of her family with no struggles."

"That was good of you."

"It was the least I could do," he mutters, grabbing some eggs and shutting the fridge door. "You don't really have much in there."

"I need to go grocery shopping." I grab the loaf of bread from the cupboard. "Are you okay with an egg sandwich?"

"Sounds perfect."

I get to work, frying up the eggs and toasting the bread. I pull out the butter from the fridge, slathering a generous amount on the toast before building the sandwiches.

"Voila," I say, setting a plate down in front of where he sits at the small kitchen table. I don't have anything to drink except bottled water at the moment, so I set one of those down next to his plate too.

He smiles up at me. "Thank you."

I plop down in the seat next to him, taking a big bite of my sandwich. We eat in comfortable silence. The feelings of nostalgia wash over me. You never realize how much you could miss sitting down and sharing a meal with someone. It seems so insignificant, and yet this moment means everything in the world to me.

We eat quickly and it's not long before we are settled on the couch and I can tell my little bubble of happiness is going to be momentarily popped by all the information Roman is about to throw my way.

Roman stares at me, eyes roaming over my face like he's memorizing every detail.

"Are you okay?" I ask.

He sighs, leaning back heavily into the couch. "Yes, just preparing myself for everything I need to tell you."

"I'm ready to listen, whenever you're ready," I say quietly, pulling my legs up to my chest and resting my chin on my knees.

"This may not all be easy to hear," he says, expression looking stricken.

"That's okay. I need to hear it."

He nods, inhaling deeply before releasing it.

"Okay, so let me start from the moment you were kidnapped."

ROMAN

Chapter Forty-Three

"*Tell me the time and the place.*"

His sinister chuckle meets my ears. "*Excellent.*"

I turn calmly towards Sawyer as I hang up the phone with Lorenzo.

"Sawyer, I need you to call and get the plane ready, I want Alex and Lacey to go to Fiji tonight. Make sure you get their passports and ensure Alex has full access to my offshore account. Once you do that, meet me in my office."

Sawyer nods, already pulling out his phone. "On it, boss."

I go into the closet and grab a duffel bag and run out of our bedroom quickly, needing to get to my office.

I press the hidden button on my desk and the picture covering my safe on the wall opens. I type in the combination and listen for the click, then toss the wads of cash into the duffle, along with multiple jewels and other valuable items that were inside.

Once the safe is almost empty I grab the folder tucked towards the back and walk to my desk, not even bothering to shut it.

I set the duffle down, alongside the folder, grab my cell phone and scroll down to Mateo Stephano's number, then press call.

The phone rings twice before his gruff voice sounds through the line. "Roman."

"Mateo, I want to make a deal."

Silence meets my ears and I'm half expecting him to say no before he finally speaks.

"I'm listening."

I walk into Mateo's office, flanked by his bodyguards.

"Roman, good to see you."

Mateo Stephano; the head of the third family in Vegas. With his balding head, and oversized stomach, he is a replica of the Spiderman comic character Kingpin.

He motions for me to step forward as he stubs out his cigar.

I do as instructed, setting the duffle on his desk, unzipping it to show him what all is inside. "Money, plus some. It's all yours."

I pull the folder from where I had it tucked into the back of my pants and lay it out in front of him.

"This is every contact, contract, and business of mine. You can have them all and take over my entire section of the three."

I go through and break down every business, every investment, my employee list, and who owes me what. Everything. I literally give him everything.

He eyes me curiously, absently rubbing his thumb and forefinger over his chin.

"Are you sure you want to go through with this? Once you are dead Roman, there is no coming back."

I can't help the chuckle that escapes my lips. "That is the idea."

Mateo nods, stands, then motions for his guards.

"Get all of my men together. I want everyone here in the next hour. Tell them no exceptions."

The guards leave and he turns towards me once more.

"All of this for a boy?" I can see the distaste written across his features. Usually that comment alone would have earned him a bullet hole but nothing could possibly pop my bubble right now.

So, instead I level Mateo with a hard stare. "He's not just a boy. He's my everything."

I watch Sawyer carry off a distraught Alex and it takes everything inside of me to not chase after him. I want to kiss him and tell him everything will be okay, because it will.

Just not right now.

But I can't, I have to stay focused and remember the bigger picture. A future. A different life.

My body hits the dirt as Lorenzo's guards start kicking me, and I let them.

"Enough, let him up. I don't want this one to die quickly," Lorenzo says, voice sounding smug.

If only you knew.

"When do I get my money?" A voice I know all too well reaches my ears, and my gaze snaps up as I take in a sweaty, worried looking Randal.

What the fuck?

He stands next to Lorenzo, a couple of feet away and he looks terrible.

How had I not noticed how bad he looked before? His blond hair is dirty and sticking to his sweaty forehead. His eyes are sunken with dark smudges beneath them. He looks like he's just come back from a week long bender.

"Randal? You were the rat?" I question in surprise.

He refuses to meet my gaze as he shuffles from foot to foot. Fucking coward.

"It wasn't personal. I just needed the money." He turns to Lorenzo once more. "When can I get my money?"

This fool. I can tell by the look on Lorenzo's face that he isn't giving him jack shit.

Lorenzo's sinister laugh reaches my ears before he whips out his gun and shoots Randal in the head. It happens so quickly that I barely have my eyes shut when the warm blood splashes against my cheek.

Randal's lifeless body falls to the ground with a thud while Lorenzo and all his lackeys stand there laughing at his expense.

Every dog has its day. Is my last thought before the chorus of gunshots ring out in the shipping yard.

The sounds of pings as they tear through the metal containers is my cue and I roll underneath the nearest car. Lorenzo rips out his gun and begins shooting blindly, the look of confusion and panic obvious across his face.

The loud screams of men reaching their impending death and the booming of guns as their bullets were released from the chambers was music that sounded through the air.

This is what war sounds like. True terror and fear. While people destroy one another in the hope of becoming the last man standing.

The good thing though, is in this war, I already know how it ends.

Lorenzo's lackeys go down quickly and soon enough it's just him standing alone, spinning in circles with his gun hand shaking so badly that he couldn't aim now even if he wanted to.

I slide from underneath the car and Sawyer reaches my side, gun pointed at Lorenzo. Sawyer assesses me, eyebrows raised in question.

I shake my head, doing my best to wipe away the dust on my suit pants. "I'm good."

"Roman," Lorenzo releases a nervous chuckle. "Let's talk about this."

Oh, you want to talk now, huh?

"That won't be necessary," Mateo says, as he steps behind Lorenzo. "No conversation is needed."

A gasp tears from Lorenzo's throat as he turns towards Mateo. Mateo's guard reaches forward, snatching the gun from Lorenzo and snapping his arm back at an awkward angle. His loud cries fill the space around us and my monster relishes in the noise.

"I don't understand," he croaks. "You are siding with this...this...abomination?"

Mateo tsks, "You still cannot see."

Lorenzo looks even more confused now when he says, "See what?"

"I don't want to split Vegas anymore." Mateo pauses, leaning forward slightly. "I want to rule it all."

With that, he raises his gun, putting an end to that miserable sack of shit. Lorenzo gasps and sputters as blood drips from his lips; blood pours from his chest where the bullet ripped him open. He chokes, falling to the ground as the life leaves his body.

Good riddance.

I turn towards Sawyer. "Keep him safe for me."

"Like you have to worry with Lacey around," he says, a smile playing across his lips.

I can't help but return the gesture. "Good luck with that one.'

He sighs, "I'm going to need it."

I reach up and give his shoulder a squeeze before taking a step towards Mateo.

Sawyer turns, leading my men away from me. Several of them look back at me with admiration and concern. I motion for them to continue on with Sawyer.

I had a little pep talk with them before we arrived, informing them that I was not making it out of there and they were now obligated to follow Mateo. There was some protest but I simply reminded them of their duty.

The only thing my men know is that Lorenzo took my husband and I am paying for his safety with my life. Everything else that will come to pass is between me and Mateo, and the two remaining guards he has with him.

"Are you sure?" Mateo asks, when I'm about ten feet away.

I have questioned so many things in my life. Have gone to Hell and back, but nothing has ever given me this level of clarity.

"I have never been more sure about anything in my life."

"Very well."

Mateo raises his gun and I shut my eyes, letting my mind wander to Alex. I think about his sweet, sleepy smile when he wakes up in the morning. I think about his whimsical laughter as he watches a comedy on TV. I think about his eyes, glazed over with desire the moment before I slide inside his body.

I'm so lost in Alex, drowning in the memories of him, that I don't even register the sound of the bullet exiting the chamber, nor do I so much as flinch when the first bullet slams into my shoulder. Two more shots fire, grazing the side of my thigh and hip.

I release a sigh and my body finally surrenders to the pain. I fall to my knees, letting this new found calmness settle over me. I chuckle lightly as I lie back meeting the hard earth.

Peace, this is peace.

For the first time in my life; I'm truly free.

Chapter Forty-Four

I'm reeling from all the information. I bite down on my thumb nail as I absorb everything he just told me.

"What happened after you were shot?" I ask, voice barely a whisper.

"Mateo and his men left me there, but called an ambulance to come pick me up. I needed it to be news. Ground breaking news. I was rushed to a hospital where they did surgery to remove the bullets and repair any damage that occurred."

"The papers all said you died. I checked the internet. You even had a funeral."

He nods. "I paid the head surgeon and Detective Dominic Valentina a lot of money to make that happen."

Right. Money makes the world go round.

I run my fingers over my thighs, biting down on my bottom lip.

"Why didn't you come to me sooner?" I finally manage to ask.

He slides forward, tilting my chin up to meet his gaze. "Believe me when I say I wanted nothing more than to come to you sooner. I had to be sure you were safe from those who might be looking for you, but also I wanted to make sure you would be safe from me." He sighs, rubbing his thumb over my lip, "I went to therapy. I had to fix myself. I had to make sure I could be the man you needed. I wanted to be the man you deserved."

My lip wobbles and I crawl forward, settling on his lap. I bury my face into his neck, wrapping my arms around him as tightly as possible.

"I heard the gunshots," I mumble into his skin. "I heard what I thought was you dying and it broke me inside. I hated that I couldn't get to you. Couldn't help you." I pull back cupping his face with my palms.

"I was so devastated. I never thought I would ever be able to do this. To look you in the eyes when I tell you that I forgive you. That I love you."

He gasps, eyes welling with tears. "Oh, baby." He presses his forehead against mine, soaking in my warmth. "I don't deserve you. I never have, but I swear I will spend the rest of my life trying. If you let me."

I smile, enjoying the feel of his body pressed against mine.

If I let him?

Pft, it's not even a question. I already lost this once; I won't ever let it slip through my fingers again. I lean back holding his gaze, running my fingers through the soft strands of his hair.

"Forever sounds really good to me."

The smile that blooms across his face is radiant. I want to kiss it. I want to feel that smile.

So I do.

I lean in and kiss his lips. Savoring the feeling of having his mouth pressed against mine. Lazily running my tongue across his lips, begging for entrance into his mouth. We kiss for long minutes, hands searching, hearts healing, and souls colliding.

Yes, forever sounds really good to me.

ROMAN

Epilogue

I stand on the beach near the shore enjoying the feel of the water as it runs across my bare feet.

Today is the day; the first day of the rest of our lives. I'm nervous and excited all wrapped into one.

"Are you ready?" the officiant asks.

I nod, smiling wide at him as the beginning chords of *Thinking Out Loud* by Ed Sheeran begin to play.

I look towards the end of the makeshift aisle where Alex is walking towards me, with a sobbing Lacey on his arm.

Who would have thought that after every fucked up thing I've done or gone through, my life would lead me here? Standing at the end of the aisle about to marry the man of my dreams and the keeper of my heart...again.

I never thought Alex would give me a second chance. But I thank the powers that be every single day that he did.

Alex's smile is huge as he takes the last few steps to get to me and I soak in all the love pouring from him. We did it. I interlock our fingers as we turn towards the officiant. Ready to say our vows and truly commit to one another. Commit to a life built together on a foundation of love, loyalty, and honesty.

I was told once that when you shake hands with the devil you accept that he is in control. I have to say that is probably the truest thing I've ever heard.

From a small child I was raised to believe I had to be a certain way in order to live the life that was planned out for me. I had to sign my soul over and be a man I hated, in order to live up to the expectations laid out for me by men with a God-like complex.

I lived in Hell for so long, accepting my fate like the good little soldier I was expected to be. The thing is, even the devil was once an angel; so it's important to remember you can't trust everyone. Sometimes that means even the people who are supposed to have your best interest at heart.

I fought my way back from Hell somehow and now am here. On the cusp of redemption, holding the hand of the man I love more than life. So happy to be alive.

My pesky monster is long gone and it leaves me with so much hope for the future.

Alex and I exchange vows and rings, sharing smiles and this is a moment that will stick with me for the rest of my life. I lean in to brush my lips across his, enjoying the feel of his soft lips against mine. *My husband.*

We pull back slightly breathless, expressions equally heated.

"Let's get out of here, husband," he purrs, waggling his eyebrows at me.

I laugh, nodding my head enthusiastically. We practically run across the beach, the sounds of Sawyer and Lacey's laughter meeting my ears.

And I think perfect, everything is just perfect.

THE END

"The devil whispers to the warrior, 'You cannot withstand the storm.'
The warrior whispers back, 'I am the storm.'"

THE
REDEMPTION
OF ROMAN

THANK YOU

Writing a book is harder than I ever could have imagined and I couldn't have done it without so many amazing people in my corner.

To my sweet Pineapple, you know who you are.

Taylor Griffiths, thank you for your constant help in keeping me grounded and taming the chaos in my brain. I would be lost without you.

Alisha Williams, I adore your vision of Roman and how you helped bring him to life for me. He is just gorgeous.

Lindsay Hamilton, Ashley Cooper, Oriane Steiner, Jennifer Storke Felderman, and Corina Ciobanu. You beautiful ladies, I cannot even express my gratitude enough. From reading my firsthand/chicken scratch drafts to the progress in making it become a completed novel. I appreciate the help along the roller coaster ride.

Amber Nicole, from the moment I said I want to write a book until the final The End you were there every step of the way, offering advice and encouraging words. Thank you for helping me bring Roman to life in the way I envisioned him.

JLCR Author Services. Jessica, Cat, and Rebecca. Thank you ladies so much for everything. The teasers, the formatting, the advice, answering all my crazy questions. Mostly thanks for having my back and being a big part of my journey in becoming an Author.

My Dehydrated B!tches. Kelsey, Bethany, Nat, Marisa, Mari, Taylor, Cat, Corina, and Amber. Thanks for the inspo pictures, all the laughs, and the constant daily support on this journey! I love you all.

My amazing ARC team- Thank you for taking a chance on a newbie Author. I appreciate you all more than you know.

And finally to my readers- Thank you, a thousand times over. I cannot express my gratitude enough.

I hope you enjoyed reading Alex and Roman's story!

ABOUT ME

T. Ashleigh is an author who loves, books, cats, and wine. Lots and lots of wine.

STALK ME

T. Ashleigh Reader's Group

Facebook

Instagram

Goodreads

Amazon

Pinterest